Praise for
New York Times and USA Today Bestselling Author

Diane Capri

"Full of thrills and tension, but smart and human, too."
Lee Child, #1 World Wide Bestselling Author of Jack Reacher
Thrillers

"[A] welcome surprise….[W]orks from the first page
to 'The End'."
Larry King

"Swift pacing and ongoing suspense are always
present…[L]ikable protagonist who uses her political
connections for a good cause…Readers should eagerly anticipate
the next [book]."
Top Pick, Romantic Times

"…offers tense legal drama with courtroom overtones, twisty
plot, and loads of Florida atmosphere. Recommended."
Library Journal

"[A] fast-paced legal thriller…energetic prose…an appealing
heroine…clever and capable supporting cast…[that will] keep
readers waiting for the next [book]."
Publishers Weekly

"Expertise shines on every page."
Margaret Maron, Edgar, Anthony, Agatha and Macavity Award
Winning MWA Past President

JACK
OF HEARTS

by DIANE CAPRI

Published by: AugustBooks
http://www.AugustBooks.com

ISBN: 978-1-942633-53-2

Original cover design by: Cory Clubb
Digital formatting by: Author E.M.S.

Jack of Hearts is a work of fiction. Names, characters, places, and incidents either are the product of the author's imagination or are used fictitiously, and any resemblance to actual persons, living or dead, business establishments, events, or locales is entirely coincidental.

Published in the United States of America.

Visit the author website:
http://www.DianeCapri.com

ALSO BY DIANE CAPRI

The Hunt for Jack Reacher Series
(in publication order with Lee Child source books in parentheses)

Don't Know Jack (The Killing Floor)

Jack in a Box (*novella*)

Jack and Kill (*novella*)

Get Back Jack (Bad Luck & Trouble)

Jack in the Green (*novella*)

Jack and Joe (The Enemy)

Deep Cover Jack (Persuader)

Jack the Reaper (The Hard Way)

Black Jack (Running Blind/The Visitor)

Ten Two Jack (The Midnight Line)

Jack of Spades (Past Tense)

Prepper Jack (Die Trying)

Full Metal Jack (The Affair)

Jack Frost (61 Hours)

Jack of Hearts • (Worth Dying For)

Straight Jack • (A Wanted Man)

The Jess Kimball Thrillers Series

Fatal Distraction

Fatal Demand

Fatal Error

Fatal Fall

Fatal Game

Fatal Bond

Fatal Enemy (*novella*)

Fatal Edge (*novella*)

Fatal Past (*novella*)

Fatal Dawn

CAST OF PRIMARY CHARACTERS

Kim Otto
William Burke
Carlos Gaspar
Charles Cooper
Lamont Finlay
Gamon Chen (called "GiGi")
Mika Chen
Ying Chen (called "Jade")
Amarin Chen (called "Alan")
Roberto "The Elephant" Rossi
Thaddeus Sydney
Eleanor Duncan
Evan Vincent
Dr. Ezra Landon
Brenda Landon
Petey Burns

and
Jack Reacher

Perpetually, for Lee Child, with unrelenting gratitude.

JACK

OF HEARTS

WORTH DYING FOR

by Lee Child

Reacher lived in a world where you don't start fights but you sure as hell finish them, and you don't lose them either, and he was the inheritor of generations of hard-won wisdom that said the best way to lose them was to assume they were over when they weren't yet.

CHAPTER ONE

Sunday, May 15
Hoover Dam, Nevada
Noon

A PASSING STRANGER MIGHT have mistaken Jade Chen for a teenage boy. The constant video surveillance of one of the country's top terrorist targets might be fooled, too.

Jade was dressed like a tourist. Black jeans and black running shoes and a black hoodie covered her body and kept her warm enough in the wind. Oversized sunglasses shielded her eyes. She'd gathered her ebony hair into a wide barrette low on her neck and pulled her hood up to cover her head.

She sauntered along the cold, narrow pedestrian walkway of the Hoover Dam bypass bridge, sweeping her gaze in all directions. The noonday sun was bright overhead and a strong breeze made the day feel cooler than the weatherman's forecast.

Jade forced herself to stare straight down through the thick concrete spindles lining the walkway as she moved. She had been afraid of heights since she was a child, three lifetimes ago.

Only with fierce concentration did she manage not to tremble.

The bridge was amazing. It soared nine hundred feet above the Colorado River. She paused at the Arizona end and stared at the ribbon of water below for a good long time, facing her fear of falling with faux courage. She no longer displayed the timidity her Thai culture had demanded. Years of hardship had forged her into steel from the frail reed she'd once been.

Her body's small tremors reminded her that she might follow her gaze, straight down to the water's surface. From this height, it would be the same as splatting on concrete.

She'd fallen off the roof of her neighbor's home when she was eight. She'd been frozen in place, staring at the terrifying drop off the roof, until her body simply fell forward and down and crashed onto the hard ground below.

Amarin had been there. He'd picked her up and carried her all the way to the doctor's home. He'd stayed with her until she was released. He'd done all he could, but it hadn't been enough.

The break had never healed correctly. Even now, she had a slight foot drop and still walked with a limp when she was too tired to control it.

But with Amarin's help, she had survived the experience.

She wouldn't survive a fall from here. Not simply because she was slight and fragile. Her size didn't matter. A giant would suffer the same fate.

No one could survive a fall from this bridge.

Jade knew that much for sure because she'd looked it up online before she agreed to meet Amarin secretly here. The prospect of facing him anywhere terrified her, which she absolutely would not reveal. Only through extreme force of will had she forced herself to come.

She'd agreed because she knew Amarin would never leave

her alone otherwise. This was her one chance to persuade him to abandon her once again. This time, forever.

Amarin had loved her once, as she'd loved him. Before she'd dishonored herself and her family. She was a sex worker now. She owned the business and employed other sex workers. She was in full control of her life.

But he was outraged by her behavior, and he'd never been able to control his anger.

Still, Jade wanted to believe he wouldn't toss her over the bridge to her death, like a discarded childhood plaything, when she refused him with iron-willed finality.

Why had he wanted to meet here? There were hundreds of safer places, surely.

Her fear insisted this would be the perfect place for him to dispose of any enemy. The body would be found eventually. The enemy's only chance would be to thwart the execution before he went over the railing.

Against Amarin, the possibility of success in physical battle was nil.

Not many possessed the strength or speed to thwart him. For Jade, it would be useless to try. She hoped she wouldn't need to.

The bridge was heavily traveled day and night, and there were always police around. A killer would need to be clever about the timing if he hoped to avoid witnesses and escape capture afterward.

Could Amarin do all of that? She suspected he could.

Amarin's combat skills had always been magical.

If one wanted to die here, the good news was that police didn't try to stop suicides. There were no suicide prevention signs or phones to call hotlines or anything like that. The prevailing view seemed to be that anyone who wanted to die would do it, regardless of efforts to thwart them.

Amarin would only need to persuade authorities that she'd killed herself. He could do that easily.

Jade began to walk from the Nevada side of the bridge. When she reached the Arizona side, she paused to look down. And then she turned and strolled back, forcing her gaze away from the magnetic pull of the abyss.

Halfway across the walkway this time, she saw him standing alone, watching her approach, waiting with infinite patience like a crouching tiger until she reached him.

Amarin was dressed almost the same as she, perhaps for the same reasons. As children, they'd often been in sync like that. Perhaps time and distance and circumstances had not severed the bond of shared history.

Jade lifted her lips at the corner in greeting. He made no effort to acknowledge her.

He leaned casually against the railing, not far from the Nevada side of the bridge, hands loose at his side. He was wearing black leather gloves. She hadn't been this close to him since they'd left Thailand for America more than seven years ago.

He looked the same but different. Partly, he'd matured. But now, he had a chiseled athlete's body instead of the lean, lithe physique of the boy she remembered. He stood with a formidable presence, a focused and threatening grace.

The physical and mental changes had no doubt developed as he'd honed his boxing skills. At last count, he'd won more than one hundred Muay Thai matches. It was the sport of his country and his childhood. He'd bested all opponents from a very young age.

His style was fast, elusive, and technical. It had made him a champion and, in certain circles, a celebrity.

All of which meant that if Amarin wanted to kill her, he

could easily do so. It would be the work of a moment to pick her up and toss her over the barrier railing and into the deep canyon. His actions were lightning fast. Tourists, focused on the magnificent views, might not actually see him do it.

Jade stopped ten steps away. After a few moments of mutual appraisal, she steadied her voice. "You look good. The mustache suits you."

He nodded. "Are you packed?"

"No," she said firmly, keeping her gaze and her voice steady. "I'm not going with you."

Amarin's eyes narrowed and he flashed the look she'd seen him use to quell an opponent in the ring just before he delivered a solid knock-out kick. "Why not?"

Jade stood her ground and firmly delivered the short speech she'd rehearsed. "My business is going well. We are thriving. Your life is not your own. You have nothing to offer us. And there's nothing for us back in Thailand. No home. No family. Nothing but shame and sorrow and loss awaits me there. I'm staying where I am."

He stared into her sunglasses for a few moments more and then he turned to lean his forearms on the railing, looking out toward the spectacular views of the Hoover Dam in the distance. Vehicles passed on the bridge behind them. A few tourists walked to and fro.

Jade stayed ten feet away and waited, afraid to move any closer. Amarin was lightning fast. Her only hope of evading him was distance. The breeze had strengthened and she felt the cold wind through her hoodie.

Eventually, he began to talk as if he'd accepted her conclusions about her future. "The journey was fine for us. Until we reached the U.S., we were comfortable."

She understood he was asking about her journey also, so she answered his unspoken questions. "We were well cared for. Our passage to America was exactly what we'd dreamed, what our families paid for. We arrived safely. All unfolded as we had been advised before we left Thailand."

"Until you reached Montana," he said firmly. "That's where things went wrong."

Jade nodded. "But even that turned out well for us. We stayed together. We were transported to Denver. We've made a good life there."

He understood she was asking about his journey, too. He nodded. "We were fine. When we made it to Montana, we were divided up. The younger boys were taken away. Our brothers. We never saw any of them again."

Amarin lowered his head and Jade did, too. Seven years later, they were older and wiser than they'd been when they excitedly boarded the boat in Thailand, headed for a better life.

They both knew now that they'd been victims of human trafficking seven years ago.

The boys were irretrievably lost, probably sold into the sex trade. Separated from each other, sent to different owners, thousands of miles apart. Some had died. Although Jade and Amarin continued to hope, there was no way to avoid the likely conclusion.

Jade sensed that he was still angry because he'd felt responsible for the boys. Jade no longer cried for them. She preferred not to think about the fate of those she could not rescue. That way lies madness and she simply didn't have the luxury of giving in to it. She had the living to consider.

They shared a few minutes of conversation about their rural village and the people they'd left behind. Friends and distant family they would never see again. Celebrations in days gone by. The usual things old friends talk about when they've been separated for many years.

A passing SUV blew its horn when another vehicle swerved into its lane on the roadway behind them. The loud noise startled them both and returned them to the present.

Jade glanced behind to see vehicles passing safely. She observed tourists walking along in small groups, pointing at the lake and the dam, snapping photos or longer videos on their phones.

A lone man approaching from the Nevada side of the bridge caught her eye. He might have been a tourist exploring alone, but something about him raised Jade's internal warning systems. She kept her wits about her these days, which was how she'd stayed alive so long.

The man strolled easily in their direction. He wore a leather jacket and dark glasses and a baseball cap pulled low on his face. One hand rested in his pocket. The other swung free and loose at his side.

"What are you looking at?" Amarin asked, turning his head to see.

A strong electrical current ran up her spine and down again, setting her nerves on fire. "That man coming toward us. Does he look strange to you?"

Amarin stared at the man and his breathing became rapid and uneven. He stepped in front of her. "Go. Get out of here. I'll contact you again. But you can't stay here now."

"Why? What's going on?" Jade asked as she tried to see around him to the man wearing the cap. "You know him?"

"He works for my boss. He's a fixer. His name is Fredo Moretti. He's not here to socialize," Amarin said sternly. When she didn't move, he said, "You're in danger, Jade. He's seen us. If he gets close enough, he'll kill you. That's what he does. There's no other reason why he would be here. Get going. Now."

Jade's heart thumped rapidly in her chest. "What about you?"

"He won't hurt me. I'm the golden ticket." Amarin gave her a hard stare. "*You're* the problem to be eliminated. Somehow, Rossi knows I came here to meet you. He's sent Moretti to deal with you. And watch yourself. Rossi will find you again."

Jade nodded, turned her trembling body, and rushed quickly in the opposite direction.

Six tourists were gathered at the welcome sign attempting to take a selfie photo and not having much luck getting their group into the frame.

Jade approached them offering to shoot the whole group together and they readily agreed. She took the phone and stepped back a few paces, ostensibly to compose the photo.

From this vantage point, she had a clear view of Amarin and the approaching threat. Mindlessly, she snapped several images of the group while she kept her gaze on Moretti.

When she finished the photos, she pulled her phone from her pocket and shot a burst of Fredo Moretti images, too.

Amarin and Moretti were arguing now, but the wind carried their conversation into the canyon. Jade tried using her video, hoping to capture the words. Their voices were raised in anger, but the dialogue was lost in the wind.

The argument turned physical. Moretti pushed Amarin against the railing.

Moretti's push triggered Amarin's fighting instincts. His lighting fast reflexes engaged.

He punched Moretti in the stomach before Moretti had a chance to deflect.

Moretti grabbed his midsection with his free hand and bent over with pain. His other hand seemed to be stuck inside his pocket.

Swiftly, Amarin lifted his leg high in the air and delivered a vicious kick.

The blow landed hard to the side of Moretti's neck and head.

Moretti crumpled against the railing, sliding toward the concrete.

In one smooth, fast motion, Amarin bent slightly at the knees, lifted Moretti as if he were weightless, and effortlessly tossed him over the railing.

Moretti didn't scream at all as he went into the abyss. Which probably meant he was unconscious. He had no chance to be frightened.

Jade gasped. Her hand flew to cover her mouth.

She stared at Moretti, falling rapidly down toward the river until he disappeared from view.

The scene had unfolded too quickly.

No one seemed to notice the fight or Moretti's pitch over the railing or anything else.

Jade moved closer to the edge and leaned to see Moretti's body as it continued to drop like an anchor all the way down.

Nine hundred feet.

By the time he hit the water, the body was a spec of darkness.

She continued to stare in horrified silence for a few moments more.

When Jade pulled her gaze away and turned toward the bridge, her brother was gone.

She sucked in a quick breath and whispered, "Amarin, what have you done?"

CHAPTER TWO

Sunday, May 15
Las Vegas, Nevada
2:00 p.m.

ROBERTO "THE ELEPHANT" ROSSI sat behind his desk in his plush office at the Snake Eyes Casino, which is where he could be found at this hour seven days a week.

The décor was mostly reminiscent of the gambling floor where Rossi had won the casino hotel from a rival years ago. Safir had been a small Lebanese with outsized ambition and annoying habits. No one mourned his passing.

The casino's logo, a pair of shiny black dice showing a single red dot on each, adorned the walls and the glassware and the table tops. The probability of rolling snake eyes was one in thirty-six or 2.777%. In other words, not too likely.

But Rossi had always been lucky and the night he won the hotel and casino from Safir had proven it. Instantly, he became the new owner, terminated his rival, folded Safir's businesses into his own, renamed the enterprise, and never looked back.

A year or so later, Rossi was able to eliminate Safir's customer, the Iranian, Mahmeini and the last of the old Duncan, Nebraska fiasco was laid to rest. Rossi moved up two places in the supply chain.

He grinned whenever he thought about the takeover. All's well that ends with Rossi in control and alive to fight another day.

Loose ends remained. For now.

He would find the rest of his property. The product he'd bought and paid for that had been stolen from him, reducing his business and his profits for too many years.

And he would avenge his soldiers who had died in the fight.

The Elephant never forgot a slight. The time for revenge would come. He had only to remain alert to opportunity and seize the moment when it arrived. Just like with Safir and Mahmeini.

Until then, Rossi spent his days at his casino. He lived here and worked here and played here. Where else would he be?

He drained the last of his private label beer and returned the empty bottle to the tray on his desk. He opened the drawer and located the gold bottle opener embossed with the snake eyes logo. He used it to pop open a fresh bottle and added the cap to the growing collection beside him. He counted the bottle caps as the day continued. Part of his inventory management system.

Las Vegas was ground zero for Rossi's diversified business operations, which had grown exponentially in recent years as he'd eliminated his competition. No violence that could be tied to him directly, of course. The last thing he needed was some misguided dope coming after him.

No, Rossi had done the job subtly over time and kept his fingerprints off the weapons. First the Lebanese, Safir. Then the Iranian, Mahmeini. The others fell, too, one by one.

His considerable bulk and power were at the top of the U.S. operation's food chain now, a position he intended to defend and never relinquish.

Which was why he needed to eliminate the girl. Jade, they called her now. She was already an issue for the boxer. Initially, Rossi had wanted her gone before she became a bigger problem.

Rossi had a sixth sense for these things. He'd ignored his misgivings during that unpleasant Nebraska business seven years ago and he'd incurred heavy losses. He'd clawed his way back, better than before. Lessons learned.

After that setback, he'd made two vows.

First, to never repeat the mistakes of the past. When his gut told him what to do, he simply made it happen. No failed partners to rely upon. No messing around. No wrestling with his conscience.

No second-guessing. Ever.

His gut said the girl, Jade, was trouble. She had to go.

Seven years had passed since the Nebraska situation and so far, so good. Following his gut was working well. Why mess with success?

The second vow he'd made back then was to hunt down and kill the son of a bitch who caused him such disastrous consequences.

Jack Reacher.

The guy was as big as a bull. He shouldn't have been that hard to find.

But he was. Seven years later, and Reacher was still at large.

He had feelers out on Reacher and sooner or later, the bastard would show up. Nobody that big and that mean could hide forever. When he surfaced, Rossi would make good on his promise. He was looking forward to it.

Meanwhile, Rossi had concentrated on rebuilding and growing his business.

Which was why he'd sent Fredo to the Hoover Dam this morning.

Rossi's best boxer was in over his head. A sign of weakness that could cost Rossi big money. Weakness his enemies wouldn't hesitate to exploit.

Messing around with that girl was a fast road to disaster. Rossi would not allow it.

Fredo's orders were simple. Kill the girl. Report back.

Should have been an easy morning.

Jade was so tiny that almost anybody could kill her and throw the body into the river. Should have taken Fredo five minutes, tops.

Rossi leaned back in his oversized desk chair and thumped the buttery soft leather with his beefy left thumb. He was barely aware of the nervous habit he'd developed in childhood, but his employees and associates had noticed. Nothing good ever happened when The Elephant's thumping reflexes ruled his reason.

He glanced again at the clock. Fredo should have returned before office hours. He hadn't.

Rossi sighed. His gut said he'd never see him again.

Not that he cared that much about Fredo.

He was a reliable soldier. Totally expendable.

Rossi could find another Fredo with the wave of his hand. Guys like Fredo stood in line simply to serve at Rossi's whim. He'd lost such soldiers in the past. Reacher had killed two of his best. But Rossi had dozens more waiting.

The problem wasn't replacing Fredo.

It was much more serious.

Rossi leaned over and pressed a button on the house phone. A woman opened the door and hurried into his office, an inquisitive look on her face.

She was a Dolly Parton impersonator in the casino lounge on weekends. All lip-synch, of course. Nobody had a voice like Dolly Parton for real. But the boobs, the ass, the wigs, the long red fingernails, the makeup. He had to hand it to her. She looked like the real deal under the soft lounge lighting.

"Dolly, first send up more beer. Then call Sydney. Get him in here."

"He's in Los Angeles. Won't be back until Tuesday," Dolly said before she noticed the thumb thumping. When she saw it, she added, "I'll call him now. Maybe he's on his way."

Mincing steps were all she could manage in the tight skirt and spike heels. But Dolly turned and dashed out as quickly as she'd arrived before The Elephant expressed displeasure with a deafening roar.

CHAPTER THREE

Sunday, May 15
Mount Rushmore, South Dakota
3:00 p.m.

FBI SPECIAL AGENT KIM Otto lay flat on her bed in the
cheap hotel staring at the ceiling. It had been a harrowing
morning. She'd watched dozens of replays on the screen. The
question was never answered, no matter how many times she
saw the plane dip into the trees before the crash.

Eye strain caused a piercing headache before Kim had closed
the laptop and then closed her eyes to rest.

The video of the plane crash looped in her head repeatedly
for what seemed like a thousand times.

Was Reacher dead? Possibly. He'd risen from near death in
the past, but he was mortal, after all. Sooner or later, he'd
succumb to the big sleep, like every carbon-based life form
before and forever after.

Kim rolled over on the bed and fumbled for the burner phone
that connected her directly to her former partner, Carlos Gaspar.

She pressed the redial. He picked up immediately.

"Still nothing to report, Sunshine. And every time you call me, I have to stop looking for new evidence to answer the phone," he said gently. "Cooper told you to cool your jets. I'm telling you the same thing."

Gaspar meant Charles Cooper, the top dog at the FBI as far as she was concerned, the man she usually thought of as The Boss.

"Cooper is not God," she said because it was something Gaspar had told her often enough.

He replied, "Let's go at this another way."

"Such as?" Gaspar was preoccupied. She heard the keys clacking on his keyboard. With his new high-tech security job in the private sector, he had access to whatever he needed to find. One way or another.

"We know Reacher was here. In Bolton, South Dakota. Seven years ago," she said, kneading the sharp pain between her eyes.

"Right. Reacher stepped off a bus. Trouble ensued. People died. Reacher disappeared. The usual," Gaspar rattled off sarcastically, laser-focused on whatever he'd been doing when she called.

She took a breath before she said, "Where did he go?"

A couple of moments of silence passed before he said, "What?"

"After Reacher left Bolton seven years ago, where did he go?"

"Why do we care?" Gaspar said, distracted.

"Someone knows. He went somewhere," she said, speaking between the lightning bolts striking just above the bridge of her nose every few seconds. "And that somewhere might have a record of whatever happened. Because, like you say, Reacher arrives and disaster follows, as surely as the day follows the night."

"Uh, huh," Gaspar said as if he wasn't really listening.

"Here's the thing, though. Reacher didn't die in Bolton all those years ago. Because if he had, we'd never have been assigned to find him. The Boss would have known he was dead already," she said tiredly.

"Yes. True. So?" Gaspar said. "Doesn't mean he's alive today."

"Right, but wherever Reacher went back then, if The Boss knows, then Finlay knows…" she allowed her voice to trail off.

Lamont Finlay, Ph.D., was Special Assistant to the President for Strategy. A Harvard man. Now the second most powerful man in the government. Which for Kim, meant the third most powerful in the world, after her Boss, who hated Finlay with a smoldering anger strong enough to radiate through the cell towers whenever Finlay's name came up.

The antipathy was mutual.

Like her Boss, Finlay knew Reacher. They'd met back in Margrave, Georgia. The experience had pushed Finlay into the limelight and shoved Reacher further off the grid. Whatever it was had also bonded the two men tighter than silver plating on a base metal.

Finlay claimed he had no idea where Reacher was or how to find him. He said they'd been out of touch since Margrave, fifteen years ago.

Gaspar didn't believe that story for a minute.

Neither did Kim.

Nor did the Boss.

Gaspar didn't like Finlay and he didn't trust the man. Every time Kim mentioned Finlay, Gaspar got his back up.

"What's your point, Suzie Wong? You're gonna just call and ask Finlay where Reacher went from Bolton seven years ago?" he replied testily. "He'll tell you in his typical oblique way. And then what? You know Reacher didn't hang around there, wherever it was. You go there, wasting your time, and you get nothing."

She shrugged, eyes closed, still watching the looping video in her head. The plane dips. The door opens. But did Reacher jump out? "That's the problem, for sure. Got any better ideas?"

"Actually, I do. But you've gotta give me a little time to work on this. It's complicated."

"Are you getting anywhere?"

"Maybe."

"How long will it take before you'll know something definitive?"

Gaspar said nothing.

"Okay. You're right. I'm tired. I need sleep. You keep looking and I'll keep waiting," she said with another deep sigh. "But not forever, Chico. If Reacher's alive, every minute that I'm not out there chasing him is ten minutes he's getting ahead of me."

"Yeah, I got it. His legs are ten times as long as yours. Take a nap. I'll call you as soon as I can," Gaspar said. "Meanwhile, try calling Cooper again. He's the man with the answers. And it's actually his job to give them to you."

"Right. And you know that if Cooper or Finlay were talking to me, I wouldn't need to be asking you." She disconnected the call.

Gaspar was right, though. She needed sleep. And calling him every hour wasn't helping either of them.

CHAPTER FOUR

Tuesday, May 17
Las Vegas, Nevada
3:00 a.m.

THADDEUS SYDNEY WAS A careful man. His lean, fit, muscular body was one of his well-maintained tools. Meticulous planning had saved him many times. He defined his goals as narrowly as possible and executed them as specifically required.

His work commanded a high price because he wasn't sloppy.

Rossi paid him well to do this job right the first time. Which suited him perfectly.

After he had wrapped up in Los Angeles, Rossi called him back to Vegas. Now in Rossi's office, Sydney heard the particulars on the new job.

Rossi said, "Moretti screwed up. I need you to fix it."

Sydney nodded, encouraging Rossi to reveal details.

"Moretti's orders were simple. Find the boxer on the bridge and kill the woman," Rossi said.

Sydney already knew the boxer had been preoccupied with

her since his last fight in Vegas, where they'd met for the first time in seven years. Rossi controlled the boxer. His body, his mind, his life.

The woman was an unacceptable distraction. She had to go. Made perfect sense in Rossi's world.

Moretti had failed and paid for it with his life. Which was as it should be. This business was always about kill or be killed.

Sydney had no illusions about the stakes. He'd been a warrior for two decades. The lifestyle suited him, kept the adrenaline running through his veins, made him feel alive every minute of every day.

What red-blooded American wouldn't love a job like that?

Rossi said, "Moretti screwed up. He lost his focus or miscalculated or something. He hasn't returned, which must mean he's dead. The woman isn't."

"Understood." Sydney didn't intend to make the same mistakes, even though his orders were more sophisticated.

"Moretti was good. He's quite a loss and she's got to pay. For that, she's more valuable alive than dead," Rossi said, laying out the rules. "I want her, and her friends, and her business, too. Find them. Bring them to me."

Sydney nodded. He paused to let the words settle in before he asked questions.

Kill or be killed was a simple plan. Rounding up a herd of women and transporting them across state lines was another thing entirely. Lots of moving parts. It required a team. Equipment. A solid schedule.

Rossi's motivation was important. Sydney needed to know exactly what he was up against. The strategy could change on the fly, but the ultimate goal must be met. Was it necessary to deliver all of the women unharmed, for example?

Sydney said, "She runs a high-class escort service. You own half a dozen of those already, right here in Vegas. Not to mention the rest of the state and the country. Why is this one special?"

Rossi narrowed his eyes and pushed his fleshy lips in and out, which was what he did when he was thinking. In this case, Sydney figured he was trying to decide how much to reveal and how much to hold back.

Sydney would do the job regardless of the risks. He simply wanted to know what he was up against. He wouldn't fail. He never had. His reputation for excellence was worth dying for.

"Her business is extremely profitable and well-managed. It rightfully belongs to me," Rossi finally said after he swigged from a beer glass. "She owes me. I'm the one who brought her to this country and gave her a chance. Everything she has, including her life and the lives of the others, she owes to me. I'm collecting that debt."

Sydney cocked his shaved head and leaned back, crossing his ankles. There was more to the story. "How does the boxer fit into this situation?"

Rossi smirked. "Didn't I mention that? The woman is his sister."

"And Moretti's situation tells us how far the boxer will go to protect her," Sydney said, the truth finally shining through the bullshit. "Which means she is an asset you can use to control the boxer. And she's more valuable as an ally or a weapon than a corpse."

"Some fates are worse than death." Rossi shrugged his fat shoulders. "One word, and she's on a slow boat back to Thailand with nothing, disgraced and shamed. She and her sister and her niece, too. Or maybe I'll deliver them to the men who would have paid for them seven years ago. Enhance my business relationships. Point is, I've got options. But I need her alive and unharmed, along with the others."

Sydney nodded, getting the whole ugly image now. The boxer and his family were illegal. They'd been trafficked from Thailand. But something went wrong and they'd avoided their fates back then. The reprieve was over. Time to complete the transaction.

He had zero qualms about that. He'd been managing human cargo for Rossi for years.

"The woman simply needs to be reminded of her reality," Rossi replied as he poured yet another glass of beer. "Make it so."

Rossi was an old-fashioned gangster. He had learned cold-blooded murder and treachery at the knee of his father and grandfather before him. His reach extended to every illegal activity currently operating in Vegas and he was well connected to similar mobsters around the country.

Which meant Rossi was a dangerous man to cross. He saw the world in black-and-white. You were either with him or against him. Sydney planned to stay on the right side of the ledger.

The woman and the boxer were against Rossi at the moment, whether they understood that yet or not. The situation was about to change.

Sydney's only life insurance was a secret escape plan that he would eventually be required to deploy. Until then, what Rossi wanted, Sydney delivered.

Sydney stood and clasped his hands behind his back. "Anything else I need to know now?"

"Sooner is better." Rossi nodded and drained another glass of beer. "Use whatever resources you need."

"Understood," Sydney said on his way out.

He made a plan and put his backup team on notice.

Military service had taught him to pack light, carry nothing traceable, and leave no evidence behind. Everything he needed was new and fit into a single small duffle. He gathered only the gear essential for the job. Even the weapons were stolen and disposable.

He didn't expect to be gone for more than a week. Less, if everything went well.

Sydney gassed up the SUV he'd collected in California and installed a different stolen license plate. The vehicle was owned by a shell corporation nested inside three others and all held by a non-existent offshore strawman.

Anybody trying to trace him or the SUV would be slowed to a standstill for a while. Which was long enough. The less time he spent in Denver, the better.

The GPS route was an easy ten hours and thirty-two minutes' drive time. Once the plan was launched, he rolled out of Vegas alone, planning to find the place and then get some shuteye.

CHAPTER FIVE

Tuesday, May 17
Nebraska
10:00 a.m.

KIM AND HER NEW partner, FBI Special Agent William
Burke, rolled into Nebraska from South Dakota when the sun
was well above the eastern horizon. Burke was at the wheel of
the rented Lincoln Navigator. Kim was belted into the passenger
seat.

She'd persuaded Burke to come along, but he wasn't happy
about it.

He had never worked off the books before, let alone as
deeply under the radar as they were operating now. He was
comfortable with easily identifiable targets and straightforward
war games. And bosses he could rely on.

The hunt for Jack Reacher was none of that. Not even close.

Two days ago, they'd hit another wall. They'd finally had
eyes on Reacher and they'd lost him. They'd been instructed to
stand down and wait for new orders.

Which meant giving up on the best lead Kim had developed since she began looking for the invisible man seven months ago.

For two days, despite her misgivings, Kim had followed those orders. Burke chaffed against the handcuffs. He wanted to get on the road and follow Reacher before they lost him again. Kim agreed although she didn't say so. Not to Burke, anyway.

But the Boss disagreed, and he might have been right. He was usually several steps ahead of his team in the field. This could have been one of those times.

Any reasonable person would have concluded that Reacher had died with the other passengers on that Gulfstream.

Thing was, Kim didn't believe it, and Burke was on the fence.

Kim appreciated Burke's bullheaded approach. In this instance.

Still, sitting in a hotel room wasn't proving The Boss's theory or advancing the search or getting her any closer to Reacher, dead or alive.

After too many idle hours with no further word from the Boss, Kim had finally received the intel she'd requested from Gaspar, her former partner.

She'd devised an alternate plan and presented it to Burke this morning with his breakfast. Not that she needed his approval. But the work was easier when her partner was on board.

"We'll go to Duncan, Nebraska. It's not far. If Reacher's injured, he might go back to a place he knows. He may have friends there," she'd said. "We'll interview witnesses he knew back then. Maybe we'll even find him lying low."

Burke shook his head and flipped his hand as if to flip off the plan, too. "I don't like it. There's no reason to believe that's where Reacher is."

"You have a better plan?" she'd asked.

He didn't.

Kim had been ordered to keep Gaspar out of the case since he'd retired. Because she disagreed with the order, she'd ignored it. Her ass was out here on the line. She felt The Boss's rules were more likely to get her killed or maimed, which wasn't at all acceptable to her.

But she didn't flaunt her defiance. She might not survive this mission, but she saw no reason to voluntarily stick her neck in the guillotine and let The Boss chop her head off. She was intrepid, not suicidal.

Burke respected the chain of command. Which meant he disapproved of her continued reliance on Gaspar. She didn't care whether Burke approved or not, but she wasn't sure he'd keep her transgressions secret, either.

"Let me try contacting Cooper again. It's been almost forty-eight hours since we've talked to him. Maybe he's got better intel by now," Burke said.

"You do that. I'm headed to Nebraska. Get in the vehicle or don't. Your choice," she replied.

By the time she'd packed up, he'd tried calling and got nowhere again. He'd left a message with The Boss and stowed his gear in the Navigator's cargo hold. Then he climbed into the driver's seat.

Mostly because he was tired of sitting on his ass waiting for orders.

Burke fancied himself as a man of action.

Sixty miles later, The Boss had finally returned Burke's call.

"We've left the hotel. Traveling south," Burke said as if the Boss didn't already know as much since he tracked them constantly. "Any further intel on Reacher?"

Cooper replied testily. "When I have it, you'll have it."

Burke offered a couple of alternatives to the sit-on-your-hands-and-wait approach. "Nothing on the satellite feeds around Mount Rushmore?"

The Boss said nothing.

"How about local doctors? He could have been injured. I can call in some favors…" Burke suggested.

"Are you unclear on your orders, Burke? Let me repeat," the Boss snapped like the drill sergeant he once was. "Keep your mouth shut and stay out of the spotlight and take orders from Otto. She's number one on the team."

This wasn't how Burke normally operated, and he clearly didn't like either the orders or losing face in front of Kim. Not even a little bit.

He frowned behind his sunglasses, and his lip curled in an ugly way. "We're losing our advantage by twiddling our thumbs instead of going after Reacher now."

"Burke! Get your head out of your ass!" The Boss shouted through the speaker, putting a loud and final smackdown on all objections. "You're no good to the mission unless you can keep your mouth shut and follow orders. If I want you using your contacts to get intel on Reacher or anything else, I'll let you know. Meanwhile, you're as invisible as possible, and you're following Otto's lead. If there's anything you need to know, I'll tell you. Period. Got it?"

Burke gripped the plastic burner phone so hard it cracked. He snapped, "Message received."

Maybe he'd damaged the phone and his final words were lost in the ether.

Or maybe The Boss had disconnected Burke first.

Either way, the conversation abruptly terminated.

Burke threw the cracked plastic hard over his shoulder. It sailed to the rear of the SUV, where it hit the window like a small-caliber bullet and fell with a brittle thump into the cargo compartment.

Kim turned her gaze toward the side window to offer him a small slice of privacy while he dealt with his frustration and to hide her amusement.

She couldn't help it. Cooper finally knocking him down a couple of notches was music to her ears.

William Burke, former SEAL, former FBI Hostage Rescue Team hotshot, was easy on the eyes and he had a voice many women would like to hear on their pillow at night. He was also used to working as head of a bigger team with access to unlimited resources.

Simply put, the guy thought he was special. Which he was.

But he had a short fuse and a demanding style that had rubbed Kim the wrong way from the start. They'd been working together for only a few days, and the situation hadn't improved with time.

Burke wasn't thrilled to be the second of two, working in the dark. He craved splashy assignments like taking out terrorists and rescuing kidnapped heads of state. Missions where he could display his considerable skills and be rewarded with medals and commendations for his successes.

Turned out, Burke was not as special as he'd thought. Not to Cooper. And so far, not to her.

His new reality seemed to sink in at the speed of a sauntering tortoise.

Truth was, Burke *was* expendable, just like Kim and Gaspar.

In half a hot New York second, The Boss would throw him under the bus or over the cliff or whatever metaphor Burke preferred.

Kim found that truth oddly reassuring. It meant Burke was in the same untenable situation she and Gaspar had been placed in. Which meant she might be able to rely on Burke more than she'd expected now that he clearly understood they were their own army of two on the Reacher thing.

"Welcome to my world." She smirked a couple of minutes after he'd smashed the phone.

Burke turned his handsome scowl toward her. "What the hell do you mean?"

What a prima Donna this guy was.

She missed Gaspar. He was competent and capable and reliable. A father of five, Gaspar also possessed an infinite supply of patience.

He had retired, sure. But to Kim, Gaspar was irreplaceable.

Kim had tried to cut Burke some slack. She hoped he might display some of Gaspar's best traits, eventually. But he shouldered an oversized ego that barely wedged into the cabin of the Navigator they'd been driving for the past few days.

She understood him.

She'd felt some of the same things when she'd come on this mission.

Only successful people became FBI special agents. That success was a foundation for everything an agent did on the job.

It was difficult to accept that no agent was any more special than the rest.

Maybe that reality was especially tough for Burke.

SEALs were trained hard and some believed they were invincible. Burke embodied the training as if he'd been born to it.

Which he probably was.

His dad had been a SEAL. And so were Burke's three

brothers. The traits were embedded in his DNA as surely as those sparkly dark eyes and that dimple in his chin.

She could wait a short while longer for him to get a handle on his new role.

A bigger problem was the trustworthiness issue.

Kim had trusted Gaspar with her life. Many times. Her trust had been well placed. But for some reason she couldn't quite define, she wasn't there yet with Burke. She was skeptical by nature. But something about the guy made her even more wary than usual.

"You know what I think? Cooper knows Reacher's still alive, that's what," Burke fumed. "Why don't we get our teams out there looking for him? Enlist the public. Get this thing on the nightly news. Reacher shouldn't be that hard to track. Especially if he's injured. We always get our man. Always. Why are we wasting time?"

All good questions, for which Kim had no answers.

She shrugged. Gaspar's all-purpose gesture. She deployed it when there was nothing brilliant to say.

Burke barely noticed her silence. He was way too chatty. "Does Cooper even *want* to find Reacher? You've been looking for seven months. South Dakota was the closest you've ever come. We *know* he was there. We *saw* him. He can't have gone very far. Why are we squandering our chance?"

Kim said nothing, hoping he'd wind down soon and they could get on with it.

Gaspar wasn't a talker. He spoke when he had something worthwhile to contribute. Which Kim appreciated, like so many of Gaspar's attributes.

By stark contrast, Burke's blather was exhausting.

Kim tuned him out.

Intense focus was one of her superpowers. Developed over long years in school, graduate school, law school, and Quantico. Growing up in a big family and even being married to a drug addict for a while had further honed her superpower.

Yep, she could focus like a laser beam.

Especially when she had only one option. When there's only one choice, it's the right choice.

She turned her thoughts from Burke's issues to the matter at hand.

Finding Reacher.

CHAPTER SIX

Tuesday, May 17
Las Vegas, Nevada
10:15 a.m.

ROBERTO ROSSI ALWAYS ROSE at eight, no matter what
time he went to bed. He had breakfast in his penthouse on the
twenty-first floor of the Snake Eyes Casino and read the
newspapers until ten.

He was a businessman. Keeping abreast of what was going
on in the world had been integral to his success from the
beginning. Enterprising journalists could be valuable assets for
criminal enterprises like his.

After breakfast Rossi spent two hours every morning, from
ten until noon, in the plant rooms in the greenhouse on the roof.

He'd read a series of novels years ago about a rotund genius
who engaged in the rather esoteric cultivation of rare orchids.
Tending orchids in a rooftop greenhouse in Las Vegas seemed
like the kind of expensive and eccentric hobby a man as
successful as he was could enjoy indefinitely.

Experienced gardeners wouldn't think of Las Vegas and orchids in the same sentence. There were ten thousand sub-species of the exotic plants, but most orchids preferred cooler temperatures, indirect light, and loads of humidity. None of which was native to the desert.

He'd hired Siegfried, an expert in ornamental horticulture with a sub-specialty in the rarest orchids, to identify and acquire his jewels, and oversee the construction of a greenhouse where they would thrive. Oscillating misters, evaporating coolers, shaded screens, and more had created a tropical environment in the desert. Money, after all, was no object.

Once the greenhouse was completed on the east side of the roof, the next step had been to fill it with orchids worthy of a man like Rossi. Nothing so common as phalaenopsis rested there.

Endangered species were his most prized acquisitions. Which was why he had been on the hunt for the ten rarest orchids in the world over the past few years. Simply possessing such plants could get him charged with several crimes in multiple countries.

Which was okay. Stealing rare plants wasn't the only criminal activity he engaged in regularly. Wasn't the worst, either. But it was the least profitable, which appealed to his cultivated eccentricity.

Rossi's enemies said his hobby was somewhat foolish. He shrugged. He had no interest in whoring or drugging. Cars and jets and yachts and villas were useless because he never traveled outside his luxury casino. A man had to spend his money somewhere.

Siegfried had returned from hunting the beautiful and bizarre *Rhizanthella gardneri* in Western Australia this morning.

He displayed the trophy to Rossi with the pride of a big game hunter.

"It's beautiful, isn't it? Even the blooms are underground," Siegfried marveled.

Rossi had peered under the light shield Siegfried had created to protect the delicate orchid that was perhaps the most critically endangered in the world.

"Only fifty known specimens exist in the outback. The five locations are kept secret because of the orchid's rarity," Siegfried said in awe. "No one would ever find these beauties without a knowledgeable guide and substantial resources. The astonishing price you paid for the guide alone! Oi! The trip into the outback to find this jewel was one of the most grueling experiences of my life."

"How did you discover my little *Ella*?" Rossi asked, in equal reverence and hushed tones, peering at the tiny purple blossom with the impossibly difficult name.

"Hours of hunting on hands and knees under shrubs. Backbreaking work," Siegfried replied, pressing a palm to his back to emphasize the pain he'd endured. "Not to mention the extra bribes it cost you to get this beauty back here. But so worth it, yes?"

Rossi smiled as he folded his hands over his ample belly. "The challenge now is to keep *Ella* alive in her new habitat."

Siegfried nodded. "And then, to encourage her to reproduce for us."

Rossi was an introspective man, much wiser than his enemies believed. Not a genius, perhaps. But close enough to have amassed an unrivaled business and a sizable fortune and a cadre of competent sycophants to supply his every whim.

For two hours, Siegfried shared the full details of his

successful search for the Western Underground Orchid. Since Rossi had read about the rarest orchids in a magazine, he'd aimed to own all ten species, which Siegfried said was akin to finding the holy grail.

Exactly the sort of goal Rossi appreciated.

Few would pursue such an impossible quest.

Fewer still would achieve it.

Upon such unthinkable successes had Rossi built his reputation. "Don't mess with The Elephant," his enemies said. "He never forgets."

Rossi listened carefully to Siegfried's story. Asking well-developed questions and gasping appreciatively at the dangerous exploits of his surrogate's adventure.

His display of admiration was cut short by an intruder.

A sharp rap on the door to the greenhouse was followed by a man's voice.

"Rossi? Are you in here?" he called out from forty feet away. He would never dare enter the greenhouse. Only two people were permitted inside. Rossi and Siegfried.

No one else.

For any reason.

Ever.

The Elephant recognized his consigliere's voice. A long sigh escaped from his lips. "I'm sorry, Siegfried. You get some rest. I shall return."

Rossi lumbered toward the doorway, moving his bulk in slow, shuffling steps to avoid jarring the delicate plants. When he reached the door, he scowled to present his displeasure fully.

Simply because the man had permission to visit Rossi's rooftop for emergencies didn't mean he should actually use it.

"I'm sorry to break up your morning," Luca said. He'd

worked for Rossi a long time. They had played together as boys. Rossi was quite fond of him.

Luca knew Rossi better than anyone on earth. He knew the routine. And he knew how much Rossi hated interruptions while he was with his orchids.

Rossi pushed Luca's apologies aside and continued around the rooftop toward the elevator lobby with mock acceptance. The entrance to the emergency stairs was across from two elevator cars resting side by side.

One was utilitarian and came up from the third floor, which housed the hotel lobby.

The other car was private and dedicated solely to Rossi's penthouse. He pressed the call button to open the doors and stepped inside. "Let's move this conversation to my suite."

The doors closed after Luca entered and the elevator car descended slowly to Rossi's apartments one floor below.

His lunch was due to arrive promptly at twelve-thirty. He preferred to eat alone while his food was fresh. Which meant he had precious little time to devote to Luca's emergency, whatever it was.

Rossi waved Luca to a chair in the sitting room and lowered his one-fifth of a ton bulk onto his enormous, reinforced seat.

"What is bothering you today?" Rossi said, after a pointed glance at the clock to suggest that Luca should get to the point and then get out.

"One of our informants at Las Vegas PD gave us a heads-up half an hour ago. Call came into the system from Jarbidge," Luca said, reciting the facts as he'd been instructed and allowing Rossi to reach his own conclusions. "They found two more bodies. Males. Small. Maybe late teens. Probably Asian."

Rossi nodded, pushing his lips in and out, thinking.

Luca said, "Took them a while to get the rescue equipment down into the canyon and get the bodies out."

"We had this issue two years ago. It wasn't a problem then. Hikers get dehydrated, pass out, die in the desert. Sad, but it happens," Rossi said.

"Right. Which is why we didn't concern ourselves," Luca replied and then finished delivering the news. "Now that they've located a total of four bodies, similar in various ways, they're mounting a broader search."

"I see," Rossi nodded. "I assume our friends are conducting this search?"

"Some are friends. Others are not," Luca said. "The story has surfaced in the media. We expect to see the grisly details on the air and in the press this afternoon."

Rossi's lips pushed in and out again and his left thumb began to tap the chair arm. Luca waited for instructions.

"What did they find with the bodies?" Rossi asked.

"Nearby, two generic backpacks. No wallets or cell phones or other identification. Empty canteens. Food wrappers," Luca replied. "The usual sort of things hikers might be expected to carry."

"Condition of the bodies?"

"No autopsies yet, but they were severely dehydrated and decomposed, according to our sources. Vultures and other predators had feasted upon them for a while," Luca said.

"Our friends will keep us apprised," Rossi said, nodding approval. The situation was far from ideal but equally far from disastrous.

Luca replied with a steady gaze directly at Rossi, "We may never know who these unfortunates were. Bodies found in the desert can remain unidentified for years. Some are never identified. But it would be foolish to continue."

Rossi nodded. He had an alternate dump site in mind already. "Thank you, Luca. Please see yourself out."

The lawyer was gone before Rossi's lunch arrived, which was perfect. He seated himself at the private table overlooking Las Vegas to enjoy his lunch and consider Luca's problem. He pulled the first bites off his fork and savored them as his mind went to work.

In the daylight, his city was sprawling and unremarkable. If he'd lived outside the Snake Eyes Casino, required to work out there in the daytime, he'd have moved on from Vegas years ago.

The nighttime was when Rossi's beloved Las Vegas thrived. When crowds filled his casino and his hotel and his restaurants.

And his live performances.

In the dark of night, his illegal Muay Thai boxing attracted the soulless cockroaches with money burning holes in their pockets.

Never satisfied with legal gambling on sports or pushing the buttons on the slot machines, or even betting high stakes on card games, they craved edgier experiences. Those depraved customers, upon which Rossi had built his fortune, paid for his orchids and his lifestyle. He understood them at the core level because he was the same.

Luca's problem carried the seeds of greater difficulty.

Rossi inhaled deeply and held the breath in his lungs for a while before returning to his meal.

Lobster salad was Rossi's favorite starter. He finished it and moved on to the delicate Dover Sole Almandine, sautéed spinach with garlic, and a side of pasta alfredo, all prepared as well as his mother had made it all those years ago.

He swallowed the first few bites with a nice white wine as his thoughts returned to his star performer.

The problem was simple.

Alan Chen was too good.

His opponents were trained in Thailand and other Asian countries where Muay Thai was popular, but none had his skill or his speed. Chen had been told to scale back, but he seemed unable to pull his punches and kicks. Delivered with lightning speed and superior force, Chen's blows landed far too well, far too often.

Which was the reason Fredo Moretti probably rested now with the fishes at the bottom of the Colorado River. Rossi had had time to reflect on the situation.

If Moretti got crossways with the boxer, he never had a chance. Not that it mattered whether the brother or the sister killed Moretti. He was too stupid to live, and now he didn't. Which was fitting.

Chen's prowess was not the problem. Whenever Chen was on the ticket, revenues from the match soared. Chen was by far the most profitable boxer in Rossi's stable. Perhaps the most profitable boxer Rossi had ever possessed.

He sopped up the last of the mingled sauces on his plate with warm bread and pushed a big wad into his mouth. The flavors satisfied distinct aspects of his sophisticated palate perfectly. His new chef was indeed a master in the kitchen.

He moved to coffee and chocolate lava cake, his favorite dessert, when he'd solved Luca's problem.

Chen wasn't the issue. He was way too valuable to be labeled any kind of trouble.

No, the trouble was Rossi's incompetent cleaning crew who had dumped the bodies where they could be found.

Which was easily solved.

The crew would be replaced. Today.

CHAPTER SEVEN

Tuesday, May 17
Nebraska
10:30 a.m.

LIKE BURKE, KIM HAD received a new padded envelope
from The Boss this morning. No flash drive filled with files was
included this time, though. Nothing but a new burner cell phone,
the same as all the others he'd sent.

It was pre-programed to call another burner. A direct line
from her to him. Like everything else about this assignment, the
need for such direct contact was frighteningly bizarre. It
emphasized the reality that the FBI definitely did not have her
back. Not in the slightest.

She'd fired up the phone and dropped it into her pocket
hours ago and ignored it.

But the wretched thing was vibrating now. The Boss was
probably calling to tell her to get Burke under control. She
wasn't ready to talk to him just yet, so she tuned him out, too.

She considered the Reacher Problem.

Burke was right about one thing. After seven months of searching, she was no closer to finding Reacher. Whether he was dead or alive right at this moment was unknowable.

Kim would never give up, no matter what happened. She'd been called stubborn all her life, and maybe she was. She preferred to call her bulldog attitude tenacity.

Even so, she felt Reacher slipping from her grasp with every passing hour. Two days of radio silence from The Boss hadn't advanced the search at all. She had long ago tired of his game, whatever it was. On that much, she and Burke agreed.

Reacher was like an enormous, predatory cat. He'd had at least nine lives already, and maybe more. Kim would never believe he was dead until she saw the body for herself. Reacher's corpse wasn't currently lying on a slab in South Dakota. Which meant she'd lost too much time waiting for Cooper to come through.

She meant to find Reacher before she lost her chance, whether Burke understood that or not.

Kim pointed to a road coming up on the right. "This is our turn. Duncan, Nebraska, is straight ahead."

Burke steered the Navigator as she'd requested onto a paved two-lane running north and south. Traffic was sparse. They'd passed few vehicles along the way, some farm trucks and a tractor or two, and a few older SUVs.

Turned out Reacher had landed in the farming community when he left South Dakota seven years ago. What followed was the usual murder and mayhem Reacher magnetized simply by walking around.

Gaspar dug up the police report from the Nebraska State Police, which was created after the fact and not filed in any digital database. Short, skeletal, to the point. And Reacher's name was listed as the prime suspect in eleven murders, several assaults, and two arsons for good measure.

Reacher had been named by a credible witness as the perpetrator of the violence. Which Kim had never seen before. Usually because the witnesses who might testify were all dead. The others were never willing to talk about Reacher's actions, for one reason or another.

Kim's intuition, supported by the additional video Gaspar located, suggested that Reacher might have gone back to Duncan again two days ago.

The video showed the man they believed to be Reacher hitching a ride in a late model Volkswagen Jetta. The Jetta's GPS traveled halfway to Duncan before the vehicle was abandoned in a strip center parking lot. Which probably meant he'd hitched another ride.

It was a leap in logic to think Reacher had continued on to Duncan, sure. But not that big a leap.

There was nowhere else around for miles between where the Volkswagen had been abandoned and Duncan, the place Reacher had stayed seven years ago, according to the witness.

Kim's immediate plan was to interview the remaining witnesses he'd engaged with back then and find out whether Reacher had come back and where he was now.

Follow the breadcrumbs. Old-fashioned bloodhound work. Nothing special about it. But the method was tried and true. Simply put, it worked if properly performed.

After Kim broke the silence in the cabin of the Navigator, Burke once again found his voice.

"It's a ridiculous operation, making us wait around for who knows what," he said, still fuming, picking up right where he'd left off. "Reacher could be anywhere in the world after two full days. He could have taken a jet to Australia by now. We're spinning our wheels driving around here on these backroads, going nowhere."

Kim inhaled deeply for patience before she replied, "It seems that way, sure. But I've been on this assignment for seven months. Reacher is not predictable. Nothing has ever turned out to be what we expected going into a new place. This could work. And if it doesn't, at least we're moving instead of staring at the ceiling twiddling our thumbs."

Burke arched his eyebrows and growled, "Do tell."

She glanced through the windshield. There was a stand of trees up ahead. She pointed. "Pull over there."

"Why?" he demanded.

"Call of nature. Too much coffee this morning," she replied.

It was possible that The Boss wasn't listening in real-time to every word they said inside the Navigator. But he recorded every last breath, all the time. If he wasn't listening now, he'd find the discussion later. The only way to have a private conversation was to get away from his surveillance range.

Burke slowed the big SUV and pulled off on the shoulder near the trees. Kim unlocked her seatbelt. She pulled both phones from her pockets and tossed them onto the floor. Then she opened the door and slid onto the gravel. She gestured to Burke to do the same.

He frowned again, but he did as she wanted and followed her toward the trees.

Kim led him to the shady center of the stand of pines. The tall trees and broad branches blocked the sun, which meant it was a little too cool. She buttoned her jacket, turned up her collar, and stuffed her hands into her pockets.

"What the hell are we doing?" Burke said, still grumpy.

"If we can't see him, he may not be able to see us," she explained, like talking to a three-year-old. "If he can't see us at the moment, he might not be able to hear us, either."

"Who the hell are you talking about?"

"Cooper. And keep your voice down."

He looked at her like she'd lost her mind, but he clamped his lips together and didn't say anything more.

"Look, we know Reacher left South Dakota seven years ago and turned up again in Duncan. We know he connected with local residents. We know one of those people is the local doctor."

"How do you know all of that? And what difference does it make now?"

"I've read the police reports from back then," she said, pausing a moment. "And Gaspar found the satellite video from Sunday. It took a while to locate, but he did."

He frowned and might have objected, but annoyance about Gaspar lost to his curiosity and his desire to find Reacher. "What's on the video?"

"If the hitchhiker was Reacher, and we're operating on the assumption that it was, he hitched a ride from Mount Rushmore and headed this way two days ago," Kim said, rushing ahead before Burke could interrupt again. "He knows there's a friendly doctor in Duncan. Maybe he needs medical attention or something. Like you said, jumping out of airplanes isn't the safest thing in the world."

Burke's eyes rounded and his eyebrows shot up. "You've been working directly with Gaspar? We've talked about this. Sharing classified intel with a civilian is a crime, Otto. Are you out of your mind?"

"Probably. You'll come to visit me in Leavenworth, won't you?" she joked.

He wasn't amused.

"We'll talk to these people, find out if Reacher was there in the past few days and where he went, and go after him," she explained patiently.

He cocked his head, unpersuaded.

She inhaled deeply. "Look, it's very likely that The Boss knows what we're doing and why. He watches every move I make. Has for months. He probably knows everything Gaspar told me, too. And he hasn't attempted to stop us."

She paused again and Burke didn't interrupt. "Which probably means he knows we're on the right track."

"If you say so," Burke said sourly, shaking his head.

"Or maybe he doesn't know that at all. In which case, I'm violating orders. I could be fired or worse. So you should exit here and hitch a ride because I'm going to Duncan." Kim's patience had been stretched way too far already. "Unless you've got a better idea. In which case, let's hear it."

He frowned and jerked his head in a sharp no.

"Just as I thought," she smirked. "Look, I can't tell you what we'll find out here in the middle of Nowhere, Nebraska. But I've got a strong feeling about this. It makes sense that Reacher might have gone back there, doesn't it? Hell, he could still be in Duncan right this minute. We're wasting time. Time he could use to slip through our grasp again."

After another moment, Burke stated flatly, "Okay. But if we find a better approach, we're taking it. And I value my career, even if you don't. So leave Gaspar out of this from now on."

Kim simply shook her head. She'd thought it would help to read him in on her plans. But she might have made a mistake.

Burke was the kind of guy who wanted to run his own show. Nothing she decided was likely to make much difference to him.

She'd figured that much out already.

They walked back to the Navigator and rode the next fifty miles in welcome silence until the GPS beeped. "Four miles from the destination," the mechanical voice said.

Two miles beyond the beep, an ambitiously large, weathered sign appeared on the side of the road. She read aloud. "Welcome to Duncan. Population 683."

"Six hundred eighty-three?" Burke snorted. "That's fewer people than my high school graduating class, and I lived in a small town."

"The sign's old. They've probably grown a bit since the last census," Kim replied.

"Yeah? By how many?" Burke grinned. "If nobody died and every female in town had at least two babies, the population would still be less than a thousand."

Duncan came into view up ahead. It was nothing more than a crossroads named after a prominent local family.

Zip codes hadn't been assigned when the post office was built fifty years ago. Like many small towns in America, the post office was a lifeline to the outside world. The place needed a name to put on mailing labels so the postal service could do its job.

Just like that, Duncan, Nebraska, was born.

The land around the crossroads was flat and empty, although Kim noticed a few signs of spring. The snow had melted and green weeds grew along the roadside. A few of the weeds sported jaunty yellow and purple blooms. In the distance, fields had been plowed in preparation for planting.

In a fit of capitalist enthusiasm probably ginned up by the new post office, the crossroads had developed a bit at some point. But the commerce seemed to have dried up before it really got started.

An abandoned gas station stood on one corner. It probably had leaky underground storage tanks that weren't worth the cost of environmental cleanup, so the station would never re-open and the land would most likely never be sold.

Another corner sported a large, poured foundation. Maybe it had been installed for a strip center that was never built. The enthusiasm for shopping had come and gone, too. Now folks probably ordered online and had merchandise delivered by the post office.

The third corner was covered in dust and weeds, plans probably abandoned when the expansion had sputtered and died.

Only one corner showed any signs of life. The whole business district was now the enterprise that had settled on that fourth corner—a retro motel that looked like a 1960s children's comic book depicting a space colony.

There was a large domed main building and smaller round buildings in steadily decreasing sizes leading out from it, all painted silver. The effect resembled a silver apostrophe but was probably intended to simulate perspective.

A late-model Chevy was parked in front of room seven, which suggested that the place was still in business.

The motel's sign sat atop a plywood rocket ship from the same era. Letters that looked like the MICR standard E13B font used to print on the bottom of bank checks since 1963 identified the place as The Apollo Inn.

The real Apollo 11 mission landed on the moon in 1969, and the motel could have been constructed in the same era.

Like everything else in Duncan, the Apollo Inn desperately needed maintenance. The paint was flaked and faded on the buildings, and the pavement in the lot was cracked and buckled and punctuated with potholes deep enough to swallow a toddler.

"We're booked there for the night," Burke dipped his head toward the motel, his lips pursed as if he was sucking on a sour lemon. "I doubt we'll have room service. Maybe not even a decent cup of coffee."

"Sometimes these places surprise you," Kim said. Not because she believed the lie. She just didn't like his superior attitude. "Let's check it out before we go looking for our interview subjects. Given the size of Duncan, the Apollo's owner is likely to know any potential witnesses. We might acquire a bit of useful information before we approach."

Burke turned into the parking lot. "And once we see the inside of the place, we might decide to keep on driving until we find a better rack for the night, too. This place probably has bedbugs."

CHAPTER EIGHT

Tuesday, May 17
Duncan, Nebraska
11:30 a.m.

BURKE PARKED THE NAVIGATOR and they walked into the main building. The sun was shining and the temperature had warmed slightly, but Kim was happy to be wearing her jacket.

Inside, the domed building was mostly open space. There was a pie-shaped slice at the back for restrooms and probably an office. A curved reception desk was close to the front at the right of the door and a larger curved bar was on the opposite side.

The rest was basically a retro lounge, as gaudy as they were back in her grandma's day. A dance floor, red velvet chairs set up in groups of four around cocktail tables with lamps and tasseled shades. The lightbulbs cast a pink glow. The domed roof's concave ceiling was awash with the same red and pink lighting that adorned the walls and the tables.

Kim half expected a Bobby Darin impersonator to emerge from somewhere singing a karaoke version of "Mack the Knife" or "Beyond the Sea." She'd seen a guy like that once when she was in Vegas on the job. The stage where he'd performed was set up something like the Apollo Inn.

There was only one person in the place, a guy behind the bar. He was somewhere north of sixty with a full head of russet hair styled like he'd been electrically shocked as a teenager and never managed to tame his hair again.

When the front door opened, he looked up with a smile as if his goal in life was to be sure every customer who walked into the Apollo Inn was satisfied. Maybe it was.

Kim approached the bar and Burke followed a couple of steps behind.

"What can I get for you?" the bartender asked, still wearing a welcoming smile.

"Got any coffee?" Kim replied, scanning the bar and the rest of the room. Nope. Not another soul in the place.

She wondered how the Apollo Inn stayed in business. The community probably supported the place, but how profitable could that possibly be?

"Let me brew you a fresh pot. How's that?" He was already walking toward the end of the bar where a service station was set up. He filled the Bunn flask, added the coffee, and pushed the button. Before he returned, the aroma of fresh-brewed caffeine filled the air.

"Passing through?" he asked.

"Not exactly. We're staying overnight. We've got business here in Duncan," Burke said.

Bushy eyebrows tinted the same russet color as his hair looked like a terrified caterpillar climbing up his forehead. "What kind of business?"

"I'm Burke. This is Otto. We're assigned to the FBI's

Special Personnel Task Force," Burke said smoothly, showing his ID too quickly for the guy to read it but slowly enough to let him see the badge. "We're completing a background check on a job candidate. He's being considered for a classified assignment."

Kim extended her hand to shake. She put a friendly tone into her voice when she said, "What's your name?"

"Evan Vincent. I'm the owner here." He wiped his hand on a bar towel and took hers. His eyebrows calmed down and slid into a normal position above dark eyes, impossible to read in the pink light. "You called ahead. Reservations for two nights."

"Yes," Burke said. "We may not be here that long. But don't worry. Uncle Sam will pay for both nights, even if we finish up early."

"Sounds good to me." Vincent seemed pleased that he'd have money coming in soon. Kim wondered how often the Apollo Inn had paying overnight guests. Not very, she guessed.

He pulled a pair of ceramic NASA mugs from the shelf and washed them. Then he filled both and slid them across the bar with great pride.

"Cream or sugar?"

"Just black, thanks" Kim replied, leaning into the bar.

Her stomach growled as the coffee teased her appetite. "Do you serve food here?"

"I've got mixed nuts if you'd like that. Otherwise, there's a diner about an hour south of here, closer to town." He found his jar of mixed nuts and poured them into a small bowl and set it in front of her.

"Seems like you'd have a lot of business if you served breakfast and burgers." Kim collected a few nuts with the spoon he'd put in the pewter NASA bowl.

"No restaurants closer off to the west?" Burke asked, tilting his head that way.

Vincent shook his head. "The road goes to gravel after about a mile in both directions. You probably came in from the north, so you know there's not much up there, either."

"Why have a crossroads here if it doesn't lead anywhere?" Burke asked.

Vincent shrugged. "People had high hopes at one time. Everything dried up. Those of us still here got nowhere better to go. No place like home, right?"

Kim swallowed and dusted the salt off her hands before she washed the snack down with the coffee, which was surprisingly good. "No other business in Duncan, then, besides the Apollo Inn?"

"Most folks are farmers. There's a trucking company folks use to move their crops to market after harvest. But that's about it. People eat at home, pretty much," Vincent replied.

"Who owns the trucking company?" Kim asked as if the existence of another business was a surprise. Which it wasn't. The company's sordid history had been included in the police files Gaspar uncovered.

When Reacher was here seven years ago, Duncan Trucking was owned by the Duncan family. Those Duncans ran afoul of Reacher for some reason the police had not uncovered at the time. And they'd failed to survive the experience. She'd assumed some Duncan family members remained in charge of the business.

"Uh, I'm not sure who owns the company now." Vincent squirmed a bit, and sweat beads broke out on his forehead above the caterpillars.

"Was it bought out by some conglomerate or something?"

Burke asked after he'd swilled the last of his coffee and offered the empty cup to Vincent for a refresh.

Vincent seemed grateful for the chance to retrieve the flask. He walked toward the coffee maker and brought the refilled cup back, giving him enough time to come up with his story.

"It's still called Duncan Trucking, but like I said, I'm not sure exactly who owns it now," Vincent said as he busied himself with small tasks.

"Where's the main office?" Burke asked.

"The depot is about twenty miles from here," Vincent replied, clearing his throat to signal a change of subject. "Let me get your room keys and we'll have that done, at least."

Burke cast Kim a questioning glance as they watched Vincent shuffle toward the reception desk, pull keys out of the drawer, and return. He placed the keys on the bar. Rooms five and six, in the middle of the curving line of small, silver pods.

"Who runs the depot if the Duncans don't?" Kim asked, picking up her rocket-shaped key ring with the shiny silver-colored key attached.

"A couple of guys. Thad Brady and Ollie Simpson. Former football players good enough for college but not good enough for pro. Cornhuskers."

Kim cocked her head quizzically.

"University of Nebraska. Duncans always hired Cornhuskers to work at the depot. When the last Duncan, uh, died, the employees, uh, stepped up, I guess." Vincent turned his head and coughed weakly to cover the lies.

"If we head out there now, are we likely to find anyone around?" Burke asked, draining his coffee and plopping the mug onto the bar.

Vincent's face scrunched up again like he was thinking hard

to come up with a plausible reply. He failed. So he said, "You'd probably have more luck early in the morning. That's generally when the shipments roll in and out if they have any. My deliveries come once a week. On Wednesday. That's all I know about the schedule."

"Maybe tomorrow, then." Kim nodded and changed the subject. "We're gathering background information, as Burke said. So we can fill in the blanks on the government forms. You know how it is."

Vincent nodded.

"The guy we're considering stopped in Duncan about seven years ago," Burke said. "He probably stayed here, given this is the only motel around."

Vincent's eyebrows were twitching like crazy now, and his Adam's apple was bouncing up and down, too. Sweat trickled down his temple, and he flipped it away with his right hand.

This was all the confirmation Kim needed that they were on the right track. She'd seen similar reactions before. Reacher had that kind of effect on people, even years later.

Usually it was because they had what her law school professors called guilty knowledge.

Meaning he knew things about Reacher that he didn't want to tell.

Burke said, "We've got four names on our list to interview. All have Duncan mailing addresses. Town this size, you all must know each other. Maybe you can help us out."

Vincent cleared his throat and tried twice before he managed to croak out, "Who are they?"

CHAPTER NINE

Tuesday, May 17
Duncan, Nebraska
11:30 a.m.

"WE'RE LOOKING FOR THE local doctor and his wife. You can't have more than one doc in this place, right?" Burke replied. "And two widows. Dorothy Coe and Eleanor Duncan."

Vincent's breathing had quickened. The dark eyes glanced everywhere but directly at Burke or Kim. His forehead and the russet hair looked like he'd stuck his head under a running faucet. Even his shirt collar was soaked.

"Let's take it one thing at a time," Kim said. "You met Reacher back then, didn't you?"

Vincent nodded like a bobblehead.

"And so did all of the others on our list, right?"

He nodded again.

"While Reacher was here, there was some trouble with the Duncans and their employees. We know all about that. We've seen the police reports," Burke said.

Vincent cleared his throat and swigged water from a glass as if his voice was too parched to speak. Then he managed to croak, "If you know all of that, what are you looking for now?"

"We need to fill in a few more facts. And to know where Reacher went when he left here," Kim said.

Vincent shook his head. "I wasn't the last one to see him before he left town."

"Who was?"

"Dorothy Coe, maybe. She's the one who talked to the police. She probably told them where he went," Vincent said, stumbling over his words as they tumbled out.

"Call her. Ask her to come over here. We'll buy her a coffee," Burke suggested.

"Dorothy died last year. She didn't have any family left. Her husband and daughter died long ago," Vincent said as if it genuinely pained him to relay the news.

He took a swig from his water glass. He staggered a bit and leaned into the back of the bar for support. His behavior suggested the clear liquid in the glass probably wasn't water.

Before she could follow up, Kim felt a cool breeze wafting through the room.

The front door had opened and four burly men tumbled inside, pushing and shoving and trash-talking, punctuated by good-natured guffaws. They were wearing faded red Cornhuskers football jerseys. They had cropped blond hair, small eyes, and round, fleshy pink faces.

Kim's lip curled. Oversized frat boys with thick necks and huge shoulders, way too old to behave like teenagers. Which didn't slow them down any. They seemed to fill up the entire place as they rolled forward, tumbling and stumbling along.

She slid out of the way to avoid being flattened like a ribbon of asphalt.

The leader pushed one of the guys aside and landed a mock punch on another's shoulder as they moved through like the tide. He shouted, "Hey, Vincent! Bring us a round of beers. Hell, bring two rounds. We're celebrating! It's Jimmy's birthday!"

He staggered toward a table at the opposite end of the bar and his buddies waddled along behind him.

Jimmy, the birthday boy, was too drunk to walk. He fell against Burke on his way past, pushing about three hundred pounds of lard into Burke's left side, pinning him briefly against the bar.

Burke grunted and shoved the guy hard in the opposite direction.

"Whoa!" Jimmy staggered and two-stepped and stuck his thick arms out for balance. He managed to right himself without falling flat on his ass.

When he realized he was still upright, he flashed a sloppy grin Burke's way.

"Sorry, buddy. My bad," Jimmy said with a giggle. "No harm, no foul, right?"

Burke gave him a steely stare and growled a warning. "Sure. Don't let it happen again."

The others had managed to plop into chairs, but the leader glanced back in time to see the exchange. He scowled and pushed himself upright and turned to face Burke from across the room.

Hands on hips, his chin pushed forward, he demanded, "What's your problem, pal?"

Vincent hurried out from behind the bar. "Come on, Brady.

Jimmy's fine. It's nothing. I don't want any trouble in here. I'll get your beers. You guys take a seat."

Brady wasn't in the mood to be placated. He had already started tumbling his bulk in Burke's direction. For a big man, he moved with surprising speed and dexterity toward his target.

He fisted his hand and used his arm as a battering ram to knock Vincent off his feet, into the air, and across the room. When he landed hard on the concrete floor, Kim heard a sickening crack, followed by Vincent's wounded yowl.

Vincent displayed an oddly swelling lump about halfway up his forearm. The damage was bad. All the vodka he'd consumed from his water glass must have numbed the nerves because he was able to form a coherent sentence. "What the hell, Brady? You've busted my arm!"

Kim grabbed a bar towel and filled it with ice. She carried it to Vincent and put the ice pack on his forearm. The unmistakably revolting scent of vodka mixed with fear sweat wafted from his body.

"Come on, Vincent," she said, encouraging him to stand up. "Let's get you to a seat and call the doctor. We don't want you going into shock."

She glanced at her new partner, and a look of understanding passed between them.

Trouble in a faded Cornhusker jersey was headed this way.

Brady was all business now. He nodded toward the biggest of his squad. "Simpson, you're with me."

Simpson lifted himself like a whale pushing from the depths of the ocean straight up through to the surface. He had already closed the distance from the table to the bar before his chair finally fell backward and clattered onto the dance floor.

Brady reached across the bar and pulled out a ball-peen

hammer and a long, two-headed wrench as if he knew exactly where to find them. He tossed the wrench to Simpson and gripped the hammer in his left paw.

"Burke," Kim warned from her position on the floor next to Vincent.

Burke nodded and backed away from the bar for room to maneuver.

Kim watched for an opening she could effectively exploit.

Brady and Simpson came within seven feet of Burke's position and then stopped, shoulder to shoulder, weapons in their outer hands.

Burke placed himself directly in front of the two guys. Simpson at eleven o'clock with the wrench and Brady at one o'clock with the hammer.

Simpson moved first. He locked his knees, grunted, and pushed the wrench swiftly backward by bending his elbow. Like his pal, Brady, Simpson was fast for such a huge man.

The force of the heavy metal arced his arm, pulling him slightly off-balance. He prepared to swing forward, intending to break Burke's left arm between the shoulder and the elbow.

A direct strike with that thing would have crippled Burke for life.

"Burke!" Kim shouted a quick warning, which was all she had a chance to do. She pulled her weapon, but she didn't have a clear shot.

Timing was everything.

Simpson was fast for such a big man, but Burke was already moving.

He swung his right foot while the Cornhusker's exposed forearm was on the backswing. Before Simpson could reverse direction to bring the wrench crushing down on Burke's arm,

Burke had kicked forward and smashed the big heel of his boot into Simpson's knee.

The big man dropped the heavy wrench onto the floor with a loud thud, grabbed his ruined knee with both hands, and howled. He went down, landing on his back, rolling on the floor, howling like the hounds of Hell were gnawing his enormous belly.

Burke stepped aside and around Simpson, coming up behind Brady as if he'd practiced the move countless times, and his body operated on pure muscle memory.

He never took his eyes off Brady, who stood holding the hammer, unsure what to do with it.

Brady was still facing forward. He'd had no time to change his stance.

He could try to twist his body around before Burke attacked from behind. Or he could trust his judgment. Seemed like he had minimal confidence in his judgment.

He made the wrong choice.

He flailed the hammer behind him, hoping for a lucky contact. He missed.

Burke planted his feet, and jerked from his waist, and drove his palm into Brady's elbow like a ramrod.

The sound of bone and cartilage dislocating came quick.

The hit was not hard enough to maim Brady forever. But it was hard enough to put him out of commission for a good long while.

Kim scrambled forward along the floor and grabbed the wrench. The damned thing weighed a ton. Even a glancing blow with it that connected in the right spot could do plenty of damage.

She watched the other two Cornhuskers, expecting a second wave, daring them to make a move.

Jimmy seemed rooted to the spot.

The other one, John, wasn't as smart. He displayed a loopy grin before he opened his arms wide and ran at Kim, chest first, eyes bulging, nostrils flared like a charging bull.

Coming straight at her.

She braced her feet, held the wrench firmly, stared straight into his eyes, and waited until she was sure he couldn't stop.

John came closer. Closer. And reached to grab her with both arms as if he could pick her up like a child's toy.

At the very last possible moment, she ducked under his left arm and pushed hard with both feet, harnessing the energy to move to one side, passing swiftly on his left.

Too swiftly for John to react.

He tried to stop his forward momentum and pivot, but he couldn't make all that bulk respond fast enough.

While he was flailing his arms to regain balance, Kim raised the wrench and swung with all her strength like hitting a line drive to center field.

The wrench landed a solid, sickening blow on the back of John's elbow.

He howled like a wounded animal and grabbed the destroyed joint with his right hand, pulling it close to his chest.

Which screwed up his balance. He tripped over his own feet and went down hard.

The left kneecap landed on the concrete and took all his weight. The bones and ligaments in his knee snapped and cracked.

John rolled onto his back on the floor, grabbing his ruined knee with his right hand while his left arm fell uselessly by his side, baying and crying until the pain overwhelmed him.

He passed out and continued to whimper even as he was unconscious.

John's vocals distracted Brady, who glanced away from Burke at precisely the wrong moment.

Burke finished Brady off with a hard fist to the solar plexus, punching air from his lungs. Brady doubled over and dropped onto the floor next to his buddies.

Jimmy was still standing at the end of the bar, mouth open. Kim pulled her weapon, just in case Jimmy was even dumber than she'd given him credit for.

Burke sent her a questioning glance and she nodded, breathing heavily. She was okay. Burke had handled himself as well as any man she'd witnessed, and she'd seen plenty of bar fights.

He could have done more damage. Maimed these good ol' boys for life or simply killed them and ended their interference forever.

But Burke wasn't a barbarian. And he wanted to keep his job.

"How about you?" Burke asked, staring at the last Cornhusker.

When Jimmy shook his head rapidly, Burke's lips turned up slightly at the corner.

Kim holstered her gun and said, "Okay, get your pals out of here. They'll need a hospital. Closest one is about an hour south, I hear. You'd better get going."

Jimmy had sobered up fast.

Kim watched as he struggled to get Brady, Simpson, and John out the door.

Just before he left, Jimmy, who had said almost nothing during the entire encounter, paused to glare at Burke with as much menace as he could muster.

The message was weak but simple enough. "I'll be back."

Burke smiled more broadly. "Yeah, you do that."

When the Cornhuskers got outside, and the door had closed behind them, Burke turned his gaze toward Vincent, the immediate problem.

Kim called Dr. Landon and spoke to him briefly while she checked the ice on Vincent's arm. He said he wouldn't need an X-ray to diagnose the break. The arm was out of commission for a while, for sure.

"He's on his way over," Kim said when she hung up.

Burke replied, "Is he bringing his wife? I'd just as soon get these interviews over with and head out before the Cornhuskers call in reinforcements."

CHAPTER TEN

Tuesday, May 17
Duncan, Nebraska
1:45 p.m.

WHILE THEY WAITED FOR the doctor, Kim tried interviewing Vincent. Partly to keep his mind off the arm and partly because his pain might keep his answers honest. His skin was clammy and his breathing rapid. He was still slightly intoxicated, too. Otherwise, he seemed in control of his mental state.

"Tell me about Dorothy Coe," Kim said. "She worked as a maid in the motel, didn't she?"

Vincent nodded and winced, changing the position of the ice pack over the growing lump on the top of his forearm. "She did for a while, yeah."

"She worked here when Reacher was in town, though."

"Dorothy and her husband," Vincent winced and readjusted the ice pack. "When their daughter disappeared, all the joy disappeared with their little girl."

"Did Reacher know about that?"

"Dorothy had a really hard time." Vincent shook his head and blotted the sweat from his forehead with his sleeve. "Reacher helped her, uh, deal with the loss. But after that, she didn't seem to have a purpose anymore. Long before she had the stroke that killed her, Doc Landon said her spirit had died of a broken heart years ago."

"A lot of people died while Reacher was here. The police report said ten dead and at least six seriously injured. A few locals, mostly all named Duncan, and some guys from out of town," Burke said. "What do you know about that?"

"It was a long time ago." Vincent shrugged, which jarred his arm, and he winced again. Burke waited and Vincent filled the silence. "Seems like the Duncans had a business deal go bad. Not sure exactly what it was all about. I try to keep my head down, you know? Stay out of trouble."

"And Dorothy Coe? Did she keep her head down and stay out of trouble?" Kim asked.

"Wish she had. Dorothy didn't deserve what happened to her." Vincent shook his head slowly. "Look, some pretty bad dudes came into town, looking for the Duncans. They all went at each other for a while. Dorothy and a few others got caught in the middle."

"Including Reacher?" Burke asked. "Did he get caught in the middle? Or was he more proactive?"

"Kinda both, I guess. He didn't start the trouble. But when the smoke cleared, the only Duncan left standing was Eleanor, and she wouldn't have survived without Reacher." Vincent glanced toward the door as if he was willing the doctor to materialize. "So if you're looking for a guy to complain about Reacher, you've come to the wrong place. Far as I'm concerned, he done us all a public service."

Burke frowned and narrowed his gaze toward Vincent. "Seems like a lot of violence for a dispute between a rural trucking company and its customers, doesn't it? What exactly were they hauling, anyway? Drugs?"

Vincent closed his eyes and slumped into his chair as if the story was too much to tell.

"When was the last time you saw Reacher?" Kim asked, following her hunch. If Reacher came back here two days ago, Vincent might admit it, considering the state he was in.

He moaned and closed his eyes. The glass door opened and an average-sized man ambled in. He was carrying an old-fashioned doctor's bag in his left hand like the kind Kim used to see on television shows when she was a kid.

She would've guessed his age at about fifty, give or take five years. He was wearing a threadbare tweed sport coat with frayed leather patches on the elbows. He peered into the pink-washed interior, spied them in the bar, and made a wavy line for Vincent.

"Dr. Ezra Landon?" Kim asked as he approached. "I'm the one who called. We had a little trouble here with a couple of drunks, and Vincent seems to have suffered the worst of the damage."

"Hey, Doc," Vincent said sheepishly.

Kim and Burke stood aside. Landon approached Vincent, setting his bag on the floor. "Show me the problem."

Vincent removed the ice and the towel and displayed the lump on his forearm. Landon prodded and examined the injury while his patient winced and moaned. After a few minutes of checking vital signs and the like, Landon looked up into Vincent's distressed face.

"It feels like you may need surgery. Can't say for sure without some imaging. I'll wrap the arm to try to keep the swelling down. But we need to get you to a specialist at the hospital if you want to keep full use of your hand and arm," Landon said, looking into his bag for an elastic bandage. "Brenda can drive us. We can lock up until you get back."

"How long will I be gone?" Vincent asked. "These folks have reservations for two nights. There's nowhere else for them to sleep."

"Depends on when they can do the surgery. Couple of days at the most, I'd guess," Landon replied. He'd finished the elastic wrap. He grabbed his cell phone and speed-dialed his wife.

Kim said, "Don't worry about us, Vincent. We'll be okay here on our own. You already gave us our keys. We'll leave them in the rooms when we check out."

Vincent nodded. With his arm in the elastic bandage, he was able to move around. He staggered slightly on his way toward his rooms in the back. "I need to pack a bag. Not sure I can do it with one arm."

Kim tilted her head toward Burke, who followed, saying, "I'll give you a hand."

When Landon finished his call, he dropped the phone into his pocket. "Thanks for helping Vincent. Good of you to stay, too. He can use the revenue."

Kim nodded. "Actually, we were on our way to talk to you anyway. Do you have a minute?"

He cocked his head. "Me? What about?"

She showed her badge wallet. "We're looking to fill in some missing background on a job candidate. Guy's name is Jack Reacher. You know him, don't you?"

Landon's face blanched. He cleared his throat and glanced around the bar as if he'd mislaid something. "I wouldn't say I know him, exactly."

The way he answered the question sounded odd. "How would you describe your relationship?"

He looked away from her steady gaze. "Doctor-patient, I guess. What kind of background are you looking for?"

Kim's heartbeat quickened. "When did you see him last?"

Landon loosened his shirt collar as if it was too tight all of a sudden. "A few days ago, I guess."

"Reacher was here two days ago?"

Landon nodded and frowned. "I thought that's why you came."

"You said your relationship was doctor-patient. Was he injured?"

"I can't talk about my patients," Landon said. "Privilege and privacy and all that, you know."

"I can get a court order if you like," Kim replied, even though she knew for sure that she couldn't. The Boss would never allow it. "If it was something so serious or sensitive that you feel like you need to cover your ass."

He considered things for a second before he shrugged. "Nothing like that. Hairline fractures of a couple of small bones in his left wrist. He fell on it pretty hard, he said. He let me cast it up."

"Was it a bad break?"

He shook his head. "It would have healed on its own. They don't even treat fractures like that in Europe. It's mildly painful. Sometimes it doesn't heal well and the wrist can be deformed. Which he didn't seem to care about. I really had to talk him into the cast. So no, nothing so serious or sensitive that I'd need a court order to cover my professional lapses."

"Is he here now?"

Landon shook his head. "Headed to Denver."

"Why Denver?" Kim asked. "Is he still there? And do you have an address?"

Landon lowered his head and stared at the carpet for a few seconds. Vincent and Burke walked toward them, Burke carrying a small duffle bag in one hand. Two quick beeps from a car horn sounded in the parking lot out front.

"That'll be Brenda," Landon said. "You ready to go, Vincent?"

"I'm as ready as I'm going to get," he replied, taking the duffle from Burke and giving him a brief grin. "Thanks for your help."

"Hold on a second," Kim said, grabbing Landon's arm. "Why was Reacher on his way to Denver?"

Vincent's eyes widened and he began to cough uncontrollably. Landon patted him firmly on the back with the flat of his hand until he finally stopped.

"We need to go. The hospital's more than an hour's drive from here," Landon said, moving Vincent toward the door with a firm hand on his bicep.

Kim attempted to delay them briefly. "As I said before, I can get a court order. Or we can take you in for formal questioning if you'd prefer."

Empty threats. The doctor might have known as much.

"It's a long story." Landon sighed as if he'd always known the day would come when he'd be required to answer questions about Reacher. "Once I get Vincent settled, we can talk. There's nowhere to get a meal around here and my wife's a good cook. We'll feed you dinner. How's that?"

Vincent started another round of coughing and a worried look crossed Landon's features. He didn't wait for Kim to answer his question. He pushed Vincent out the door and into the Chevy SUV waiting out front.

"I'll call you from the road when I'm headed back," he said, just before he climbed into the passenger seat and closed the door.

CHAPTER ELEVEN

Tuesday, May 17
Denver, Colorado
3:00 p.m.

SYDNEY BEGAN WATCHING THE restaurant as soon as he'd rolled into town. Slumped into the driver's seat of the green SUV, window cracked for ventilation, engine off, he had an unobstructed view of the main entrance.

He'd had little sleep, but he wanted to get the lay of the land before he checked into a hotel. Sydney was a nocturnal animal, but he preferred to complete extensive recon before he approached any target. Recon was easier in daylight, which was another good reason to do it first.

This assignment required more finesse than his bread-and-butter enemy assassinations. He'd be exposed to the target instead of hidden in the shadows. Which meant he could be identified. Theoretically, anyway.

From his vantage point now, he could see Orchid Thai Bistro's posted hours of operation for lunch and dinner.

Business men and women in groups of two and four had stalked in looking hungry and sauntered out wearing satisfied smiles.

The parking lot had filled and then emptied as the lunch service ended, but a few diners still lingered inside.

Dinner service was scheduled to begin two hours after the lunch service. Sydney would take a break from his surveillance during the bistro's downtime.

Rossi had collected more information about the woman. She was called Jade now. He provided photos and a background check. He traced her contacts, which had led Sydney to the bistro.

A skeletal plan had begun to form in his mind as he reviewed the photos.

He'd been told that his target often strolled over for dinner before her business activity picked up at night. She'd even lived here above the Bistro for a while. Her bond with these women had been forged hard as steel by shared experiences, good and bad. Bonds like that were hard to break. The bistro's dinner hour was as good a place as any to begin.

He might simply abduct Jade while she was out in the open if she showed up tonight. He could scoop her up and toss her into the SUV without breaking a sweat. She probably didn't weigh a hundred pounds, fully dressed and soaking wet.

But she'd put up a fight, and Rossi was adamant that she should not be harmed.

Rossi's order left persuasion as Sydney's only available weapon. Unless she refused to cooperate, and Rossi would authorize force.

Rossi was a blunt instrument. Effective and brutal. Working for him was generally a simple matter of applying the right amount of force against weak resistance until the target was destroyed. Which Sydney greatly preferred.

Like many Asian women, Jade was a fragile thing. Even in the photos, her bones seemed visible beneath the translucent skin that barely concealed them. Straight black hair tumbled down her back like a midnight waterfall, easy to grab. Subduing her should be simple enough.

Many men found Jade enchanting.

Sydney did not.

She was a target.

Eliminating her would be one of the easiest kills ever.

Too bad he wasn't authorized to do it. Yet.

The point was simply to send the message Rossi wanted delivered, which should persuade her to come along peaceably. Simply put, Sydney's job was to be sure Jade understood that she and everything she owned belonged to Rossi. Rossi expected no resistance, but Sydney was a careful man.

He studied the restaurant's structure carefully. Orchid Thai bistro was located in a busy neighborhood closer to Golden than downtown Denver. The three-story building was relatively new and had been specifically constructed to house the bistro. The spacious parking lot suggested a prosperous enterprise often filled to capacity.

The owner and the employees lived in apartments above the restaurant. That was the good news. It meant he could handle several problems with one bold solution, which was his preferred method of operation.

He made a mental checklist.

Tonight, he'd come back for a personal look at the bistro's interior and to observe the woman.

He'd gather the equipment and tools he'd need to complete the first phase of the job.

Then, he'd execute.

CHAPTER TWELVE

Tuesday, May 17
Duncan, Nebraska
6:30 p.m.

THE NAVIGATOR'S GPS ROUTE located the home of Doctor
Ezra Landon and his wife, Brenda, south of the Apollo Inn.
Which wasn't surprising. Seemed like everything in Nebraska
was south of the crossroads that led east and west to nowhere.

The land between any two points was flat and infinite on all
sides. Cornfields. Acres of them. They had seen more cornfields
today than either had seen in their lifetimes before.

Burke drove past a cluster of three burned-out homes set
close together at the end of a long, shared driveway. The charred
houses were surrounded by the remains of a sturdy post-and-rail
fence that had once created some sort of compound.

Kim made a mental note to ask about the owners, simply to
confirm that each house had been owned by a Duncan.

"Looks like country living isn't all that great when your
neighbor has a house fire," Burke said sardonically. "We've

been driving all over this area today and haven't seen a fire department or a hydrant or even a lake. Once a fire gets started, no way to put it out."

"Yea, no kitchen fire extinguisher would do the job," Kim replied.

Burke turned right and left and right again along the boundaries of yet another cornfield until they reached a newer ranch-style house set on a couple more flat acres. The GPS announced they'd arrived at the destination.

Kim spied a satellite dish on the roof and the nearest neighbor was more than a mile away.

The doctor and his wife were not gardeners. There were no bushes, no flower beds, no hedges. Nothing but grass all the way around, set apart from the road by another post-and-rail fence, this one intact and painted white to match the house.

Burke parked the Navigator behind the Chevy in the driveway. Kim unbuckled her seatbelt and slid down onto the concrete. She'd been riding most of the day and her body felt tighter than a bow string. She reached her arms up like a cat and then bent over at the waist to stretch her hamstrings.

"You about done with the gymnastics over there?" Burke asked, closing his door.

"I hope the doctor's wife is a good cook. I'm starving," Kim said as she walked past him to the sidewalk and up to the front door. It had a peep hole, which seemed more than a little odd. Whatever animals roamed the fields were not likely to ring the bell.

"We saw that steakhouse about thirty miles south. It's probably open for dinner and maybe even some line dancing," Burke suggested, in a somewhat snarky tone.

"Who knew you could line dance?" Kim replied as she rang the bell and stepped back from the door.

The doctor and his wife must have been in the back of the house because it took longer than it should have for the door knob to turn and the door to swing back slowly.

"Come in," Dr. Landon stood aside, one hand on the door knob and the other holding a cut crystal glass about a third full of brown whiskey, no ice. He closed the door behind Burke and led them along the hardwood floor. "My wife's in the kitchen. This way."

The narrow hallway resolved into a big open floorplan that ran across the back of the house. The kitchen was on one side and a sitting room on the other. The dining table was placed between them and already set for dinner. An appetizing aroma wafted from the oven, causing Burke's stomach to growl.

A woman close to fifty, small, dark, and worried, extended her hand to each of them. "I'm Brenda Landon. Nice to meet you. Dinner will be ready soon. Ezra, get them a drink, please."

"Sure. This way," the doctor said, pointing his head toward a couple of empty chairs in the sitting room. He collected the drink orders, and his wife passed a tray of Stilton cheese and flatbread garnished with spicy chutney while the doctor delivered the glasses.

Once the hosting duties were completed, both Landons perched and conversation stalled, drifting into an unproductive silence.

Kim filled the gap. "How did things go with Vincent at the hospital?"

"He'll be okay," Landon replied, his words only slightly slurred by the alcohol. He was an experienced drinker, that much was certain. "They'll do the surgery in the morning, and he'll probably be released tomorrow afternoon."

"How did you know his arm would need surgery without an X-ray?" Burke asked, sipping beer to wash down the cracker.

"I treated lots of broken bones when I was in the army," Landon shrugged. "You get a feel for how serious things are, what needs surgery when you can just cast it up and move on."

Kim cocked her head. "And in this case…"

"Pretty obvious the break was severe enough to require surgery if you know what to look for," Landon nodded, drained his glass, and walked to the sideboard for a refill.

Burke said, "We drove by Dorothy Coe's place today. It looks abandoned."

Brenda Landon nodded, a sad expression on her face. "Dorothy and Artie only had the one daughter, Margaret. After she disappeared, Artie sort of gave up, leaving Dorothy on her own. As she got older, things got tougher for her. The only thing that kept her going was the hope that Margaret would come back some day…"

Her voice drifted off and the doctor chimed in. "Eleanor Duncan bought the place, paid the debts, and gave Dorothy a life estate a while back. Then Dorothy died and the fields have lain fallow."

Brenda finished up the little tale. "Somebody will buy the property someday, maybe."

"What about you? Don't you want more land?" Kim asked.

Landon shook his head. "I never wanted to be a farmer, and Brenda has about all the land she cares to manage."

"What about Eleanor Duncan?" Burke asked. "Why doesn't she plant corn there now that Dorothy's gone?"

Brenda and Ezra exchanged glances before Brenda cleared her throat and replied. "Eleanor left farming behind when she moved. She doesn't plan to come back."

"Where did she go?" Kim asked, but she thought maybe she knew the answer to that one already.

A timer began to chime from the oven. Brenda stood up and hurried to finish the meal, leaving the conversation to her husband to manage.

"We've read the police files from seven years ago," Kim said.

Landon nodded. "So you know what happened back then. Why are you raking all of this up again now?"

"We're trying to find Reacher," Burke said.

Landon bristled. "You said you were looking for background on the guy, not conducting a manhunt. Why did you lie to me?"

"Oh, come on. You're a smart guy. No point to gathering background intel unless we're looking to find him," Burke shot back.

Kim directed a swift frown in Burke's direction to get him to back off. "Dorothy Coe told police that Reacher was responsible for the deaths that happened here seven years ago, which is consistent with what we would expect. But the final police report ended at the point where Reacher left town. It doesn't mention what happened afterward."

Landon shook his head. "Why would it? When Reacher left, all the trouble ended. That's all we cared about. Reacher wasn't our problem. But apparently, he is yours."

"Right. And we're trying to follow up on that," Kim said.

Burke added, still annoyed. "Which is why we want to know what happened when Reacher came back here two days ago."

Landon jutted his chin forward and glared.

Kim intervened. "You said Reacher left for Denver. Did he go to find Eleanor Duncan?"

Landon's eyes narrowed. He jerked his head to one side.

"Reacher was injured a couple of days ago in South Dakota. He came here and you helped him out," Kim said reasonably.

When Landon didn't reply, she pressed again. "We're going to need the whole story. We'll stay here until we get it. All night, if we have to."

"The whole story? I don't know the whole story," Landon stood on wobbly legs, still holding onto the high ball glass. He stopped at the bar for a refill before leading them toward the table. "Bottom line? If I were you and I wanted a guy who could get things done, I'd hire Reacher. Question for you is, would he take the job?"

"Dinner's ready," Brenda called from the kitchen.

"You're saying Eleanor Duncan hired Reacher because she's in trouble and needs to get things done?" Burke asked.

Landon cocked his head and gave Burke a long stare before he shrugged and said, "Not exactly."

CHAPTER THIRTEEN

Tuesday, May 17
Denver, Colorado
7:30 p.m.

SYDNEY HAD CHECKED INTO his hotel and grabbed a couple of hours of sleep before heading to an internet café. Half an hour later, he'd completed the online research of the county building records.

Orchid Thai Bistro had originally been designed for a steakhouse chain by a licensed architect who took his permitting responsibilities seriously. Which meant that full blueprints were accessible in the database.

The original building was planned as a free-standing, three-story, multi-use building. The building was surrounded by a spacious flat parking lot. The steakhouse was planned to occupy the main floor. Residential condos filled the two floors above.

Looked like the construction hit a financing snag when the building was near completion. The original owner went bankrupt.

The building remained uncompleted for a while. Until it was purchased by a new owner and redesigned. The new owner had abandoned the plan to sell condos on the residential floors. The second-floor rooms were converted to apartments for the restaurant's employees. The new owner's apartment occupied the top floor.

The building was finished about six months later, and Orchid Thai Bistro opened successfully right from the start.

Sydney had ordered a second cup of coffee to drink while he researched the bistro's owner. She had moved to Denver to open a Thai restaurant and was lucky to find the bankrupt property in Golden, the article in the local newspaper reported.

The attached photo depicted a woman with black hair and pale skin. She had good bone structure and pretty eyes. She was slim and fairly tall, compared to the Thai women gathered around her in the photograph.

The caption under the photo identified the owner as Eleanor Duncan. Sydney had heard the name before, but the context was a little foggy in his memory. But he was starting to put the pieces together.

One of the Thai women in the photo was his target, Jade. Younger and less worldly in the old photo, but unmistakable. Long dark hair tucked behind small ears fell down her back. Her outfit was a traditional Thai dress in red and gold with bright red lipstick, meant to be a sort of costume to help sell the bistro's ambiance, Sydney guessed.

He copied the photo to his phone and did a quick search for Eleanor Duncan. He found a few local news reports about her work at the restaurant and involvement in local groups, but nothing more.

Eleanor Duncan was not relevant to Sydney's assignment as

far as he knew. He'd ask Rossi when he reported back after the task at hand was completed.

Sydney shut down his research session. He paid his bill and headed out to the SUV.

Orchid Thai Bistro was a ten-minute drive from the café. The dinner service was in full swing and the parking lot was full, with vehicles waiting in the driveway for slots to open up. The place was popular, for sure.

Sydney drove around to the back of the building.

A line of eight residential-sized parking garages faced each other near the property line. Each garage was large enough to accommodate two cars. Sixteen vehicles. The garages were numbered to match the eight apartments upstairs. The residents had a private driveway off the alley.

Closer to the back entrance of the building, near the kitchen, was a three-sided enclosure surrounding a cluster of dumpsters.

He continued his circuit around the building and noticed a vehicle reversing from its space in the front lot. He turned on his signal and waited for the sedan to leave.

From this vantage point, he could see the front of the Bistro, but his view was obscured by parked vehicles and pedestrians walking through the doors. Orchid Thai Bistro was a busy and prosperous place, even on a Tuesday night.

Two men climbed out of a late model Audi SUV near the north end of the parking lot. Illuminated by bright halogen bulbs atop the light poles, the vehicle appeared to be pale ivory, but it was probably white.

Something about the two men seemed odd. Sydney raised his phone and snapped several photos of the pair.

The passenger could have been one of Rossi's bouncers. He weighed about two-fifty, maybe six foot four. His hair was fair and closely cropped as if his barber was the U.S. Army. He pushed the SUV's door closed awkwardly, using his left hand, which was the size of a frozen turkey.

His companion was a smaller, wiry guy sporting a longish blond mop in disarray around his head and a good-humored expression.

Maybe they were just a couple of hungry Thai foodies. But years of training in the art of observing every nuance when his life might depend on it had hard-wired Sydney's lizard brain to signal visceral danger before he actually recognized it.

The little guy did all the talking. The big man didn't say two words all the way along the sidewalk to the Bistro's entrance. Perhaps the big guy was the muscle, hired to protect the little dude. Sydney had run into that dynamic before.

The big man reached out with his right hand and curled his fingers around the handle, thumb up, to open the entrance door. His shirt sleeve was rolled up, and a thick white sleeve covered his forearm from below the elbow all the way to his brawny knuckles. Sydney only saw the flash of white for a brief moment, but it looked like a hard plaster cast.

The little guy slipped inside and the big guy followed, letting the door swing closed behind them. Which meant the bodyguard hypothesis was a bust. If the big guy was hired for protection, he'd have entered the place first to assure there were no active threats to the client inside.

Sydney waited a bit longer, watching patrons come and go. He noted the time when three different groups entered and again when they returned to their vehicles, sated and happy. The bistro's dinner rhythm seemed to turn over the tables every hour, give or take.

Two hours had passed, but the big guy and his sidekick

didn't emerge. Which meant there was more to them than a couple of guys looking for a good meal.

The visceral response Sydney had experienced earlier returned. His stomach tightened. Something about the pair was definitely off.

The constant parade of diners had not slowed and he couldn't wait any longer. He had a schedule to keep.

Sydney stepped out of his SUV and walked to the entrance.

Coming directly toward him from the opposite direction along the sidewalk was Jade, arm-in-arm with Eleanor Duncan.

Sometimes, you get lucky.

He held the door open calmly as if he had no idea who they were.

As they walked through, Eleanor Duncan looked into his eyes and said, "Thank you."

"No problem," Sydney replied and followed them inside.

CHAPTER FOURTEEN

Tuesday, May 17
Duncan, Nebraska
8:00 p.m.

BRENDA LANDON'S MEAL WAS excellent, which wasn't surprising. Kim had been smelling the delicious aromas emanating from the oven since she and Burke first stepped into the house. The food was passed quietly as they filled their plates. The doctor ate very little and continued drinking, as seemed to be his habit.

"Are you staying at the Apollo Inn tonight?" Brenda asked about halfway through dinner.

"No," Kim replied, ignoring Burke's raised eyebrows. "We'll be heading to Denver."

"Tonight?" the doctor said as if she'd suggested a quick trip to Mars. "You got enough gas? You're not likely to find an open gas station until you reach the interstate."

Kim swallowed her last bite before she replied, "We'll be okay. It's a five-hour drive, right? Straight down U.S. 385?"

Landon shrugged. "If you get lucky and don't run into any trouble. It'll be pitch black out there, all the way south to Interstate 76. Which will take you into Denver. You'll have a chance of finding civilization once you hit 76. Gas. Food. Stuff like that."

"Why are you in such a rush?" Brenda asked. "It would be safer to sleep at the Apollo tonight and head out early in the morning, wouldn't it? You've had a long day."

"Maybe. But we can't wait," Kim replied. "We'll sleep on the way."

She couldn't say exactly why she felt the urgency. Perhaps because she was closer to finding Reacher than she'd been before. She wouldn't let him slip through her grasp again. Not for a night's sleep at the Apollo Inn, as uninteresting as that might prove to be.

Burke shook his head, but he didn't argue. How could he? He'd been hounding her about going after Reacher faster than they'd been allowed, and now she'd agreed. For once, he had nothing to complain about.

He cleared his throat, "Tell me again where we can find Eleanor Duncan in Denver."

"She owns a restaurant. Orchid Thai Bistro. It's actually in Golden, which is about twenty-five miles farther west," Landon said, pushing the green beans around on his plate with his fork. "You can look it up online."

"Where does she live?" Kim asked.

"Same address," Brenda said. "Eleanor owns the building. Restaurant's on the first floor. Her apartment is on the third floor."

"And what's on the second floor?" Burke asked as he ate his last bite of potatoes.

Brenda and her husband exchanged uncomfortable glances. "It's housing for the restaurant's workers. Single women. No men. If they get married, they move out."

Kim cocked her head. "That's a little odd, isn't it? Why doesn't Eleanor employ any men?"

Dr. Landon shrugged. "Doesn't need any, I guess."

Brenda frowned. "Eleanor doesn't have much affection for men anymore."

"You mean she's a lesbian," Burke said matter-of-factly. "Is that a problem around here?"

"It's not that." Landon shook his head.

Kim cocked her head and narrowed her gaze. The picture was starting to come into focus.

At first she'd wondered whether Eleanor Duncan had been one of Reacher's affairs.

Reacher preferred warriors. Strong women. Law enforcement or military, usually.

Which Gaspar insisted was the reason The Boss had assigned Kim to Reacher's case, because he thought she was tempting bait.

An army psychiatrist had speculated that Reacher's preference for fighters probably had something to do with his mother, Josephine. She'd been active in the French resistance, once upon a time. Reacher had been as unusually close to her as he was distant from his father, Stan.

Kim wasn't persuaded by the usual Freudian mumbo jumbo. Could have been Reacher's mother was the source of his sexual preferences. Or it could have been something else entirely.

"What's Eleanor's problem with men, then? Exactly." Burke pressed.

"Her husband beat her," Landon replied quietly, eyes staring down at the table, as if he was embarrassed to say. Then he looked up and stared straight ahead. "When she got free of him, she swore off men forever. Who could blame her?"

Kim arched her eyebrows and filed this new intel away with everything else she knew about her quarry.

The same army psychiatrist had said Reacher's feelings about crime victims were even more complicated than his relationship with his family. Reacher said he wasn't so much fighting for the little guy as fighting against the big guy. The definitions for these categories seemed somewhat fluid to him.

What it came down to in Kim's mind was that Reacher did what he wanted, when he wanted. As simple and unpredictable as that.

Kim spent a few moments rearranging the puzzle pieces in her head. "So Reacher killed Eleanor's husband, right?"

The doctor and his wife said nothing, but Burke's ears pricked up. He cocked his head like a watchdog who heard a strange noise in the junkyard. He didn't intend to miss anything.

"We've seen the police reports. They say a spree killer came through here seven years ago. Eleven bodies were found. Seth Duncan, Eleanor's husband, was one of the dead. Coroner said his body looked like it had been hit by a truck." Kim assumed none of this was news to either the doctor or his wife. Duncan, Nebraska, was a place where everybody knew everybody's business. "When the police interviewed Dorothy Coe, she said Reacher killed them all. Was that true?"

Landon shrugged. Brenda ate another bite of potatoes and chewed them way too long.

After a few moments of silence, Burke cleared his throat. "Tell you what I think. Reacher was a convenient scapegoat."

Brenda's eyes bulged. The doctor looked down at his plate.

"The real killer was Eleanor Duncan. Seth pushed her too far, and she wigged out and ran him over with his own truck. Battered wife syndrome. Totally understandable," Burke continued. "Sometimes, a jury will go for that idea, too. We bring Eleanor in, and she gets tried. Maybe she'll get off. Who knows?"

"Are you crazy?" Landon exclaimed as he choked on his whiskey, and Brenda spewed her mouthful of potatoes across the table. "Eleanor didn't kill anybody. She's not like that. Not at all. She's the exact opposite of a killer."

"But she had good reasons to kill Seth, didn't she?" Kim asked, now that Burke had broken through the silence. "He was a wife-beater. His father and his uncles were no better. I'm guessing one of them killed Dorothy Coe's daughter, too, didn't they?"

Burke said, "What happened? Reacher protected Eleanor and her husband didn't like it? So he took a shot at Reacher and Reacher killed him. The husband's family joined in and pretty soon, there was a small war going on?"

Brenda took a long swig of water and got herself under control. "Why are you digging all this up now? It was a long time ago. The files were closed. Dorothy's dead. Everybody involved is dead. Reacher's gone. Eleanor's gone. How can this ancient history possibly matter?"

"Good question. You tell me." Kim leaned in. "Reacher came here again on Sunday. Doc fixed up his broken wrist. Then he left for Denver, looking for Eleanor Duncan. If the ancient history is irrelevant like you say, then what new facts should we know about?"

Brenda paused, perhaps waiting for her husband to jump in. But he didn't. So she said, "Because we told him Eleanor was in trouble. He helped her before. We thought he might be able to help her again."

"You've got to be kidding." Burke's astonished face was almost comical. "Reacher went to Denver to *rescue* Eleanor Duncan? Why would anyone believe that?"

"Doesn't matter whether you believe it or not." Dr. Landon shrugged again. "That's what happened."

"Okay. Good to know." Kim nodded, sending a glare toward Burke to keep him quiet until she could tease out the truth. "How did Reacher get here? To Duncan. It's not like there's a bus stop or anything."

"He hitched a ride. Petey Burns picked him up near Mount Rushmore," Brenda said. "Drove him to Denver, too, I imagine. Petey said he didn't have anything better to do. And he had a car. Which Reacher didn't have."

Burke shook his head as if he couldn't believe his luck. He pulled out his phone and flipped quickly through the photos until he found the one he was looking for.

He held the screen up. "Is this Petey Burns?"

Landon nodded. "Why do you have his photo?"

"We've been looking for him, too. He escaped from Bolton prison in South Dakota last week," Burke said. "What kind of vehicle were they driving?"

"Petey? In prison? But he's so sweet." Brenda looked completely miserable now. As if she'd squealed on a close friend.

"Yeah, well, he's a very good car thief, as it happens." Burke scowled at her. "What kind of vehicle?"

"A white Audi SUV. It looked fairly new. Petey was talking about how he likes to drive German luxury cars," Dr. Landon said as he drained his glass again. "He didn't mention exactly how he, uh, acquired the Audi."

"One last thing," Kim pushed back from the table. "Exactly what kind of trouble is Eleanor Duncan in now? And why do you think Reacher can help?"

Dr. Landon cleared his throat. "Like I said. I imagine there's very little trouble Reacher can't fix."

CHAPTER FIFTEEN

Tuesday, May 17
Denver, Colorado
8:30 p.m.

SYDNEY WATCHED AS ELEANOR Duncan and Jade walked straight past the hostess stand, deeper into the dimly lit interior. The bistro was one large room decorated in some designer's idea of traditional Thai style.

He had never been to Thailand, but he'd visited many Thai restaurants. The décor was always similar. Red, gold, and dark wood. Carpet on the floors and dim light for ambiance, he supposed.

The hostess was a young Thai woman, wearing a long pink and gold costume similar to the ones he'd seen in the old photos. Sydney guessed she was about sixteen and cute as anything. He saw two other girls about the same age, dressed similarly and bussing tables. It was refreshing to see teens with jobs for a change instead of standing around waiting for an allowance.

"Dinner for one?" the hostess asked politely, with a smile.

When he nodded, she collected a menu and politely gestured, "Right this way, sir."

He followed her to a small table for two in a dimly lit back corner. The spot felt like a location for a romantic date but suited his need to be inconspicuous.

He sat with his back to the wall, facing the room. She left the menu with another smile and a nod before she pressed her palms together and bowed her head slightly. He assumed the gesture was a Thai greeting and sign of respect.

She returned to her station, back ramrod straight, moving with the grace of a tiny ballerina.

Sydney glanced around the room to get a better feel for the place. He'd studied the blueprints, so he knew the basic layout. The big dining room consumed most of the space on the first floor. A short corridor led to restrooms and the kitchen across the back.

A small bar area was set up across from his table on the opposite wall. Four empty bar stools had been supplied for patrons. Another smiling Thai woman was behind the bar preparing drinks that were picked up by servers and delivered to diners.

The servers were all young Thai women. Sydney had begun to wonder whether there were any men working at Orchid Bistro. So far, he'd seen none. Which was just fine with him.

Diners of all sorts continued to come and go. Tables turned over at the steady pace he'd noticed before as the servers scurried to and from the kitchen.

A four-top across the room caught his attention. It was occupied by the pair he'd seen outside. If the big dude and the little guy had eaten, the table had already been cleared. Nothing cluttered the table top now.

The giant sat in the shadows with his back to the wall,

detached but watching. The little blond guy occupied the chair next to him. From the body language, Sydney guessed they were not a couple. They behaved as if they barely knew each other. They exchanged no conversation. The big guy watched the room. The little dude fidgeted like he wanted nothing more than to leave. Thirty minutes ago.

Sydney saw that the little guy wasn't actually as small as he seemed.

One of the tiny Thai women approached the table with a round tray and two steaming coffee mugs. By comparison, the smaller guy was average-sized. Maybe about five-ten and one-sixty. Clean-shaven, shaggy hair, and a generous smile. He flirted with his server.

She looked down at the floor and blushed as she delivered the coffee. Which Sydney took to mean she found Mr. Average appealing and inoffensive. But she was careful not to approach the bigger man as if she feared him.

Sydney tucked his observations away for future reference.

Next to the petite waitress, the big guy looked like a giant. He could have crushed her fragile bones with one hand. Perhaps to avoid frightening her, he kept both hands visible on the table. From Sydney's vantage point across the room, the cast on the giant's right forearm was clearly visible.

Experience suggested a monstrous blow delivered with speed and heft had been required to fracture the giant's thick bones. Sydney shrugged. Maybe the big dude was clumsy and fell on top of his own arm.

The waitress pressed her palms together and bowed her head slightly before she departed. Sydney had seen the gesture repeated by several employees. Probably meant to foster the Thai ambiance.

The two men sat silently, sipping coffee. The big one scanned the room, watching everything that moved. Whatever he was looking for, he didn't seem to find it.

Sydney lifted his menu to obscure his face from the giant's line of sight. His server, another young Thai woman, came and took his order for Yum beef, Pad Thai, and pineapple fried rice. He was a big eater and Asian cuisine didn't stick around in his stomach very long.

She bowed and promised the food would arrive shortly before she hurried away again.

While he was occupied with ordering his meal, Eleanor Duncan had approached the giant's table. She smiled and spoke words Sydney couldn't hear across the distance.

She shook hands with the little guy as if meeting him for the first time.

And then she pulled out a chair and sat opposite the giant, still wearing the smile. Whatever had frightened the waitress about the big man didn't seem to faze Eleanor Duncan.

Sydney's internal radar pinged.

Maybe there was no connection between Fredo Moretti's death at the Hoover Dam and Eleanor Duncan.

Maybe the giant and Mr. Average were not here because of Jade and her brother.

Sydney grimaced. Yeah, maybe today was the day when a sounder of wild hogs would soar to the heavens, too.

A few minutes later, his instincts paid off.

Jade joined the giant's table. Eleanor Duncan gestured introductions. Jade shook hands with the two men. No head bowing was involved. Whether that meant no show of respect was due or that Jade had become too Americanized, Sydney didn't know.

He couldn't hear their conversation across the busy restaurant, but the giant had triggered Sydney's primordial responses. His lizard brain was jumping around in his skull like it had spied a hungry wolf approaching.

His immediate orders were clear.

Jade and her employees must not be harmed, but isolated and collected and transported back to Vegas, where Rossi would deal with them.

Orchid Thai Bistro was the instrument Sydney had chosen, purely for practical reasons. He wanted the women to be vulnerable and easier to manipulate.

Whether Duncan or Jade had hired the giant was irrelevant. Either way, he was an unforeseen complication. The cast on his arm meant he wasn't operating at full capacity. But it didn't mean he was less dangerous.

The waitress brought Sydney's food and he consumed it quickly. He tossed a few bills on the table and camouflaged his exit by mingling with a group from a nearby table on their way out.

There was no reason why anyone should give him a second glance, but Sydney was still alive precisely because he was a careful man.

Before he went any further, his first task was to identify and assess the giant and his sidekick.

Sydney scanned the parking lot, located the Audi SUV they'd arrived in, and made his way to the vehicle. He pulled a small tracking device from his pocket and casually installed it in the front left wheel well, where it would remain undetected.

He adjusted the app on his phone and snapped a few shots of the passenger door where the giant had shoved it closed with his left hand. He might be able to get usable fingerprints using some new software Rossi had acquired. A guy like that was likely to have prints in some database somewhere.

He took similar photos of the driver's door for the little guy's prints and the Audi's license plate before he sauntered toward his SUV.

On the way, he called Rossi. "Boss, we might have a problem."

Rossi's long stream of curses could've been heard from Vegas without the phone.

CHAPTER SIXTEEN

Wednesday, May 18
Las Vegas, Nevada
12:10 a.m.

WHILE HE LISTENED TO Sydney on the speaker phone, Rossi counted the gold beer bottle caps on his silver tray. He'd restricted himself to six bottles after dinner. The temporary limit was both an annoyance and a challenge.

He normally denied himself nothing. This was a device to motivate himself to solve at least six problems in the evening. Tonight, he'd solved four, so far. It was a small thing, but the gamesmanship amused him.

"Did you send me photos of this dynamic duo?" he asked, waking his computer to check.

Rossi hated computers with a white-hot passion. Avoided them whenever possible. Digits and data and gadgets were for little minds. No man with a brain needed to rely on the crutch of technology.

"Half a minute ago," Sydney replied. "You should have them now."

Rossi pushed the enter key on the keyboard, one of the few keys he ever touched, and the monitor sprang to life. Four photos filled the screen. He pressed the enter key again and the photos popped up individually.

He ran through the four images. Two men. Two photos each. One big guy and one much smaller. Rossi had never seen the smaller man before. He looked vaguely like a celebrity. Maybe he worked as a lookalike somewhere. But not at the Snake Eyes lounge.

The other guy, the big one, seemed vaguely familiar, too. Rossi narrowed his eyes and peered at the screen as if seeing a slice of the guy might revive his memory. Didn't work.

Maybe he'd never seen the man before. There were a lot of big guys in Vegas. Some were footballers or wrestlers. Some were bouncers. Some tourists. Didn't matter. They were irrelevant. Rossi paid little attention.

"What are their names?" he asked.

"Don't know yet. I'm running them through facial recognition. As soon as I get a hit, I'll pass it along," Sydney replied.

No sooner than the words had left his mouth, Rossi heard a ping of the kind that electronic devices made when something was received.

Sydney said, "Got it. The little guy's coming up in several recent news stories. His name is Petey Burns. Looks like he escaped in that South Dakota prison break last week."

Rossi's thumb began tapping the buttery leather chair arm. The prison break had been the lead story in all of the newspapers Rossi read for a few days. That's why the little guy looked familiar.

If he'd recalled the man, he could have rewarded himself with the fifth beer. Since he hadn't recognized Burns, he'd failed. The delayed gratification was becoming more annoying. Rossi rarely denied himself anything he wanted. Perhaps this six-problem challenge should be revised.

"What about the big guy?" Rossi asked. He'd been thinking about Reacher. Wouldn't it be nice if this big guy turned out to be him? He shook his head. Not likely.

"Nothing's popped up on him so far," Sydney said. "An anonymous tip to the authorities on Burns might be all we need to fix this."

"Fix what, exactly?" Rossi asked, eyeing his four bottle caps wistfully.

"Hard to say. These two had dinner with Duncan and Jade. Something about them triggered my instincts. Which, as you know, are pretty damned reliable," Sydney said.

"If Duncan or Jade have hired these two for muscle, that suggests they know they've got difficulties ahead," Rossi said. "We tip the feds to Burns, and we won't find out what those difficulties are."

"Possibly they don't know what problems they have. Or who they need protection from," Sydney replied, a hopeful note in his voice.

Rossi pushed his lips in and out, thinking things through. "No. Let's find out more before we make the call to one of our friends at the FBI."

"Okay by me. I've got plenty to do tonight anyway," Sydney replied.

Rossi smiled and opened another beer. Five problems, five solutions. Only one more to win, and that would happen shortly.

Dolly knocked on the door and stuck her head inside his office. "Alan Chen's here."

Rossi nodded. "Wait a minute and then send him in."

When Dolly backed out and closed the door, Rossi said, "Sydney, I have to go. Keep me apprised. I want to know who the big man is, too. I think I've dealt with him before."

He disconnected and closed the screen half a moment before Chen knocked twice and opened the door.

Chen walked into the room like a man who feared nothing. He carried himself with the kind of assurance borne of extreme competence in close-quarters combat. He believed, with good reason, that nothing and no one could best him.

So far, his confidence had proven true.

Which meant Alan Chen walked through life uncowed and unafraid.

It was a stance Rossi fully understood because it was also ingrained in him.

His confidence was well placed while the boxer's was foolhardy. It was well past time to deliver that message to Chen and make him believe it.

Rossi waved his open palm toward a chair on the other side of the desk. Chen moved with the easy grace of a dancer as if he could sit and spring up again without effort. Which he probably could.

"Thanks for coming in," Rossi said hospitably as he poured his fifth beer into a chilled glass. He did not offer Chen a beer. Rossi never shared his beer.

Although he'd never met Chen in person before, the civilized greeting was mere theater. Chen was Rossi's property, pure and simple. Whatever Rossi wanted, Chen supplied. No questions asked.

Facts Chen seemed to have failed to grasp.

Chen nodded politely. Quietly, he said, "How may I be of service to you this evening, Mr. Rossi?"

Rossi's thumb was tapping slowly on the chair arm, like a metronome, keeping the conversation moving at the tempo Rossi preferred as he savored the fifth beer and anticipated the sixth.

"I wanted to give you some good news," Rossi said.

Chen's demeanor remained unchanged. "Good news is always welcome."

"You've been with us a long time. Despite your advancing age, your performance remains at the highest level. We appreciate your focus and your dedication," Rossi said as if he was planning to name Chen boxer of the year or something.

Chen nodded. "Thank you."

"I'm afraid I have some disturbing news as well." Rossi frowned, lowering his neck to display his triple chin. "You must have heard the reports today about the bodies found in that desert canyon up north."

Chen did not reply.

"The young men have not been positively identified. So far."

Chen nodded as if he was following along. Perhaps he was.

"There is no reason to believe you'll be questioned in connection with those deaths," Rossi said, matter-of-factly, as the statement wasn't a thinly veiled threat. "If you are approached with questions, you must let me know immediately."

"Of course." If the suggestion that Chen might be deliberately fed to the authorities as the perpetrator of those deaths bothered him at all, he gave no indication.

Illegals sometimes got crazy notions about whistleblowing and human rights and other crap they were fed by the press. Rossi wouldn't stand for such nonsense.

Chen should harbor no illusions about his situation.

He was totally expendable.

He'd been treated well because he'd performed well and because he was extremely profitable for Rossi. An astonishing number of gamblers were willing to pay to cheer a fight to the death. Rossi had made millions giving his customers exactly what they craved.

But Chen was a prisoner here and he shouldn't forget that. Not even for an instant.

"You must also know that if those bodies are tied to you, your association with us will be terminated immediately." Rossi paused to let the euphemism settle in firmly. He didn't mean Chen would simply be fired. "We shall have no choice. You understand?"

Chen nodded. "Yes."

Rossi continued to watch Chen for a few moments as he sipped the beer. It was important for Chen to absorb that he could lose his life at any moment.

Chen remained as poised as before, but when Rossi became satisfied that Chen understood the precariousness of his situation, he offered a final curt nod and moved on to the next topic.

"I'm hoping you can help me with another small problem. One of my men has gone missing. Fredo Moretti," Rossi said, tossing the bait into the calm water and watching for the widening ripples on the surface of Chen's implacable expression. "Moretti is one of the bodyguards we provide for you. You've been seen talking with him."

Chen didn't flinch. He displayed iron-willed self-control, as always.

"Perhaps you didn't know, but Fredo is one of my cousins.

I've known him all his life. His family is asking about him. My family." Rossi continued to sip the beer as he waited for Chen's reaction, which Chen failed to supply. "Fredo said he was meeting you on Sunday, and he hasn't returned. It's been two days. This is unlike Fredo. He's always reliable."

Chen said nothing.

"I'm worried that something untoward has befallen my cousin. You know how this town can be. People get hurt here. Killed, even." Rossi found the young man's composure infuriating. His thumb had increased its tapping tempo as Rossi's internal temperature rose with Chen's impertinence. "Did you see my cousin on Sunday? Do you know where he is?"

"I do not." Chen didn't break a sweat. No twitching or blinking or other signs of agitation. He was as calm now as he was every time he delivered a hard knockout in the ring.

Rossi had questioned many evil men over the years. None had exhibited such complete self-control over their autonomic reflexes, even when they had the balls to lie to his face.

Chen was a cold-hearted killer, as well as an effective and efficient one. Now Rossi knew he was a stellar liar as well.

A momentary, slight, niggling doubt about Fredo Moretti's disappearance passed through Rossi's mind. Could Chen be telling the truth?

True, Fredo's body hadn't been discovered. And he could be a little flaky sometimes. He might have found a woman he'd wanted to party with for a few days before coming back to work. It had happened once before, and Rossi had disciplined him severely. Fredo had promised never to stray from his orders again.

"Did you kill my cousin, Chen?" Rossi asked outright.

Chen said nothing. Simply sat as still as before.

But now Rossi knew for sure. Chen was a sociopath and Fredo Moretti wouldn't be back. Problem solved.

"Thank you for coming in," Rossi said, nodding toward the door. In one fluid, graceful motion, Chen rose from the chair, turned toward the door, and left the room.

Rossi drained the fifth beer and opened the sixth with a smile.

CHAPTER SEVENTEEN

Wednesday, May 18
Golden, Colorado
3:30 a.m.

BURKE WAS SLEEPING IN the Navigator's passenger seat when Kim pulled into Golden, Colorado. Following the directions in the GPS, they'd made good time on the drive from Nebraska.

As Dr. Landon had warned, there had been nothing but darkness between Duncan and the interstate. But once they'd hit I-76, the drive had been easy. Light traffic. Dry weather. Ideal conditions, for the most part.

Kim had connected with I-70 northwest of Denver. An exit ramp dumped them not far from Orchid Thai Bistro, located on the north end of Golden. Five minutes later, instead of a typical town's nighttime quiet, the Navigator approached what had the look and feel of a full-on crime scene in the typical early stages of chaos.

"Wake up, Burke." She reached over to give his arm a sharp poke. "Something's going on here."

"What the hell?" he said, sitting upright and rubbing the sleep from his eyes.

From four blocks away, Kim saw the fire illuminating the darkness and the smoke rising to the sky. Two empty police cars blocked the street at the corner, and she could drive no closer. She parked the Navigator and shut off the engine.

"Looks like Orchid Thai Bistro is ablaze," she said, slowly reporting her observations to settle the situation in her mind. And because The Boss was probably listening, which would save her from filing a formal report. "It's a free-standing building. Surrounded by its own parking lot."

"Which means the fire shouldn't spread too far," Burke said, still gazing at the burning building, mesmerized.

"Right." Kim unlocked her seatbelt and opened the door. She slid off the leather seat and settled her feet firmly onto the pavement. "Don't get too close. We don't have the proper equipment. And there's nothing we can do to help anyway."

The fire's acrid odor was heavy on the air. It was a stench she remembered from childhood and had become all too familiar with over the years. The scene conjured an eerie sense of déjà vu.

When construction and household materials burned, the combination produced toxic fumes that could kill you if you inhaled them full strength. The scent itself clung to clothes and furniture and never dissipated.

The unmistakable stench lingered indefinitely. She could still smell it in her parents' home after all these years.

After a school dance when she was fourteen, she'd returned to find her family home surrounded by fire trucks, lights flashing in the darkness. No one had been injured, but the house was damaged and later repaired.

The noxious fumes had irritated her nostrils, then and now. Kim wrinkled her nose against a round of sneezes. A mask would have been a helpful filter. "Are you coming?"

"Yeah," he said, climbing out on the passenger side and closing the door.

The night air was cold. Forty-five degrees and a slight breeze, which was a mixed blessing. The breeze carried the worst of the fire's smoke and scent away, but it also fanned the flames.

Firetrucks and other emergency vehicles surrounded the scene. Red and blue and white and yellow lights flashed, bouncing off nearby structures. Firefighters, police officers, paramedics, and more first responders scurried around like well-choreographed dancers on a stage.

Kim shivered, turned her jacket collar up, and stuffed her hands into her pockets.

She scanned the personnel, looking for a senior police officer in charge who could brief them on the situation. She didn't find one.

Burke moved them along the sidewalk to get a better view of the Bistro. Kim stopped when she could feel the heat.

The building's windows had blown out, leaving gaping holes on all three floors. Bright red and orange flames lapped the oxygen like a giant, thirsty dragon's tongue.

The blaze spread quickly as it consumed all the fuel inside the building, burning hotter by the minute. A moment later, with an ear-shattering blast, the fire broke through the roof and exploded up toward the heavens like holiday fireworks.

Firefighters battled the conflagration with hoses aimed at the structure from all sides, but the heat seemed to absorb the water and kept on burning. If they couldn't put the fire out soon, the entire building would be nothing but charred rubble before daylight.

Another screaming siren traveled toward the inferno from the west, horns blaring when it slowed at the intersections until the firetruck pulled up on the side of the building and stopped.

Personnel jumped out and went directly to work, joining the fight. They unfurled another fire hose and set it up to blast the west side of the bistro.

Kim watched with a mixture of horrifying memories and professional detachment.

"Coincidence?" Burke asked.

"Orchid Thai Bistro just happens to burst into flames thirty minutes before we arrive here?" Kim replied. "I think not."

"It's convenient that Reacher's in the vicinity when Eleanor Duncan's place is torched, huh?" Burke said.

"So you're thinking arson?" Kim asked, cocking her head. "Reacher set Eleanor's place on fire? Why the hell would he do that?"

"Can't be anything else, can it?" Burke replied.

"Of course it can." Kim turned to look at Burke directly. "Maybe this is the trouble Reacher came to help Eleanor with, is just one possibility."

"Not likely." Burke frowned. "Arson for insurance money. Reacher torches the place, and Duncan gets rich. Makes total sense."

Kim jerked her head in a quick negative shake. Not because the idea was stupid. It wasn't. But they had zero evidence to support the plan. Last the Landons knew Eleanor Duncan was already rich. Why would she want to torch her own business? Not to mention her home?

Which was when Kim noticed a group of Asian women

dressed in silk pajamas clustered together at the corner of the sidewalk, staring at the Orchid Thai Bistro, watching everything they had in the world go up in flames.

Kim counted twelve in the huddle, their distraught, tear-stained faces illuminated by the warm and brilliant firelight. Eleven of the women were Asian-looking. About half were teens. The others were mid-twenties. From the looks of them, a few were probably mothers and daughters.

The twelfth woman was Eleanor Duncan. No doubt about it. She stood ramrod straight, fists clinched at her sides, and stared into the fire with the kind of impotent anger Kim recognized.

Eleanor Duncan was seriously pissed off.

CHAPTER EIGHTEEN

Wednesday, May 18
Golden, Colorado
4:00 a.m.

SYDNEY WAITED IN THE shadows. He lifted binoculars to his face to check the fire's progress.

The blaze burned nicely. Even with several fire companies doing their best, Orchid Thai Bistro would be rubble before daylight. Exactly as Rossi wanted.

In Sydney's experience, persuasion was a fine art, not a blunt instrument. Just the right amount of pressure would achieve the desired result. He'd been told to send the woman a strong message, to make her pliable. Not to kill her.

He'd counted the residents as they fled the burning building. Twelve in all.

Eleven Thai women, who rightfully belonged to Rossi. There had been sixteen in the original shipment. They had escaped before because someone had protected them. Now there were eleven here and five elsewhere. Probably with Jade, along with the rest of her employees.

Soon, they would all be together again and returned to Rossi, where they should have been all along.

Without the bistro as a safe haven, Sydney expected to round them up and herd them back as easily as a border collie with a flock of sheep.

The twelfth woman was Eleanor Duncan, a do-gooder who'd already meddled too much in Rossi's business. Sydney would kill her in good time. Rossi wanted her to suffer for a while first.

The Thai women stood shivering on the sidewalk in the frosty morning air. Thin nightclothes were no match for the cold Rocky Mountain springtime. They had not thought to grab coats on the way out of the burning building. With the sprinklers and the alarms blasting, awakened from a sound sleep, they barely had a chance to think at all.

Sydney clicked his tongue against his teeth as he shook his head. Eleanor Duncan was a whole different level of problem. She was too warmed by her anger to shiver in the cold.

Eleanor Duncan was experienced in all kinds of ways. She knew how to thrive in colder temperatures than these. She'd been raised in Nebraska and lived there most of her life. She was bundled into a heavy barn coat with her hands shoved into slanted pockets, which pushed her elbows akimbo.

She was also directly responsible for Rossi's heavy losses seven years ago. No other conclusion was remotely possible. The Thais would not have escaped without Eleanor. They couldn't think ahead far enough to grab a coat. They surely weren't capable of getting themselves from Nebraska to Denver, finding work, and thriving all these years.

Rossi was The Elephant. He had a very long memory. Seven

years was nothing to him. He felt the damage as keenly as if Eleanor Duncan had stolen his property and destroyed his business yesterday. Rossi would pursue her forever until one of them no longer drew breath.

Sydney's money was on Rossi. No matter how clever Eleanor Duncan was, she didn't have Rossi's frigid heart. She'd give up eventually. They always did.

Sydney saw that a bevy of professionals had joined the fire scene, increasing the volume of choreographed chaos. Cops, firefighters, emergency medical personnel fairly swarmed the parking lot, surrounding the burning building on all sides, weaving around each other like footballers on the field.

And then he noticed two others he couldn't immediately categorize.

They'd arrived in a civilian SUV, a dark colored Lincoln, black or navy or charcoal, maybe. A man and a woman wearing civilian clothes stood transfixed by the fire. No parkas, hats, gloves, or boots.

She was petite. Asian looking, too. Maybe one of Jade's women? But not Thai. He was no expert, but she was probably some sort of mixed race. It was impossible to tell in the dark from this distance, even with the binoculars and the orange flames lighting her features.

The man was taller. Six feet, or thereabouts. Square-shouldered. Trim. Fit. He carried himself like a military man. Sydney understood the military mind set. He recognized it when he observed others.

The two stood watching the fire and the scene with professional interest. What were they doing here?

He used the binoculars to scan the area again.

Sydney hadn't expected Jade to be inside when the alarms sounded, and as far as he could tell, she wasn't.

But these women had immigrated with Jade. They were the closest friends she had in this country. She had bonded with them through extreme stress and hardship.

Jade might show up and offer her friends a place to stay, at least. The fire was meant to render them homeless and without alternatives to Rossi's plans. Which it surely had achieved.

Sydney twisted at the waist and peered through the binoculars to make one last sweep around the building.

If the big guy and his sidekick from the Bistro last night were hanging around, they were invisible now.

Perhaps Sydney had been wrong. Maybe Eleanor Duncan had not hired the giant to provide security. Which was good for Sydney and Rossi. Bad for Duncan.

He smiled as he collected his gear. There was nothing more to do here.

Sydney carried the heavy black duffle through the alleys, moving from one shadow to the next, avoiding security cameras perched on corners and poles. Six minutes later, he approached the stolen sedan he'd parked four streets away.

He stashed the duffle in the trunk and slid behind the wheel as another firetruck's wailing siren headed toward the bistro. He barely noticed the flashing lights and blasting horns as the truck sped past.

He found the fresh burner phone in his pocket and fired it up. When it connected to the towers, he dialed another burner sitting at the Snake Eyes Casino in Vegas.

Rossi picked up on the first ring. "Yeah."

Sydney heard the unmistakable noises he associated with Rossi's favorite pastime. Cheering crowds. Muffled punches followed by grunts and heavier thuds. Screaming spectators. Noise exposure levels sufficient to cause post-match hearing loss, according to the experts Rossi hired to ramp up the excitement at his Muay Thai boxing matches.

Chen was heavily favored by the oddsmakers to win tonight. Which was why Rossi wouldn't tell him about his sister until tomorrow. Or maybe the next day.

When the noise abated slightly, Sydney said, "First phase is done."

"Keep me posted." Rossi disconnected. His mind was already focused on what came next.

CHAPTER NINETEEN

Wednesday, May 18
Golden, Colorado
4:30 a.m.

KIM GLANCED AROUND THE parking lot again. Her view was blocked by vehicles and first responders of all sorts. The bright flames engulfing the building were simultaneously a help and a hindrance. The light illuminated the shadows but blinded her night vision. She could see the building afire, but nothing around the darker periphery.

"We're wasting time. Are we interrogating Eleanor Duncan or just standing here with our tongues hanging out?" Burke asked.

"She isn't going anywhere for a while." Kim stuffed her hands into her pockets. "Let's take a quick walk around the perimeter first."

"What for? Reacher won't be standing out in the open where we can easily see him after he torched the place," Burke replied, but when she stepped away, he hurriedly followed. "Sure. Why not. A brisk walk will warm us up, if nothing else."

Kim ignored his sarcasm and moved toward the fire. The heat radiated outward, warming the frigid night. She didn't know exactly what she was looking for, but the flames drew her nearer even as the cacophony overwhelmed her senses.

When she cleared the nearest firetruck and moved inside the perimeter, the parking lot was as cluttered as an obstacle course. Equipment deployed everywhere. Firefighters scurried hither and yon, adjusting and resetting and shouting to be heard.

They had fought to save the building, and that battle was lost. The fire had been too hot already when they'd arrived. The inferno had spread too quickly from the ground floor.

Now they were fighting to keep the conflagration contained to the Orchid Thai Bistro instead of consuming the entire neighborhood when the breeze lifted burning embers and carried them to new sources of fuel.

A police officer noticed Kim and Burke standing closer to the blaze. He hustled over with his arms outstretched to herd them back. "Sorry, folks, we need you to move away from the building."

Kim nodded toward Burke and replied, "We're FBI."

Burke flashed his badge wallet. The fire glinted off his shield.

"Enrico Mendez. Golden PD," the officer replied. "We've got this under control. We didn't call for FBI assistance. Why are you folks here?"

Kim shrugged. "We saw the fire. Thought you might need help."

"Step over here, please. Let's give these guys room to do their work," Mendez said, gesturing to the open space beyond two vehicles blocking bystanders from a full view.

"Seems like a hot fire," Burke said as he moved out.

Mendez nodded. "Yeah. Too hot. Fire chief figures arson. We won't know for sure until we get it extinguished and forensics can analyze whatever's left."

"Everybody get out okay?" Kim asked, continuing to look for Reacher.

"Far as we know," Mendez replied. "All residents are accounted for. We've been told there were no visitors inside the building."

"Have you interviewed them yet?" Kim asked.

"I was the first officer on the scene. I talked to the owner. She didn't seem to know anything helpful. Neither did the others. But we'll do more investigation later. When we have more facts," Mendez replied, twisting his neck around when someone called his name. "That's my partner. I've gotta go."

"You think everyone got out, for sure? This wasn't a break-in, burglars still inside?" Kim asked. "No homeless people sleeping too close on a cold night? The arsonist didn't screw up and kill himself?"

Mendez frowned and shook his head. "We haven't found any bodies yet. Doesn't mean we won't, though. You think an arsonist might be in there?"

Kim pulled out a business card and handed it to him. "Call me later, when you can. After you get a good look around the debris tomorrow."

He cocked his head, a quizzical expression on his face. He put the card in his pocket. "Probably be a few days before we know much more than I've already told you."

"That's okay. If there's a body, you'll find it sooner. Otherwise, I can wait. Thanks," she said, as he nodded and turned to trot into the melee.

"Now what?" Burke asked sourly. "Like he said, it'll be a

while before we get any forensics. Petey Burns isn't the brightest bulb, but Reacher seems too smart to screw up an arson or to stick around waiting for us to find him. And you don't think he did this anyway."

Kim nodded, turned her jacket collar up to battle the cold wind, and headed toward the far corner of the lot where the knot of women were still huddled. Nautical twilight brightened the sky enough to dilute the shadows, but beyond the firefighting equipment, the parking lot was flat and smooth and free of tripping hazards.

Eleanor Duncan continued to stare at the fire as if transfixed by the disaster. Kim had seen victims unable to turn away from ruin, and she remembered all too well how it felt to find your home aflame.

First came bewildered astonishment, followed shortly by disbelief, and then anger that could grow hotter than the fire. The anger lasted a good long time. Some crime victims never recovered from it, and anger defined them ever more.

Eleanor Duncan had survived much worse. But would she recover from this disaster, or would it be the last straw that broke her?

"Mrs. Duncan?" Kim asked as she approached. Eleanor didn't flinch. "Mrs. Duncan, I'm FBI Agent Kim Otto. This is my partner, William Burke."

Eleanor stood as stiff as if she'd frozen in place.

One of the Thai women looked into Kim's gaze. She was young and pretty, and her long black hair was held at the base of her neck with a pale pink ribbon that matched her silk pajamas. She had to be freezing cold, but she barely shivered.

She spoke boldly, in a clear voice, without hesitation. "I'm Anchara. People call me Angel."

Kim nodded to acknowledge her. "Mrs. Duncan, we have a vehicle over here. We need to talk with you. Come sit inside, where it's not so cold."

Eleanor offered a glassy-eyed stare as if noticing Kim for the first time. Which she probably was. "Can all of us fit inside?"

"Maybe. We can try." Kim shot Burke a meaningful gaze. "If not, you can take turns getting warm. Or we can drive you somewhere. Is there a hotel nearby?"

Eleanor nodded, giving her blessing to the plan. Angel herded the women toward the Navigator, with Burke, a foot taller, in the lead, gliding like a row of mallards on a placid lake. Eleanor didn't move. She turned her gaze to the fire once more, entranced.

Kim moved closer. The alternating shadows and brightness of the firelight revealed that Eleanor's nose had been broken and healed with a couple of extra bumps. Her cheekbones were slightly deformed. And her lower jaw rested off-center. The combination gave her an oddly fragile vibe while at the same time suggesting Eleanor was much stronger than she appeared.

"Aren't you curious about why we're here?" Kim asked, attempting to snag Eleanor's attention.

"Does FBI have jurisdiction for arson?" Eleanor asked without turning her head away from the flames. "If so, I'd like you to find the bastard and shoot him."

Kim raised her eyebrows. Eleanor looked harmless enough, but her anger was as hard as the concrete she was standing on.

"Arson's not our jurisdiction, I'm afraid. Not without more context, at least. If it's a federal crime, we could become involved," Kim replied. "At the moment, it looks like you've got a capable team handling the fire."

Eleanor said nothing.

"Why do you believe this was arson? Did you receive threats? See someone setting the fire? Smell accelerant? Anything like that?" Kim asked.

"The building is new. It's equipped with the best fire prevention and suppression equipment available. We heard nothing. Saw nothing. Smelled nothing. No alarms, no sprinklers, nothing at all." Eleanor shook her head, her tone bitter and resigned. She waved toward the fire with an open palm. "Yet there it is, a pile of rubble. You tell me how that could possibly happen unless the fire was deliberately set, huh?"

"Why would anyone want to burn your business to the ground?" Kim asked. "The investigation will start there and fan out. Business rival? Personal vendetta? Insurance fraud? They'll need names and contact information to speed things up."

Eleanor nodded as if she'd been thinking about the questions already, but she didn't answer them. "Why are you here?"

"I'm looking for Jack Reacher," Kim said simply, sensing that she'd get nowhere with this woman by being subtle.

Eleanor didn't flinch and she offered nothing in response.

"Has he been here?" Kim asked.

"Haven't seen him around tonight." Eleanor shrugged. "Unfortunately."

Which was almost an admission that Eleanor *had* seen Reacher. Kim cocked her head and took a deep breath to settle the flutter in her stomach. "Why do you say that?"

"Because if Reacher had been here, he'd have caught the bastard who torched my building before it burned to the ground," she replied, a deep thread of anger in her tone.

"Reacher's been here, though, hasn't he?"

For the first time, Eleanor turned to gaze fully into her face. "Why are you asking?"

CHAPTER TWENTY

Wednesday, May 18
Denver, Colorado
5:00 a.m.

JADE STOOD AT THE window of her penthouse apartment
staring toward the promised sunrise. The clear eastern sky had
brightened enough to reveal the first hints of daylight to come.
Wearing white silk pajamas and a matching silk robe that
caressed her skin like a lover, she held sweet, creamy tea in a
crystal mug between tiny bare hands and worried about what the
day would bring.

This apartment was her hard-earned refuge from a world that
had never provided her sanctuary. Her intention was to create a
haven where her now much smaller family of three could be
themselves. Or at least, the selves she wanted to believe they
were now, seven long years since they'd left Thailand in search
of a better life.

That promise had ultimately been fulfilled, although not in
the ways she had expected.

Since Sunday, her lost family had fully occupied her mind once again. She recalled how her father had worked so hard for them all after her mother died. The years leading up to the long journey, as she thought of it now, had been exceptionally hard ones. Her father had tried his best to give his children what they wanted and what their mother had wanted for them before she died.

Her brother was two years older and her childhood hero. He had protected her and her sister and their two younger brothers. When their father finally saved enough money to send them all to America, where they'd been promised jobs and prosperity, he had expected to join them here.

He'd sold everything they owned to buy them a safe passage. Unfortunately, his savings didn't stretch far enough to allow him to complete the journey with them.

They had been six in all. Her older brother, Amarin, two younger brothers, and her sister's husband had traveled from Thailand with twelve other men, separated from the six women and ten girls, which was only proper.

They were to meet up again at the end of the trip in Montana. From there, they would begin new lives together in America, the land of opportunity.

At a young age, Amarin was already showing promise as a Muay Thai boxer. He and the younger boys were apprenticed to a boxing promoter known around the world. Over time, Amarin's reputation grew. He showed promise. His skills might one day feed them well.

The famous promoter wanted Amarin, but her father had negotiated with his local Thai representatives until futures for the children were assured. He would never have allowed them to go otherwise.

Too many Thai people were taken in by unscrupulous thieves. Thais were persuaded to emigrate for work, but once they left Thailand, their passports were stolen, and they were sold into one sort of slavery or another. Her father would never allow his family to suffer such a fate.

Jade had been promised a job with a famous ballet company. Her sister, GiGi, was to work at a multi-national consulting firm. Mika was only eight, but she'd shown promise with her watercolors. She'd been enrolled in private lessons with a teacher who would assure her a place at Interlochen Arts Academy when she turned twelve.

Of course, none of that happened, and Jade had not seen her brothers since they departed from Thailand.

Unlike many Thais who emigrated temporarily for work, seeking only to get home again, Jade and her family had never planned to return. Years passed before Jade learned her father had died just a few weeks after his family sailed, well before the first leg of their long journey ended.

Which meant there was truly nothing left for Jade in Thailand. Her only sister and her niece were here. Her brothers were lost. She had no family back there. No job. No home. Nothing. For better or for worse, America was her home now.

Jade refilled her teacup and allowed her mind to return to the past.

She had been called Ying Chen then. She and her sister, Gamon, landed in Canada and then traveled on foot with Gamon's young daughter, Nan, and the others across the border. They were all excited to experience their amazing future. Still nervous but living in happy anticipation, all sixteen, six women and ten young girls, piled into the back of the dirty gray van like well-behaved sheep.

They ended up in Duncan, Nebraska, where Eleanor Duncan climbed behind the steering wheel to commandeer their lives.

From the moment she stepped into that gray van in Montana, Ying Chen no longer held any illusions about her life. She was not a citizen here. She was illegal. She would do whatever it took to stay here. Which meant she lived in the shadows. She never intended to do anything else. But after years of relying on her father to take care of her, after more years of fending for herself after her brothers disappeared, she meant to be her own master.

Eleanor had been blunt with them. They had paid handsomely for the journey, but the men who took their money and promised them bright futures intended to sell them to the sex trade. All sixteen of them. Eleanor thwarted that plan, and while some of the women were grateful to her, Ying Chen felt just as enslaved in the new life as she had been in the old.

Perhaps that was when the embers of Ying Chen's anger began to warm the pit of her stomach and later, to flame and consume her entire being.

Ying Chen and her sister Gamon had no money and nowhere else to go, so they stayed with Eleanor for three long years.

She was a good woman with a good heart. She meant well. And she was devastated by their plight and the role she and her husband's family had played in it.

So Eleanor wanted to help. She honestly believed she was helping.

Eleanor encouraged them to change the names their parents had so lovingly bestowed upon them at birth. Eleanor said Chen was a common enough name to suffice in America, but their first names were too foreign.

Which was how Ying Chen became Jade. Gamon Chen became GiGi, and her daughter Nan became Mika Chen. Eleanor acquired false documents with their new names that somehow kept them from being questioned or deported.

But Jade had never intended to work in a restaurant. Her training as a dancer proved to be a set of useless skills for a food server. GiGi's accounting education was more practical, but profits from the bistro would never have made her independent.

Jade and GiGi, and later Mika, had toiled at Orchid Thai Bistro until they saved enough money to escape the existence they'd never intended to live.

Jade could have asked Eleanor to help her again. But she felt Eleanor had already done way too much. Jade had lived among Americans long enough to know that women could take care of themselves here.

She funneled her rage into gaining her freedom on her own terms.

Working at Orchid Thai Bistro, she learned how desirable Asian women were to certain men. She was astonished to discover how much the men were willing to pay for sex. For the first time, she understood why the men who trafficked them here had been willing to risk their lives.

Money. Lots of money. More money than Jade had ever seen or was likely to see in her lifetime.

Which was when she'd made her choice.

Jade saved her wages from the restaurant, hoping to rent a one-room apartment. She flirted with the men who came into the bistro. Inevitably, a few would offer to pay her much more for sex.

Her overhead was low and her prices high. Soon, she'd collected enough cash to fill a shoebox. Which was when she quit her job at the bistro and moved to her first small apartment.

Eleanor was, of course, appalled. GiGi, too, at first. But Jade would not be dissuaded. She branched out to escort services as well as sex. Walking around in public as some man's arm candy before sex increased her revenue exponentially. Her business flourished, and soon all her nights were booked with paying clients.

When she'd saved enough to rent a two-bedroom apartment, she offered her sister the second room. Between the two of them, they made twice as much money, and GiGi's accounting skills seemed to multiply the cash like the cockroaches Jade sometimes noticed under the sink.

GiGi suggested they expand. Jade persuaded three of the Thai women they'd traveled with to join the business. After a year, two of them made enough money to return to Thailand with their daughters. Jade never heard from them again.

Which didn't matter at all. Jade found more Asian women willing to work easily enough.

Within two years, they moved to bigger and better quarters. She and GiGi had built a thriving high-end escort business, the finest in Denver, and Jade was proud of it. She smiled. You gotta love America. Land of opportunity, indeed.

They dreamed of branching out to larger cities. Jade had her eye on Las Vegas, where there was even bigger money to be made. Vegas seemed like a faraway theme park to her. She couldn't wait to move there.

That had been her goal until last week. Jade's features clouded.

How quickly things can change when you're making other plans.

CHAPTER TWENTY-ONE

Wednesday, May 18
Golden, Colorado
5:05 a.m.

SYDNEY FOUND THE SPECIALLY equipped black luxury van Rossi had delivered, six blocks away from the Orchid Thai fire, ready and waiting exactly where he expected. The van was identical to two others. One owned by Jade's escort service. And the one manned by two of Rossi's enforcers.

Sydney tossed his bags into the cargo hold and fished the burner cell phone from his pocket as he climbed behind the steering wheel.

The backup team had been scheduled to arrive twenty minutes ago. The two Callo cousins Rossi had imported from New York should be in position, awaiting Sydney's signal. They had experience in short-haul human trafficking, so they'd know what to do.

Sydney pressed the speed dial on the burner.

"Yeah?" Little Tony Callo spoke in a thick New York accent he'd acquired in childhood. "Whaddaya got?"

"Twelve units, ready for pickup in—" Sydney said, glancing at the clock, "thirty minutes, give or take. I'll let you know as soon as the call comes. Wait for my signal."

"Twelve units? No way," Little Tony replied. "Me and Big Tony got seats for nine, and that'll be tight. Eleven hours back to Vegas with twelve of them and us packed in like sardines? Nine's the best we can do. You and Jimmy Prime gotta handle the rest."

"No. Rossi said you take twelve. I'll pick up the others at the brothel. Like Rossi planned." Sydney rolled the big SUV south six blocks before he turned east, giving the fire at Orchid Thai Bistro a wide berth. "You've gotta get the first eleven into your van and get on the road. We can't wait. They're small. Squeeze them in together."

Little Tony said, "Whadda'm I gonna tell 'em? Jam in there and shut up aboud it?"

His accent was so thick, Sydney had to take a moment to process the noise into a language he could comprehend. "Tell them they're not going far. You're taking them to Jade's place. Thirty minutes. They can cozy up together for warmth. They'll be fine."

"This is crap, what this is," Little Tony said, cussing a blue streak.

Sydney held the phone away from his ear and waited for the stream of profanity to subside. "Okay, look. Just take the eleven for now. I'll call Rossi. We'll get another van to meet you about an hour out of Golden. You can offload half. The second van can follow you the rest of the way to Vegas. Can you do that?"

Little Tony thought about it. Sydney heard nothing but

heavy breathing for a while. He turned north and drove toward the meeting point. He saw Little Tony's van ahead. He parked well back on the street to wait.

This was the weakest link in the plan. Because he couldn't know for sure that Eleanor Duncan would call Jade for help. But it was a solid bet.

Duncan was a fugitive herself. She wouldn't risk calling the law.

And Jade knew these women. They were like sisters to her. She knew they needed to stay under the radar because they were illegal.

Besides, Jade and Duncan were as thick as thieves. Who else would drop everything to help Eleanor Duncan in the wee hours and keep quiet about it?

"I'm parked half a block behind you, on the right. I'm flashing my lights once," Sydney said.

"Yeah, we sees ya," Little Tony said.

Sydney nodded. "There's a total of thirteen women. Twelve Asians. Eleven in pajamas. One in a black suit. One older white woman wearing a barn coat. You take the pajamas. Ask the other two to wait."

Little Tony didn't respond.

"You screw this up, and The Elephant won't like it. And he never forgets, Little Tony. You know that," Sydney said as he pulled up behind the first van. "Far as he's concerned, he's retrieving his stolen property."

Little Tony said nothing, which meant he'd dug in his heels and wouldn't budge.

Sydney played his trump card. "You screw this up, and God knows what will happen to you and Big Tony, too."

Big Tony was Little Tony's younger cousin. They were a

matched set. Could've been twins. Born on the same day to sisters. Little Tony came out two ounces smaller but three minutes ahead, which made him the older one and thus responsible for the younger cousin's life. A responsibility he took seriously.

Little Tony never replied, but another cousin opened the side door of the first van and stepped out. The younger, smarter, more handsome cousin they called "Joey Prime" Callo hustled back toward Sydney's SUV.

"Little Tony says he don't like it, but okay. They'll take the girls in pajamas. He says let them know where to meet up and hand off half, like you suggested," Joey Prime said as he opened the passenger door and slid inside.

Sydney nodded. Big Tony was driving the first van. He took his foot off the brake and slid the transmission into park. Sydney glanced at the clock on the dash, waiting for Duncan's call to Jade.

He'd wait exactly ten minutes after the call to alert Little Tony. Big Tony would drive up to the Orchid Thai parking lot, the women would pile into the van, and he'd pull away.

Ten minutes later, Sydney would pull up to collect Eleanor Duncan and the woman in the suit.

He didn't know if the suit belonged to Rossi or not, but he was sure Rossi wouldn't object to another asset. He could always sell her if he didn't want her once they got her back to Vegas.

It was a solid plan. Little Tony was objecting to the extra cargo for no good reason. Rossi wouldn't like it. Not even a little bit. Rossi demanded immediate and uncomplaining "can do" attitudes from his soldiers.

Sydney didn't plan to tell him there would be no second van. Little Tony could take up his objections with Rossi when he rolled into Vegas with the cargo.

Joey Prime settled firmly into his seat. "So we're taking the Duncan woman and the other Asian girl to Jade's place. We get there and round up Jade's girls. What is that? Five more? Six?"

Sydney stared ahead, watching Big Tony's van. "She's got six, total. Including her. We add Duncan and the other one, and we'll have eight. Little Tony will have twelve."

Joey Prime shook his head. "Man, it's gonna be crowded in here, too. We shudda brung a bus."

"Think about how happy Rossi will be. He'll get rid of Duncan. He'll have two dozen new girls. He'll make a fortune," Sydney said, explaining the facts Little Tony was too thick to work out, but Joey could comprehend. "We add another team, another van, we slow down the drive. All that costs Rossi money and makes him nervous. Money he takes out of our cut. Nerves he takes out on us, too. You wanna do that, Joey?"

Joey Prime was smarter than Little Tony, but not a lot. "Nah. It's eleven hours. These women are tiny. We can do it."

Sydney smiled. "You've got your head on straight, Joey. I've always appreciated that about you."

"Okay, Big Tony's driving. He goes first. Picks up the first batch. We follow. Collect the last two. Head over to the brothel and collect the rest. Drive straight to Vegas. Piece a cake," Joey Prime said, slouching into the passenger seat, bouncing his legs. He was antsy. Ready to go.

Sydney slid the transmission into drive and rolled the van closer to the flames, clearly marking the Orchid Thai Bistro fire up ahead.

The scanner he'd set up on the dashboard came alive. Eleanor Duncan dialed her phone and the scanner intercepted. She was talking to Jade. Sydney and Joey Prime listened to the brief conversation.

When she hung up, Sydney called Little Tony again.

"Wait ten minutes. Then roll out," Sydney instructed. "We need to get in, scoop them up, and get out before the real van arrives."

"Yeah, yeah. We know. We're not stupid," Tony replied before he hung up.

Sydney turned to Joey Prime. "After Tony tells her there's not enough room, Duncan will call a second car. We'll pick up her call and then block her phone after that."

"What if she's got a second phone?" Joey Prime asked as if he was actually interested in the tech.

"We've got a signal jammer for the whole SUV. Only certain signals can get in or out or be traced," Sydney said. "We'll clone her phone, which I'll then use to text Jade for the next phase."

"Meaning?" Joey Prime asked, cocking his head like he couldn't quite wrap his mind around it. Which he probably couldn't. He was smarter than Little Tony, but none of the Callos were brilliant.

"Just take my word for it that we won't have a problem and follow my lead," Sydney said, watching the traffic and keeping an eye on the fire's glow in the distance.

"Sounds good to me," Joey Prime said, settling his bouncing legs and slouching deeper into his seat. "I'm more than ready to get back to Vegas. It's too damned cold here."

CHAPTER TWENTY-TWO

Wednesday, May 18
Golden, Colorado
5:15 a.m.

"I'M—" KIM ALMOST RATTLED off the official answer about doing the Reacher background check in response to Eleanor's question, but her frank expression demanded an honest answer.

The few facts Kim knew ran through her head like a relay racer from one touch point to the next.

She might get further along the road to finding Reacher with intel from Eleanor Duncan than she'd ever managed to get from any witness before.

This woman had been viciously brutalized. She'd gone through hell and found her way back, and Reacher had helped rehabilitate her somehow. He'd headed here again to help her with some kind of serious trouble.

According to Dr. Landon, Eleanor's husband had been the world's worst bastard. Not one person had ever said Seth Duncan, his father, and his uncles had not deserved to die. Even the

Nebraska State Police report she'd read didn't suggest the dead Duncans had been upstanding citizens.

All of this meant that Eleanor Duncan was more than just another of Reacher's long list of women. She was no better or worse, but she was as formidable as the others in her own way.

Yet, Eleanor was different, somehow. A strange quality had drawn Reacher to her, although Kim couldn't quite put her finger on the precise nature of that trait yet.

"We need to find Reacher. He was on his way here to see you. Are you saying he never arrived?" Kim said, sensing that Eleanor was too strong. Pussyfooting around with this one would get her nowhere.

"Is this where you tell me it's a crime to lie to an FBI agent?" Eleanor smirked, which brought on a bout of coughing.

"No need to tell you since you already know," Kim replied.

Eleanor smiled, which accentuated the odd asymmetries of her face. "Right at the moment, I might enjoy being a guest of Uncle Sam. As you can see, I have nowhere to sleep tonight."

"The only people who say things like that have never seen the inside of a federal prison," Burke said sharply. He'd walked up just in time to hear their last exchange. "Guess that means we don't have to check your criminal history."

Eleanor's eyes narrowed. She pursed her lips and clammed up again.

"We could catch you in a lie, which would put you on the wrong side of the law. Then we'd arrest you and take you in for questioning. Or we can do this the easy way. Let's try that first, shall we?"

Eleanor stood ramrod straight and glared directly into his eyes.

"So here's the truth we already know to save you from trying to lie about it," Burke pushed on as if he was oblivious to Eleanor's resistance. "We know Reacher was on his way here. We know he's traveling with Petey Burns. They're driving a stolen Audi SUV. What we don't know is why they came here in the first place. And we don't know where Reacher is now. Can you shed some light on that?"

Eleanor's eyes had narrowed to mere slits and her nostrils flared like an angry bull. Burke was baiting her. She knew it and she didn't bite, no matter how much she wanted to.

"As it happens, I'm with you. Your building was torched. Destroyed. Best guess? Reacher is your arsonist. The guy knows his way around accelerants and destruction." Burke barreled through whatever resistance Eleanor had left. "Question is, did he just do you a favor by getting rid of the place because he's such a nice guy? Or did you pay him to do it? We'll check your bank records to confirm. Don't think we won't."

Eleanor coughed and scowled as Burke talked, and then her expression lightened as he finished. She grinned and shook her head.

"What's so funny?" Burke demanded, jamming his hands into his pockets.

"Have you ever *met* Reacher?" she asked as if the question contained its own answer.

"Matter of fact, I have," Burke replied.

"Then you must be as thick as a brick if you think Reacher would take money from me to burn down my building with all of us inside." Eleanor's grin broadened and she laughed, which brought on yet another bout of coughing.

"Why do you say that?" Kim asked. Although she privately agreed, she didn't need an all-out war with Burke's methods right now, either.

"When you find him, you can ask him yourself," Eleanor replied angrily again, staring them down. Her moods seemed to whipsaw faster than her gaze. "If you've got evidence that Reacher torched my building, then let's have it. Call the police over here and I'll make a full statement. I'll be more than happy to help you catch him. You won't have to ask me twice."

Her demands were met with belligerent silence from Burke this time.

"Just as I thought. You let me know when you have answers instead of questions, Agent Burke. Meanwhile, I've got to find my tenants a place to sleep tonight." She pulled her cell phone out of her pocket, turned her back, and walked away to make her call, coughing as she went.

"Nice job, Burke," Kim said when Eleanor was out of earshot. "Let's hear your next brilliant idea."

"Reacher is here. Somewhere. Either he set this fire or he knows who did," Burke said stubbornly, with way more certainty than the facts supported. "And he might be smart enough not to get caught. But what about Petey Burns? He's no brain trust. He'll make a mistake sooner or later. When he does, we'll catch him."

"So your plan is what? Stomp around the ashes looking under debris until you find them?" Kim replied, making it clear what she thought of such a plan. Which earned her another scowl from Burke. "Makes more sense that Reacher will approach Eleanor again at some point. He came here to help her, according to Doc Landon. He won't leave before he connects with her again."

"Maybe. We're both reading tea leaves at this point. But since there're two of us now, you stay with Duncan. She seems to like you. Maybe she'll give you some actual intel we can use to find Reacher."

"And what are you planning to do while I'm babysitting?"

"Look around, see if I can figure out where Reacher went." Burke didn't wait for her answer before he stomped off toward the south end of the burning building.

Kim watched him go, shaking her head, wondering when he was planning to start performing like a partner instead of a damned prima donna.

CHAPTER TWENTY-THREE

Wednesday, May 18
Denver, Colorado
5:35 a.m.

JADE HAD BEEN INVITED by one of her clients to attend a Muay Thai boxing match in Vegas. He, of course, had paid all expenses. A first-class trip to Las Vegas with a big spender to cover the bills had seemed like an amazing chance. She had not left Colorado since she'd arrived here in the back of that gray van seven years ago.

Jade's father had loved Muay Thai. It was a popular sport back home and her big brother, Amarin, was so good at it that he'd been recruited from Vegas to fight in the best matches. Amarin was destined to become a star.

Her father had beamed with pride when he told the story to everyone in their village.

Like everything else her father had been promised, the man had lied about the promoter's plans for Amarin, too.

Jade felt twinges of nostalgia for her childhood and her

homeland as soon as her client offered the trip to Vegas. She hadn't witnessed a live Muay Thai match since she'd watched her brothers in the backyard in Thailand.

Emotional baggage, she knew. GiGi told her to stop being foolish. They had much better lives here than anything they might have expected back home, she said.

Jade agreed. But something pulled her toward the Muay Thai match in Vegas anyway.

She had paid no attention to the scheduled boxers. The fight was illegal, the gamblers who crowded the venue were criminals, and she didn't care about any of it. She only wanted to feel like a carefree young girl watching boxing with her father again.

Her escort was paying a lot of money to show her off as his date, which was really all that mattered to him. Jade was getting paid, and she'd told GiGi that was the most important thing. Even though they both knew it wasn't only the money that had drawn her.

The star fighters for the night had been brought into the ring.

As soon as Jade saw the headliner, Alan Chen, she recognized him as her brother. Amarin was unforgettable. His image had been imprinted on her heart before she was born, and it remained there still.

She wanted to speak to him. To connect to her old life once more.

After he won the fight in a quick knockout, the handlers hustled him off the floor. Jade slipped away from her client and followed Amarin through the corridors.

When her brother's handlers slipped out of his room, Jade slipped inside. He was lying on a sofa, eyes closed.

"Amarin," she said quietly.

His eyes popped open in surprise. No one had called him that name in years.

"Ying? Is it you?" Amarin was astonished to see her.

Like Jade, he'd learned American ways. He jumped off the sofa and hugged her, lifting her into the air as he'd done when they were children.

He blinked back tears as he held her close. "They said you died on the long journey from Thailand. Gamon and Nan, too."

Brother and sister cried, hanging onto each other as if they might vanish at any moment. When Amarin separated for a closer look, he said, "Where is our sister, Gamon? And Nan?"

Before the conversation could go further, a sharp rap on the door was followed by a harsh command. "Chen! Three minutes!"

Unlike Jade, Amarin's life was not his own. He was expected to entertain the gamblers and then to join them for dinner. So they dried their tears and made secret plans to meet at the Hoover Dam the next day.

Thinking about it now, Jade bowed her head. That meeting had ended in disaster. She'd had no choice but to flee.

Amarin had killed a man that day. Someone who was connected to his boss. She didn't know whether her brother had survived or not.

When she returned from Vegas, she'd told GiGi everything. Neither sister knew what to do about the situation, so they carried on as if the disastrous trip to Vegas had never happened.

Then GiGi could no longer stand the stress. She told Eleanor about Amarin. Eleanor asked around and learned that the boxer Alan Chen was owned by Roberto "The Elephant" Rossi.

GiGi researched Rossi and his Muay Thai boxing schemes. Knowing her brother's boss was the notorious gangster and Moretti, the dead fixer, was one of Rossi's men was too much for Jade and GiGi to handle.

Jade's nerves were at the breaking point when Eleanor

Duncan came to her rescue again. Eleanor had friends in high places. Low places too, it turned out. Somehow, Eleanor hired Reacher and that silly man who drove him everywhere, Petey Burns.

Jade and Eleanor had dinner last night with Reacher and Burns. She had never seen anyone as big as Reacher in her life. Her reaction to him was mixed awe and terror. Added to the anxiety she'd been unable to overcome since Amarin threw that man over the bridge, Jade could barely function.

At the restaurant last night, Eleanor had explained the situation while Jade twisted her hands in her lap and kept the same stoic expression she wore whenever she was forced to endure situations she could not control.

Reacher had listened, asked a few questions, and said he could take care of it.

"What will you do? Rossi's a gangster. He'll kill you without a moment's hesitation," Jade said, distraught.

Reacher said nothing.

Jade wasn't sure what Reacher had planned, but after all these years of taking care of herself and the others, she was happy to hand off her troubles to such a giant. Surely he was big enough to handle Rossi.

Reacher exuded absolute confidence, and she wanted to believe him.

Eleanor, always reliable, assured her that Reacher could take care of everything. Jade chose to believe them both. What alternative did she have?

That was last night and Jade hadn't slept at all since the dinner. She had no idea where Reacher was or what he might be doing. She'd canceled her clients last night and stayed home, doors locked, waiting for disaster to strike.

As the sun peeked above the horizon, Jade heard her cell phone vibrating on the table nearby. She owned several phones, but this was her personal number, which was private and only shared with a limited few.

The ringing jarred her from her constantly repeating memories of Amarin and the bridge and the man falling swiftly to his death at the bottom of the canyon.

Jade swept up the phone, thinking the caller was probably her sister. GiGi often awakened early in the morning.

She raised her eyebrows when she saw Eleanor Duncan's name displayed on the caller ID. She cleared her throat and tried to speak normally. "Good morning. This is pretty early for you, isn't it?"

"We had a fire at the restaurant." Eleanor paused to cough for a long few moments. The cumulative effect of the smoke and the night air had settled in her lungs.

Jade blinked as if the meaning of the words escaped her. "What? A fire?"

Eleanor tried to control her coughing, managing only a quick short sentence before another paroxysm attacked her. "The building is destroyed."

"The whole building?" Jade asked, a tremor in her voice. She wrapped a shaky arm around her body for warmth.

Nighttime fires in rural Thailand were often fatal. Her mother had perished in such a fire years ago. The visceral memory attacked her body with a fit of uncontrollable shaking even as her mind attempted to separate the old horror from the new one.

"Is everyone…all right?" she said, her voice shaky.

"Do you have room for us?" Eleanor managed to say between bouts of coughing. "We have nothing. And nowhere else to go. We'll find another place as soon as we can. But for now…"

Without a moment's hesitation, Jade said, "Of course. You must come here. Where are you now?"

Jade had no empty guestrooms, which mattered not. She couldn't possibly turn Eleanor and the others away.

Sixteen of them had lived together in a shipping container for weeks once. They could certainly pile into her penthouse suite and sleep on the floors until different arrangements could be made.

"Thank you," Eleanor said with a catch in her voice that Jade had never heard before, not even once. Eleanor was never emotional. Yet her gratitude was palpable.

Jade waved her feelings aside, even though Eleanor couldn't see the gesture. Given everything Eleanor Duncan had done for her and the others, no refusal or hesitation could possibly be justified.

"Do you need me to send the van for you?" Jade asked.

"That would help. Everything we owned was inside our rooms. It'll take a couple of days to get ourselves together. Hell, we're all in our pajamas. We have no cash or credit cards…" her voice trailed off into the ether.

"Where are you?"

"At the bistro. Outside. Watching the last of the embers die." Eleanor coughed again as if she'd been standing in the cold and too near the smoke for a while.

"Okay, I'll send the van. Text me when you get here and we'll come down to help you all get to your rooms upstairs," Jade said. "You can stay here as long as you want, you know that. You're all closer than sisters to us."

Eleanor coughed again, but the cough had a different quality this time. As if she was holding back emotions she didn't want to release. Jade squeezed tears from her eyes, too.

When her coughing subsided, her voice even huskier than before, Eleanor said, "Is Reacher with you?"

"Haven't seen him since dinner."

"We need to find him. He can find out who the son of a bitch was that burned down my restaurant," Eleanor said angrily as she hung up.

Arson. Jade's breath caught in her throat. Her hand flew to cover her mouth.

Someone burned down the restaurant. But why? Who would want to hurt Eleanor Duncan? She was one of the best souls Jade had ever known.

Her thoughts swung immediately to Reacher. Whatever the bond he had with Eleanor was, it was strong and solid. Jade had sensed that anyone who harmed Eleanor was surely walking dead already. Reacher would see to that.

But as quickly as the questions raced through her head, the answers chased behind like a taser charge through her body.

Eleanor's trouble was about Jade. It had to be. No one would want to harm Eleanor otherwise.

Amarin had killed a man on Sunday because of Jade. A fixer for a Vegas gangster. Rossi.

She didn't know much about gangsters, but she'd seen plenty of movies. Even if the movies exaggerated a gangster's ruthlessness, Amarin's worried expression when he first saw the fixer coming toward her on the bridge had been all too real.

Jade looked out toward the sunrise and noticed the bright orb ascending steadily. Daylight. Never a good time for her. She preferred to move under cover of darkness.

She sensed that Reacher did, too.

Where had he been last night, if not watching over Eleanor?

Jade swallowed the big lump that still blocked her breath. Reacher hadn't been there for Eleanor because she'd hired him to protect Jade, GiGi, and Mika. He'd taken his eye off the real target because Eleanor had asked him to.

She texted a quick message about the fire and Eleanor's plight to Petey Burns. He had a phone. Reacher didn't.

Tears leaked from Jade's tightly closed eyes as she called GiGi, who lived in the apartment immediately below with Mika. The others lived on the floor below GiGi, where the clients were entertained seven nights a week.

GiGi answered with a cheerful "Good morning."

"Get dressed," Jade said shakily, wiping her tears as she walked toward her bedroom closet. "Eleanor and our sisters are in trouble."

"Oh, no! What kind of trouble?" GiGi asked as if she suspected the danger was related to them. Which they both knew it absolutely had to be.

"They're all terrified. I'm sending the van. They are coming here." Jade said as she pulled jeans and a sweater and underwear out of her dresser. "They've never been here before, so we'll meet them downstairs and bring them up to their rooms."

"We'll be ready. Call me when they get here. I want to come with you," GiGi said before she hung up.

Jade dialed her car service and ordered the van she used for bachelor parties to collect Eleanor and the others at the bistro. The dispatcher said the van could be there in thirty minutes or less.

Then she tossed the phone on the bed on her way to the bathroom to get dressed.

CHAPTER TWENTY-FOUR

Wednesday, May 18
Golden, Colorado
5:45 a.m.

KIM KEPT ELEANOR IN her periphery as she scanned the parking lot and peered into the shadows. The cold had seeped into her bones, numbing her fingers. She stamped her feet and wiggled her toes to keep the blood flowing.

Burke had melded into the bedlam surrounding the fire. A few shivering bystanders dressed in their night clothes had gathered in small groups at various points on the sidewalk to watch the show.

She saw no sign of Reacher on this side of the chaos. Which meant nothing.

Eleanor completed her call. She approached her employees and huddled with them. She seemed to be unusually close to these young women, which was odd. In Kim's experience, employers rarely displayed such open devotion to employees, even amid disastrous conditions.

Which made her wonder why Eleanor was so concerned about them.

Beyond that, why had no one else arrived to help these women? No husbands, boyfriends, parents?

Kim had worked fires and explosions in multi-occupancy buildings before, even a few on college campuses. Family members were called immediately and swarmed the victims like mother hens, usually. But in this case, the only protector around was Eleanor.

Kim's cell phone vibrated in her pocket. She fished it out and took Gaspar's call. "What's up?"

"I've located the Audi. The SUV Burns stole in South Dakota when he ditched the Jetta," Gaspar said to be clear as if she'd asked him about more than one Audi or suffered from amnesia or something. "No way to know whether they're still using it, though."

"Where is it?"

"Until about ten minutes ago, it was parked in back of a residential building in Denver. Right now, it's speeding expertly in your direction," Gaspar replied. "Which probably means Burns is driving. Reacher's a notoriously bad driver, remember."

"Right."

"Looks like he's doing seventy in a thirty-five at the moment. When he hits the expressway, he'll have more room to move. At the rate he's going, he'll be there in twenty minutes. Maybe less," Gaspar said.

"Is he alone in the vehicle?"

"Can't tell. The Audi has illegally tinted windows. Burns could be solo. Or he might have a passenger."

"So you don't have eyes on the vehicle now?"

"Not yet."

"Can you access communications inside the Audi's cabin?"

"Under normal conditions, we could. Turns out, Petey Burns is not only a clever car thief and a better-than-decent driver, but he's also pretty good with the tech. He's disabled the GPS, Bluetooth, and a couple of transponders," Gaspar's tone reflected something like appreciation for Burns's demonstrated skills. "He's communicating with the outside world, but not over the vehicle's internal tech."

"Okay." Kim saw movement from Eleanor's group in her periphery and turned her head.

A charcoal gray luxury van pulled up nearby, metallic paint sparkling in the cone of the streetlights. The driver lowered his window and said something to Eleanor. The van's automatic side door opened. The eleven bistro employees piled into the van, the door closed, and the driver pulled away, leaving Eleanor on the sidewalk.

She pulled out her phone and made a second call before dropping the phone into the big pocket of her barn coat. Then she stood on the curb watching the northbound traffic lanes.

"See what you can find out about the employees living in the Orchid Thai building, will you?" Kim said. "There's something weird about this situation. Whatever it is might give us better intel about Reacher."

"What are you thinking?" Gaspar asked, still clacking the keyboard. "Illegals?"

"Maybe," Kim said slowly. "Is it crazy to think they might have come with Eleanor from Nebraska?"

"Trafficking Thais for agricultural or domestic workers is common in Asia. Trafficking Thai restaurant workers in the U.S., not so much," Gaspar replied. "Besides, how would Eleanor Duncan from Nowhere Nebraska get hooked up with something like that?"

"Not sure. Just a hunch. Could be way off-base. But it's weird. We'll talk more later. I've gotta go. Keep me posted." Kim disconnected Gaspar's call, stuffed her cold hands into her pockets, and approached Eleanor, still waiting near the curb. "What's going on?"

"One of my former employees offered us a place to stay in Denver until we can get something better sorted out. The van wasn't spacious enough to hold us all. I sent the others ahead and I've called another ride," Eleanor said, shoulders hunched inside the barn coat as if she'd finally noticed the temperature outside the cone of warmth from her blazing building. "The second driver was in the vicinity. He said he'd be here shortly."

"Sounds better than waiting for the first driver to make a return trip," Kim said, nodding.

Gaspar had said the Audi had been parked near a residential building in Denver. Could be a coincidence. But the smart money was on a connection between the Denver building, the Audi, and the bistro. Which meant a connection between Reacher and the Denver building, too.

It was a better lead than she'd had in the past three days. No reason to ignore it and every reason to follow up.

Less than five minutes later, a black luxury SUV drove slowly along the street. The driver stopped at the curb, lowered the window, and pushed a button to open the door automatically. Same as the van driver had done.

"Sorry to keep you waiting, Mrs. Duncan. You called for a ride to Denver?"

"That's right," Eleanor said and gave him the address. She glanced one last time toward the ashes of her world and then hiked over to the SUV. She ducked her head and climbed in.

Kim slipped inside behind her.

Eleanor flashed a surprised expression. "Where are you going?"

"We didn't get a chance to finish our talk. Burke can pick me up when he's done here," Kim said, already appreciating the warm comfort inside the vehicle.

Before Eleanor could object, the driver closed and locked the automatic door locks.

The cloying stench of the fire embedded into their clothing hung like a cloud. Kim pressed the button to lower the window for fresh air, but the window didn't open.

A second man was belted into the passenger seat. The driver's eyes were reflected in the rearview mirror. He said, "I've got a trainee with me tonight. I hope that's okay."

It wasn't really a question and the vehicle was already moving. What were they going to do, kick the man out?

The passenger nodded toward them and offered a friendly wave without looking back. The two women slid more comfortably into their individual seats and snapped seatbelts into place. The driver raised the privacy glass, effectively creating a separate room for Eleanor and Kim.

Eleanor gave Kim a curious stare. "Aren't you worried about getting into a strange car with a woman you don't know?"

"You bet. It's my job to worry about everything," Kim quipped.

She could take care of herself. Her service weapon was holstered under her arm. The Boss's steady surveillance of every move she made and Gaspar's watchful eye were all the backup she needed.

All of which meant Kim was as safe as she ever was while hunting Reacher. She didn't mention that, either.

Adrenaline, anxiety, and ambition constantly ran through her veins, powering her through. The pole position shifted based on conditions on the ground. She called the mixture her standard triple-As.

Ambition was strongest at the moment. She wanted Reacher. And she was *so* close. She could feel it.

Allowing Eleanor to ride away in an unfamiliar vehicle to an unknown destination was simply not an option.

Besides, she'd heard Eleanor relay the address to the driver. The Boss and Gaspar would have heard it, too.

CHAPTER TWENTY-FIVE

Wednesday, May 18
Denver, Colorado
6:15 a.m.

AFTER SYDNEY HAD RAISED the privacy windows, he and Joey could talk freely. Normal conversation in the front of the SUV could not be overheard in the passenger compartment. He'd turn on the intercom to hear Eleanor Duncan's conversation with the other woman soon, but more pressing matters came first.

"Let's go over this again," Sydney said.

"What for? I got this." Joey frowned and tapped his temple with two fingers. "You think I'm stupid?"

Sydney ignored the question.

Joey shook his head and then repeated the plan. "We entice the women to come outside and approach the SUV. When they do, we'll shove them inside and lock the doors. Then we drive away."

"Basically, yes." Sydney inhaled deeply and then shoved the air through his nose. "There'll be six women and—"

"Yeah, I know. But they're tiny," Joey grinned. "Easier than dwarf-tossing. I'll bet you a thousand bucks each that I could pick them up and toss them in the back in thirty seconds or less."

"Let's save that for plan B." Sydney shook his head. "You could damage the cargo. One's a girl about twelve years old. They're all fragile. We'll try another way first."

Joey laughed. "You're afraid you'd lose the bet, aren't you?"

"It's already after six o'clock. The sun is up. People might be walking around in that neighborhood. The Thais might scream. Somebody could call the cops." Sydney paused and gave Joey Prime a frank glare as he listed all the problems with Joey's idea. "Shall I continue?"

Joey shrugged. "We'll try it your way. But any little thing goes sideways, and we're grabbing them and getting the hell out."

"Right. So, to recap. We'll be sure there's no reason to abort the plan. Then I'll send the text. I'll open the doors to the second and third seating compartments. They'll climb in voluntarily. I'll close the doors and take off," Sydney finished with a worried frown. Joey Prime had always been a loose cannon. Sydney hoped he could be trusted to follow orders.

"And what if they don't just climb in?"

"They will."

"But what if they don't?"

"Then we'll do it your way," Sydney said. "But then we do it fast. We'll have five seconds or less to get in and get out."

Joey jerked his thumb over his shoulder. "How do we keep these two quiet in the meantime?"

"Leave that to me." Sydney nodded.

He had already raised the privacy window behind the first row of seats, separating it from the rest of the cabin.

The space where the two women sat was now airtight as well as soundproofed and bulletproofed. They could scream their fool heads off, and no one would hear them. He'd had a guy try to shoot his way out once. The guy ended up with a bullet wound because of the ricochet, but he didn't escape.

Sydney had used this SUV and this precise method of abduction before when Rossi sent him to terminate rivals. Rossi had obtained the drugs from an associate in Moscow after he'd read about a terrorist incident at a Moscow theater. The method proved high risk. The terrorists were neutralized, but several hostages died.

"Any more questions?" Sydney asked. Joey shook his head.

Sydney glanced in the rearview mirror. The two women were talking. He flipped the switch to open the listening devices in the backseat. Their disembodied voices flooded the cockpit.

"Why are you looking for Reacher? You don't believe he set fire to my building, surely," Eleanor Duncan said to the other woman.

"Tell me why you think he didn't do it," the other woman replied in a Midwest American accent.

The little hairs stood up on the back of Sydney's neck and his nerves hummed along his spine. He cast a quick side-eye to Joey Prime, who seemed oblivious to the impending disaster.

Sydney had spent plenty of time around Asian illegals. If Rossi had trafficked this woman like the others, she wouldn't sound American. Not even remotely.

Which meant she wasn't like the others.

Which was a serious problem.

Sydney slammed his palm into the steering wheel.

Trafficking Asian illegals was one thing. Scooping up the woman who stole Rossi's property was another thing.

Kidnapping an American citizen and transporting her across state lines was something else entirely. Right off the top of his head, Sydney could think of two dozen terminal consequences that could befall him for this single mistake.

But the worst and most immediate problem was The Elephant. Rossi would be far from pleased.

Anger boiled in his veins and threatened to erupt like a volcano. Only because he couldn't swear and listen at the same time, he swallowed the spew of curses that sprang to his mouth, which made him feel like his head might literally explode.

"You said Reacher came here to help me. And then in the next breath, you claim he destroyed my place of business, leaving all of us homeless and destitute," Duncan said, head cocked as if she was truly puzzled. "That makes no sense, Agent Otto. Aren't FBI agents supposed to make sense?"

Sydney's mouth dried up. His heart had been pounding hard already, and now it slammed into his chest with the force of Thor's hammer. The second woman was an *FBI agent*? How could that be true?

Joey Prime glanced over. "Whoa! Sydney! Are you stroking out on me here?"

Sydney jerked his head to signal a quick no. He didn't reply. Deafening blood pulsing in his ears made it difficult to follow the quiet conversation in the back already. He strained to hear.

"Dr. Landon said you were in trouble," Otto replied. "Whether Reacher's methods make sense depends on what kind of help you need, doesn't it?"

"I don't need insurance money. Or at least, until tonight I didn't." Eleanor Duncan sighed and shook her head. "Ezra and Brenda Landon are my friends. I don't know what they told Reacher. Do you?"

Sydney wondered who Reacher was and why the FBI was looking for him, but the more he heard, the worse the situation became. He'd kidnapped an FBI agent working on an active case.

Which meant the other guy she'd arrived with back there at the fire was probably her partner. The only thing worse than one FBI agent was two of the cockroaches.

The partner would come after her. No doubt about it. He might be on his way already.

Soon, Sydney would have a whole raft of feds chasing him. They'd be after Rossi, too, once they connected the dots.

Stories about the relentless FBI searching for gangsters of all types were the stuff of legend. Because they were true. Sydney had seen it firsthand. Joey Prime, too.

Otto shook her head. "You must have told the Landons something that concerned them. What was it?"

Duncan sighed. "It wasn't about me. I told them that one of my former employees has a brother. He's in trouble."

"Does Reacher know either of those people? Has he ever dealt with them before?"

"He knows me. He's helped me before. Back in Nebraska. Which you probably already know. Maybe he was headed toward the restaurant tonight. I don't know," Duncan shrugged. "You'll have to ask him."

"I have to find him first," Otto replied.

Sydney flipped off the intercom. He'd learned as much as he needed to know for the moment.

He'd kidnapped an FBI agent. That was all the bad news he had the stomach for.

Sweat ran down his forehead and into his eyes. He felt dampness under his shirt and in the crotch of his pants. He was a wet, stinking mess.

He glanced at the clock. The SUV had been traveling easily in light traffic. They were ten minutes away from the brothel.

Sydney opened the console and found the remote for the pressurized cylinders. He triggered the release of the fentanyl-based incapacitating agent as he slowed the SUV to turn the last corner.

The dosage was tricky. Too little, and the drugs would fail to do the job. Too much, and the women would die.

In this case, more was better. He gave it two long blasts and two short ones for good measure. He hoped he'd got it right.

Worst case, these two died.

But he'd have the next six in the vehicle without incident.

Including the eleven in the van, even if the suit died, Rossi would have a total of seventeen new money makers. Which might buy Sydney some mercy.

Meaning Eleanor Duncan's death by poison was a risk Sydney was willing to take. Rossi couldn't use her, anyway.

And the other one was supposed to be a bonus for Rossi. He didn't even know she existed. Yet.

If the FBI agent didn't make it to Vegas, Rossi wouldn't be short on his inventory. Not that Rossi's money was his main concern right at the moment.

He kept his finger on the trigger. As the gas released into the passenger cabin, Sydney watched the images on the security camera mounted in the back. After a few moments of breathing poison, the two women slumped into their seatbelts.

Joey nodded approvingly. "Nice job. That's impressive stuff. Where'd you get it?"

Sydney said nothing. He had more pressing matters on his mind.

He'd cloned Duncan's phone onto a burner. He created a

simple text and sent the fake message to Jade's phone. "We're here."

She texted back. "We're coming now."

"Get ready," Sydney said.

Joey grinned. "I was born ready."

"Stay alert. Watch the monitors," Sydney ordered gruffly. "We need to deliver this batch to Rossi alive and unharmed."

"How do you know the gas won't kill them? You ever used it on tiny Asian women before?" Joey asked like he was asking about a favorite barbeque sauce.

Sydney shrugged and said nothing.

He waited until he saw Jade and the others rush outside and onto the sidewalk.

Then he rolled up to the curb, stopping in the blind spot where the cameras he'd located wouldn't capture the next few minutes of activity.

When he was sure he'd parked in precisely the correct location, he pushed the buttons to open the second and third doors.

There were five females with Jade. One was supposed to be only twelve years old, but they were all slight of stature, so it was hard to judge their ages. Combined, they probably weighed less than The Elephant.

The six females rushed headlong into the limo to rescue the others they believed were arriving with Eleanor Duncan, as expected.

Sydney closed the doors and pulled away from the curb before they realized their sisters were not inside.

Simultaneously, careful not to overdose Rossi's property, he pushed more buttons on the remote to dispense lighter doses of the fentanyl gas into the second and third enclosures.

The six females sank slowly into the seats and onto the carpet. Before the SUV had traveled two blocks, they were all unconscious.

Joey had been watching the monitors closely until the last one fell into what looked like a deep sleep. "How long will they be out like that?"

"Long enough," Sydney shrugged.

"Man, you are *good*!" Joey Prime punched Sydney on the arm and gave him a sloppy grin.

Sydney offered a weak nod as he clawed back the bile that rose in his throat and turned the SUV onto the entrance ramp for the westbound interstate toward Vegas, worrying about the suit.

CHAPTER TWENTY-SIX

Wednesday, May 18
Golden, Colorado
8:15 a.m.

GASPAR HAD HACKED INTO traffic and security cameras surrounding the Orchid Thai Bistro. On his monitors, he'd had a partially obstructed remote view of the fire since shortly after Otto and Burke had first arrived.

Firefighters had been battling for several hours, and the blaze was mostly under control. Smoldering embers might flare up again, but for now, the scene had settled into a somewhat predictable routine.

A while ago, the Audi had circled the block a couple of times before it raced away again, still headed west. Gaspar continued to trace it until it pulled into a busy parking lot two miles away and stopped.

He sipped a big mug of sweetened Cuban coffee with milk and tried pinging Otto's phone again. As before, her signal didn't show up on any of his searches. He tried twice more. No luck.

He frowned, drained the coffee, and pulled up the surveillance video surrounding the bistro fire. He scrolled to the time just before his last conversation with Otto and ran the video forward.

The charcoal van came into view. It was relatively new, possibly manufactured within the current model year. Eleven restaurant workers piled into the open maw and the door slid closed. Eleanor Duncan stepped back and the van drove away.

Gaspar paused the video and clipped stills of the rear license plate before he returned to the unfolding situation.

Soon afterward, the black stretch SUV rolled into the same spot. The images snared Gaspar's memory. He narrowed his eyes and looked closer until he realized what was strange about the boxy vehicle.

The oversized limo moved oddly. It lumbered slower than it should have. The engine was too loud as it labored harder than the manufacturer intended, too.

Gaspar cocked his head and rewound the video for another look.

He had seen that pattern before. On vehicles that had been bulletproofed or outfitted with special heavy equipment. Like politicians and third world drug lords and gangsters used.

Extra weight impacted speed, efficiency, and maneuverability. The differences weren't obvious. Unless you were attuned to the variances and looking from the right angle, you could miss it easily enough. No reason why Duncan or Otto should have noticed.

Gaspar watched them climb into the passenger compartment of the SUV. He paused the video and captured the rear license plate on the limo, too.

The driver moved the limo eastward, toward Denver. Gaspar

left the video running and turned his attention to the license plates.

Neither the van nor the SUV bore a front license plate. Which might have been okay, but it made Gaspar a little twitchy. Or maybe it was the caffeine. He grinned.

Not all states required front plates. He ran a quick check on the rules for Colorado.

Front plates were easier than rear plates to track on toll roads. A bean counter in Denver had calculated the potential lost revenue from tolls if front plates were eliminated. Turned out it was way more than the cost of making and distributing front plates. The potential lost revenue proved too much for the state government to ignore.

So front plates were necessary in Colorado. And neither the van nor the SUV displayed one.

Commercial passenger vehicles like these two were not likely to ignore such rules, putting fines and operating licenses and the like at risk while they drove the local roads all day, every day.

Now, the missing front plates made Gaspar a little more twitchy. He pushed his coffee mug aside and focused on the rear plates.

At first glance, they seemed normal enough. Nothing to draw undue attention from law enforcement or traffic cameras. Which meant there was no reason for Otto to be unduly suspicious of them, either.

Both vehicles sported standard Colorado issue plates. Classic white mountains and a green border. Gaspar's quick online search revealed that the same generic mountains had been used on Colorado plates since 1960.

Each had two stickers, the white one in the lower-left corner and the colored one in the lower-right corner, where they should be.

He enlarged the images.

The three-letter, three-number combination on both of these plates had been discontinued a while back. Colorado plates were issued with four letters and two numbers now.

Which meant both of the plates were several years older than the van and the SUV to which they were affixed.

But they could have been legally transferred from an older vehicle.

Gaspar ran the plate numbers through a couple of databases. Both plates had been renewed within the past twelve months. One was registered to a Toyota Camry and the other belonged to a Honda Accord. Neither had been legally transferred to the van or the SUV. Neither was reported stolen. Yet.

He tried pinging Kim's phones again. She carried three phones with her. One was personal. One was a burner issued by Cooper. The third was a burner she used to connect to Gaspar. None of them returned a signal.

One failed signal could have been harmless. Three missing signals was definitely not okay.

Gaspar sat up straight and stared at the screen as if the problem might lie with his tech. He triple-checked to be sure his equipment was operating as it should.

Then, he searched through recent calls on all three numbers until he found one that could have been made to Burke on Kim's personal phone. He pinged it.

The signal triangulated at the Orchid Thai Bistro parking lot. Gaspar accessed the security cameras in the vicinity until he located the phone. It was weaving between emergency vehicles, probably resting inside Burke's pocket.

"Lucky guess," he murmured before he placed the call.

"FBI Special Agent William Burke," he said when he picked up the unfamiliar number. The noise of the fire fighting continued in the background. Although the fire was under control now, personnel and equipment defeated the normal early morning quiet.

He cut right to the point. "Burke, it's Gaspar. Do you know where Otto is?"

"Not that it's any of your business," Burke replied gruffly. "She was with Eleanor Duncan on the other side of the parking lot last time I saw her."

Gaspar clenched his jaw. "She's not there now. Where was Duncan going next?"

"No clue. My impression was that she had someplace in mind, though. Did Otto leave with Duncan?" Burke's responses were not focused on the conversation at hand. He was preoccupied with something.

"Listen up, Burke. Your partner's in trouble. It's your job to make sure that doesn't happen, and you've already failed." Gaspar's judgment was harsh. He didn't approve of Burke. Hadn't from the start.

"Yeah? Well your job is to butt out, Gaspar. Cooper has made that clear. To me, to Otto, and my guess is, to you. Why don't you get that?" Burke lashed back.

Good. At least he was finally paying attention. "What the hell are you doing that's so damned important?"

"Hunting Reacher. Which is my job. You should try doing yours," Burke replied.

"You think Reacher is hanging around that fire site? Why would he? The fire's done. Even if he's your arsonist, he's not the type to stand back and admire his own handiwork like some kind of fire bug," Gaspar replied.

"That so?" Burke could have hung up, but he didn't. Which probably meant he'd already concluded the same thing.

"The proof is in the pudding, as my grandmother used to say." Gaspar shook his head. This guy had a lot to learn. "You didn't find Reacher, did you?"

"What the hell do you want, anyway?"

"I've been trying to reach Otto. She's not picking up her phone."

"Voicemail exists for that very reason," Burke quipped in response as if he was unconcerned. But he was moving toward Otto's last known location at a slow jog. Gaspar saw him on the traffic cams' live feed.

He pressed the mute button on the call and took several deep breaths.

Burke was the agent on the ground. His response time should be faster than getting another team out there. Which meant he was stuck with Burke for now.

Gaspar had broken one of his own rules. He didn't have a plan B for this situation. He'd read Burke in and hope for the best.

But he'd have a plan B for next time. He wouldn't make the same mistake twice.

Gaspar opened the line again. "Look, Otto requested intel from me. I called to give it to her. The call went to voicemail. She didn't call back. I tried to ping her phone. No luck."

"There's nothing to worry about. Otto can take care of herself, which we both well know." Burke had come around the firetrucks and should have a clear view of the vacant parking lot where he'd left Otto standing.

After a brief pause, Burke asked, "Why wouldn't her phone ping? There's a harmless answer to that question, right?"

Gaspar's jaw worked as he ground his teeth. He flared his nostrils and snorted angry hot air. "Under these circumstances, there is no harmless reason to explain why I can't find her phone."

He knew what he had to do. He didn't like it. And it wouldn't help Otto right this minute, anyway. But it would help for next time.

And with Burke, there would always be a next time. Gaspar knew it as well as he knew the sun would rise in Miami tomorrow.

Gaspar said, "She got into a limo. The plate on the vehicle is stolen. Not traceable. I've found the SUV on the traffic cams."

Burke was hoofing it toward the Lincoln Navigator he'd been driving. He opened the door and started the engine. "Which way?"

"I suspect they might be headed to a residential building in Denver. Try that first." Gaspar gave him the address and directions. "I'm still tracing the limo through the traffic cam video, but it's slow because of the transfer from one camera to the next."

"Why do you think the SUV is going there?" Burke asked.

Now that he was inside the Navigator, Gaspar knew Kim's boss would be listening to every word and tracking Burke, too. Which, for once, wasn't a bad thing.

"The Audi was parked there earlier. The one Petey Burns stole."

"The one Reacher has been riding around in, you mean? Are you kidding me?" Burke shouted angrily. "You knew where Reacher was and you didn't give us a heads-up? Whose side are you on?"

Gaspar ignored the ranting as he fast-forwarded the video and tracked the limo with maddening slowness. The Audi could wait. Burns had abandoned it in a parking lot.

Probably because he'd stolen a different vehicle.

Which meant he was driving something else now, anyway.

Possibly with Reacher in the passenger seat.

Or not.

None of which was pressing.

What he needed to know right now was the address of that Denver residence.

Finding Otto was more important than finding Reacher. Gaspar didn't give a crap about Reacher. Never had. When he was still on the FBI payroll, he'd done his job. Those days were over. Reacher was no longer his problem.

But Otto was wired differently. Finding Reacher drove her relentlessly now. She would never stop until she found him.

Or died trying.

Which was what truly frightened Gaspar.

CHAPTER TWENTY-SEVEN

Wednesday, May 18
Las Vegas, Nevada
8:45 a.m.

ROSSI'S BREAKFAST HAD BEEN delivered promptly to his rooms as expected. He was dressed and seated at the table, six newspapers neatly folded beside his eggs and waffles. The coffee was prepared precisely as he preferred.

He began to eat his first bites as he opened the Las Vegas newspaper to the broader state news which was printed in a separate section near the back. The publisher's market research showed that readers of the Vegas paper were more interested in local news, sports, and entertainment than news of the world, the nation, or the state of Nevada, curiously.

Section D was a slim few pages, easily missed by most readers and thrown out with the daily trash. The story Rossi wanted was reported in two column inches on page seven, near the obituaries, which was probably appropriate.

No photos of the bodies or the possessions found with them

were printed with the story. Rossi read the six short paragraphs through twice. The headline was brief. "Two Male Bodies Found in Jarbidge Canyon."

The report ran without a byline. It contained only a few facts, none of which were particularly troublesome. The bodies had been found by hikers. Neither the bodies nor the hikers were identified. Cause of death was presumed to be dehydration and exposure. Autopsies were still pending. The piece ended with a plea to the public for any possible information that might help to identify the two men.

Short and to the point. No speculation. Just the kind of news report Rossi appreciated.

Nothing was mentioned about more bodies found a couple of months back in another remote area of the canyon, either.

He should have chosen a better dump site for these two males because of the prior discoveries. But anybody actually finding all four bodies was an example of the fluke factor at work.

Jarbidge Canyon was a perfect dump site. It was the most remote place in Nevada. His helicopter could fly there, dump the dead meat, and get back in less than three hours.

Only a fluke had revealed the first two bodies. But with the discovery of the second two, he was now forced to change the dump site.

He'd been considering that knotty problem since Luca brought him the news yesterday. Fights to the death appealed to a certain segment of Rossi's clientele. Dead boxers were common. The high stakes matches produced one or two a month.

Until he found another dump site, dead boxers must remain in the Snake Eyes private cold storage. Which wasn't ideal, simply a solid short-term solution.

He'd begin his research for a new site today. But there was little urgency, given the facts.

The chances that these two bodies would be positively identified were slim. After all these weeks, determining the exact cause of death should be challenging as well.

Chen had killed them with clean kicks to the neck at the side of the head, two nights apart. But that was months ago.

Eight months in the hot, dry desert canyon where vultures and other carnivores roamed freely wouldn't have left much forensic evidence to evaluate.

Dental records would be no help. Both teens had been trafficked from the poorest rural areas of Thailand. Neither had ever sat in a dentist's chair.

The medical examiner, if he was exceptionally thorough, might notice evidence of similar blunt force trauma on both, but tying that trauma to Rossi's Muay Thai boxing matches two hundred miles south in Vegas was extremely unlikely.

Luca was worried for nothing. That's how lawyers were. Professional worriers. After reviewing the newspaper reports, Rossi's day was already looking brighter.

He thumbed through the remaining five newspapers. None of the others had picked up the report on the bodies. Which was to be expected. Poor immigrants without identification were not top priorities for law enforcement. Nor should they be.

He'd take it one day at a time. Chen could live to box another profitable night, which to Rossi was good news. Chen was perhaps the best boxer Rossi had ever owned. Terminating him would be a pity when the time came.

But that time was not today. Rossi grinned.

He finished his third cup of coffee and returned to his leisurely breakfast while his eggs were still hot. He read the remaining newspapers as he usually did. He found nothing reported about the restaurant fire in Golden, Colorado, which was good news, too.

Rossi swallowed the last bite of waffle with a coffee chaser seconds before his phone rang. He glanced at the caller's name before he answered.

"Good morning, Sydney. Siegfried is expecting me shortly. We can talk more later. But let's have your progress report before I journey upstairs."

Sydney got right to the point. "We have good news. And a potential problem."

Rossi sighed. "There's always problems in life. Bad news can wait. Tell me the good news. Do you have the woman?"

"We do."

"Excellent. When will you return?"

"We should reach Vegas before dinner."

Rossi beamed. He glanced at the clock. Siegfried was waiting. His time with the plants had been cut short yesterday. He meant to spend at least an extra hour this morning fully appreciating his new jewel while the victory was still fresh in Siegfried's mind and every exciting detail could be breathlessly conveyed.

Rossi said, "I shall see you in my office for a full report. Deliver the woman. Then call Dolly to schedule."

He hung up the phone feeling mighty pleased, indeed. The final chapter of what he privately thought of as the *too many women saga* had ended well. Earlier failures were mere inconveniences.

The beauty of his long memory allowed him to appreciate delayed gratification. He smiled.

He had paid for sixteen Thai females seven years ago. They

were transported across the ocean in perfect condition, as ordered. Then the Duncan woman and Reacher had stolen his property.

With the females once again within his purview, along with the additional prostitutes, his fortunes were about to improve dramatically. Funds for acquiring expensive orchids would be flush once more.

With Jade Chen under his control, Rossi felt confident that his plans for Alan Chen would move smoothly forward as well.

As long as no more bodies were found.

He frowned slightly, pushing his lips in and out.

If more dead boxers turned up, Chen might need to be sacrificed to the authorities. But that was a concern for another time. Such thoughts should not spoil his morning with the orchids.

Beaming with satisfaction, he waddled to the elevator and stepped inside for the short ride to the roof.

CHAPTER TWENTY-EIGHT

Wednesday, May 18
Denver, Colorado
9:15 a.m.

GASPAR DISPATCHED BURKE TO the address of the Denver residence where he had spotted Reacher's stolen Audi earlier.

While Burke was on his way, Gaspar continued to trace the black SUV that swallowed Otto. He'd confirmed that the vehicle had traveled directly to the unimaginatively named Denver Tower, with Otto and Eleanor Duncan still inside.

Which was the only good news so far.

The van that had collected the bistro employees a few minutes before Otto disappeared did not arrive at Denver Tower. Gaspar would need to go back to the traffic cams around the bistro to trace the van. He put that task aside for now and concentrated on finding Otto.

He watched the video recording again and checked the time clock.

The black SUV had parked for less than five minutes at the

200 | DIANE CAPRI

curb in front of the Denver Tower building and then left again. Plenty of time for Otto and Duncan to emerge from the vehicle. But did they? He didn't have a clear view of the doors.

Gaspar spent another ten minutes searching for better video views, but none of them showed Otto and Duncan leaving the SUV's passenger cabin. All blind spots converged on the passenger doors of the vehicle.

The SUV arrived. Parked. Departed.

But where was Otto?

"How convenient," Gaspar murmured under his breath as he pressed the redial for Burke's cell phone.

"I'm just pulling into a parking space around back of the Denver Tower building now," Burke said when he picked up.

"Did you call your boss?" Gaspar asked. "Tell him to get some agents out there to find Otto?"

"Tried. Got voicemail. Left a message," Burke replied. "But he wouldn't send agents after her, even if I asked. Which I'm not doing."

Gaspar said nothing, but Burke must have felt his disapproval two thousand miles away.

Burke kept talking. "Look, there could be a thousand reasons why she's not communicating with us. Regardless, we're playing without a net here. You know that. So what've you got?"

"Not as much as I'd hoped. Can't confirm that Otto and Duncan exited the SUV at the residence. Or that they went inside. But they could have. The vehicle stopped there long enough," Gaspar replied, still searching the available views, hoping for a more definitive answer.

"That's just great," Burke's tone was snide.

"Look, I don't need your help. Can *you* find her without *me*?" Gaspar challenged, already tired of his prima donna attitude.

He didn't reply and Gaspar let it go.

Burke shut off the engine and hopped out of the Navigator. Gaspar heard the chirps when he pressed the door locks on the key fob. "Let's assume they got out. Where did they go once they entered the building?"

"Again, not sure," Gaspar replied. "But I traced Eleanor's cell phone activity. Located the phone she called from the bistro parking lot."

"Find anything helpful?" Burke sounded slightly winded as if he was hoofing it in a hurry. Good.

"Dunno. The phone belongs to a woman named Jade Chen. Turns out Chen was an employee at the bistro until a few years ago. Her residence is on the top floor of the Denver Tower building. Penthouse C," Gaspar gave him the physical address.

"So you think Otto and Duncan are up there with this Chen woman?" Burke asked, already hustling toward the entrance.

"Chen's phone is still there. She could be home," Gaspar replied, flipping through the pages of data as they popped onto his screens. "But Duncan's phone signal fell off my system at the same time Otto's did."

"What do you mean, fell off? Like they were tossed in a signal-blocking bag at the same time or something?"

Burke came into Gaspar's view on the security cameras aimed at the building's entrance. He yanked the door open and rushed inside.

Gaspar changed cameras to an interior view in time to see Burke flash his badge at the doorman's desk as he rushed past and then impatiently punched the button to call the elevator about two dozen times.

The private elevator car to the penthouses slid open and Burke stepped inside. The car whooshed up fifty-two floors in less than one minute.

Gaspar switched cameras again, this time hacking into the security systems inside the top floor where several penthouse apartments were located. Residents in such places typically went overboard on security cameras. Which was always a good thing for hackers.

Burke exited the elevator and strode swiftly toward Penthouse C on the building's east side. He stood out of the line of fire, just in case, and rapped forcefully on the door. He didn't shout his identity, which was a good way to go in a high-end residence like Denver Tower.

"Is anybody inside?" Burke asked, still wearing his earpiece and speaking to Gaspar.

"Dunno. Can't see. Haven't located any cameras inside the apartment. Try knocking again," Gaspar replied.

Burke rapped on the door a little harder and more insistently the second time.

In Miami, Gaspar glanced swiftly toward another monitor on his desk. The video recorded earlier this morning of the black SUV's path continued to roll at an annoyingly slow pace.

After it pulled away from Chen's apartment building, the vehicle had merged onto Interstate 70 and headed west.

"Heads up," Burke said quietly as Chen's apartment door swung slowly open.

His body was blocking Gaspar's view of the interior. He hoped no one was standing on the other side with a loaded Glock aimed at Burke's gut.

His gaze fell downward and stopped at a location about four feet off the floor.

He cleared his throat. "Is your mother home?"

Gaspar heard a young girl's voice reply, "No."

He had four daughters. From experience, based on her height

and the tone of her voice, he guessed the girl to be about eight years old. Unless she was Thai, like her mother. Then she was probably older.

"Is there an adult here with you?"

"No."

"May I come in?"

"No."

Gaspar grinned. Smart girl. His daughters would have refused a stranger entry into their home long before they were eight years old. Of course, they wouldn't have been allowed to open the door to a stranger at that age, either.

"Burke, can you step aside so I can see the girl and get a headshot. I'll run her through facial recognition," Gaspar said quietly into his headset.

Burke shifted aside slightly as he sighed and ran a flat palm over his head. "Look, I'm trying to find a friend of mine. Her name is Eleanor Duncan. I thought she was coming here to visit your mother."

The girl was young, just as Gaspar had expected. Maybe twelve? She was pretty and slender, but her face was maturing into womanhood. He captured her image on video and snapped a few stills, giving the facial recognition software somewhere to start.

The girl said, "My mother doesn't live here. She lives downstairs. But Mrs. Duncan isn't here yet. Sorry."

"Okay. So I'm confused. Your mother is not Jade Chen?"

"Auntie Jade is my mother's sister," the girl replied with a smile.

"I'm Will Burke. What's your name?" Burke asked smiling, trying to be casual and friendly, as he should have been from the outset.

"I'm Mika." She put her palms together and bowed slightly in greeting.

"Very nice to meet you, Mika. Can I come inside to wait for Mrs. Duncan?"

"I don't think she's coming," Mika replied, her clear-eyed gaze watching Burke's face briefly before it slid away.

"Why do you say that?"

"My mother and Auntie Jade went down to meet Mrs. Duncan and the others a while ago, but they never came back," Mika said.

Gaspar frowned again. He still couldn't see the girl well. But her tone suggested she wasn't worried in the least. Nor was she particularly cautious about Burke simply showing up at the door and asking about her mother.

He didn't know enough about Thai culture to put his finger on the problem, but the vibe was off, for sure.

Burke nodded. "What others were coming with Mrs. Duncan?"

"The women who work at the restaurant. They had a fire. They were coming to stay with us. We've been expecting them for a while. But I don't know where they are," Mika explained, glassy tears pooling in her eyes. "My mother and Auntie Jade have been gone a long time."

"Do you have any idea where they might have gone?" Burke asked.

"Las Vegas?" Mika said, with a lilt. "They were talking about Las Vegas. They've always wanted to go there. Maybe they did."

Gaspar spoke into Burke's ear. "Ask her if there's someone she could call to stay with her until her mother comes back. A friend from school, perhaps?"

Burke nodded and relayed the question.

Mika shook her head. "I am home schooled. My mother wants me to learn Thai ways as well as American."

Gaspar said, "No neighbors?"

Burke asked, and Mika shook her head again.

Gaspar said, "She's twelve. She seems like she can take care of herself."

"Will you be okay here alone until your mother and your auntie get home?" Burke asked.

"Oh, yes. I have plenty of homework to do," Mika said.

"Let me come and look around. I'd feel better. I wouldn't want to leave you here without making sure you'll be okay. Mrs. Duncan would be really angry with me if I did that," Burke said, finally tuning in to the girl's unspoken signals somehow.

She opened the door wide, and he stepped through. Gaspar lost visual with him inside the apartment. But voice communication remained open.

"Jade Chen's cell phone is still pinging in what is probably her bedroom. See if you can snag it without alarming the girl," he said in Burke's ear.

Buke kept up a steady stream of chatter with the girl as he walked from room to room. "Does Auntie Jade live here alone?"

"Yes," Mika replied. "But she entertains a lot."

"A couple of my friends might have visited recently," Burke said.

"Auntie Jade has a lot of guests. What were their names?"

Burke said, "The big guy is Jack Reacher. And Petey Burns. Did you meet them?"

Mika replied, "I don't think so. I usually go to bed pretty early."

Soon, Burke returned to the open entrance door and stepped into the lobby again.

Mika stood in the doorway, her hand on the knob. "I will tell Mrs. Duncan you came to see her."

"I'd appreciate that. But you shouldn't open the door to strangers, you know. Keep the door locked until your mother comes back, okay?" Burke said.

Mika nodded and closed the door as if the conversation had ended. Burke stood still, probably waiting to hear the door lock and the deadbolt slip into place.

"I'll trace the limo. See if we can find Otto," Gaspar said.

"Okay," Burke replied, standing nonchalantly near the elevator as he pressed the call button. "What can I do in the meantime?"

"I'll text you the location of the abandoned Audi. Since Reacher was riding around in it for a few days, we might get usable DNA," Gaspar said.

"Good thinking," Burke replied. "I'll head over there now."

"And Burke?"

"Yeah?"

"Keep this to yourself. Meaning, don't tell Cooper," Gaspar said.

As Burke stepped into the elevator and pressed the button for the first floor, Gaspar noticed that Jade Chen's phone pinged in his pocket. He checked the monitor where he'd kept her account data running in real-time.

The text came from a cell phone in Vegas.

CHAPTER TWENTY-NINE

Wednesday, May 18
Unknown location
11:15 a.m.

KIM ROLLED OVER ON the cold, hard ground and squinted toward the sunlight before she turned her face away and closed her eyes again. A breeze gusted across her body, sweeping dirt and debris over her. She moved her swollen tongue inside her mouth, searching for enough saliva to soothe her parched throat.

Her head felt thick as if she'd been injected with expanding foam. She was sleepy. Maybe another nap would help. Her respirations slowed along with her heart rate. She relaxed into slumber again.

When she awakened the next time, the sun had moved higher in the sky. How long had she been sleeping here? Where, exactly, was *here*, anyway? She didn't recall lying down on the ground to rest. Or traveling to wherever this place was, for that matter.

Her service weapon still rested in the holster under her arm. Slowly, she patted her pockets. Three phones. One badge wallet. Two dozen antacids loosely arranged. A few bills and a few coins. Same as always.

She was confused. She had no idea where she was or how she came to be lying stiff and weak on the dirt. Or how long she'd been asleep or unconscious or whatever.

She pushed herself into a sitting position. Shielding her eyes from the sun's glare, she squinted into the distance. The sun was rising, not setting. Which meant it was still morning. Had she slept here overnight? More than one night?

She fished inside her pockets and pulled out the three phones, all with a solid charge. Two were burners. One connected her to Gaspar, and one went straight to The Boss.

First things first. She chose her personal phone and hit the redial to call Burke.

Where was he, anyway?

She lifted the phone to her ear. The call was dropped. Or it had never connected. Either way, Burke didn't pick up. She shielded the screen from the sun's glare. Dammit. No bars were showing. Which meant no cell service.

She pressed the talk button on each of the burners. Nothing.

No cell towers close enough to establish a connection, so no incoming or outgoing calls were possible. No texts, either. Which might be the reason the phones were still charged since she couldn't use them to connect to the world.

"Now what?" she murmured as she dropped the phones into her pockets and pushed herself upright.

Her legs were stiff and weak, but after a couple of moments of standing, they held her upright. She patted her pockets again. No sunglasses. She must have left them in the Lincoln.

She shielded the sun's glare with her hands and looked around.

"Where the hell are you? And how can you get out of here?" she whispered and discovered her mouth was too dry for audible conversation even if anyone had been around to hear.

She turned slowly, three hundred and sixty degrees.

Nothing. As far as she could see. In every direction.

Well, not exactly *nothing*. If she literally saw nothing, it would mean no light perception at all, like a blind person. Which would have been like sitting in an empty black room in the dark.

Which was definitely not where she was.

Rather, she saw no buildings, no roads, no signs of human life at all.

Sunlight and a desert landscape on all sides. Scrubby green and brown grasses. Sand. In the distance, natural sandstone structures too far away to distinguish.

The brain fog had slowly begun to clear. She identified elements of her surroundings. She was in the desert. It was May. Which meant that daytime temperatures were still comfortably cool enough that, without exertion, heat exhaustion shouldn't set in any time soon.

Kim didn't want to think about what the nighttime would be like.

It was already too late to implement the first rule of survival in the desert, never to go out there alone. If you screwed up that first one, none of the other survival options were likely to succeed.

She took a few shaky steps. She had no water or food, but if she could find shade, she might delay death by dehydration and exposure, at least for a few more hours.

Fifty yards ahead, a large rock formation protruded from the desert floor. She moved toward it, slowly, carefully. By the time she reached her destination, she was exhausted. She leaned against the rock and slid down the shady side onto the ground, away from the relentless sunlight.

Now, she couldn't be attacked from behind, at least. If a predator came at her from the front, she'd shoot it. Which gave her a ridiculous feeling of control.

After a bit, the fogginess had lifted enough to remind her of things she knew about the technology she carried in her pockets. The easy stuff.

Burke had walked away from her, looking for Reacher, hours ago. By now, he'd be trying to figure out where she was. He'd start with The Boss. Would Cooper want to find her? Would he bother to try?

If so, he had access to powerful government technology that should make the task doable, given enough time. After all, they found Bin Laden. Only took them ten years to do it.

She wouldn't last ten years. Maybe she'd last ten more hours, give or take.

How long had she been out here, anyway?

She was sunburned but not blistered. How long did it take to get blisters? She wasn't totally dehydrated, either.

She nodded. Not too long, probably.

Which didn't matter much. The question wasn't how long she'd been here already. The issue was how she could get herself rescued.

If Cooper wasn't so inclined, her ace in the hole was Gaspar. He always had her back. Always.

Gaspar knew she carried three phones. He could locate the three numbers easily enough. With all three signals, he could probably pinpoint her exact location.

What she needed to do was to sit still and give him a chance to perform his magic. She had absolutely no doubt that he'd be working on it.

As soon as he realized she was missing.

How long would that take?

She closed her eyes and tried to recall how she'd ended up here.

The fire at the Orchid Thai Bistro. When was that? Just this morning? Or was it days ago?

She remembered Eleanor Duncan shepherding the bistro employees into a van. The van pulled away, headed west.

"Okay," she croaked around her dry vocal cords. "Then what?"

After a few blank moments, she recalled climbing into a limo with Eleanor. They'd talked a few minutes. She couldn't recall the conversation.

After that, she remembered nothing at all until she'd awakened here.

Kim searched her brain for more about the limo ride, but it was like her memory had been chemically erased.

The random thought sparked an unwelcome epiphany.

Her symptoms were not caused by exposure and dehydration. At least not totally. Her memory *had* been chemically erased.

The symptoms she'd experienced since she woke up were familiar. Drowsiness, confusion, dry mouth, and the rest.

She'd worked a lot of drug cases over the years. There were other possibilities, but given the nature of drug trafficking these days, she suspected hers were symptoms of a fentanyl overdose.

Somehow, she'd been drugged. How? She didn't recall ingesting anything. Maybe she'd remember later.

How it happened was academic.

And then, after some period of time, probably hours and not days or weeks or years, she'd been dumped here.

Why would Eleanor Duncan have done that?

Kim tried to work through the puzzle, but her logic remained too muddled.

"You'll be okay. It takes longer to die of dehydration," she rasped aloud, ignoring the missing hours. How long had she been here anyway? She kept coming back to that.

She'd read statistics on dehydration deaths in the Grand Canyon, but her memory was still too fuzzy to recall the details. The gist of the important part was that the park service rescued hikers daily and sometimes deployed a medivac helicopter.

Which meant someone might find her before it was too late.

If they were looking for her now.

Gaspar would be looking for her, she hoped.

If she could stay alive until he found her, she'd be okay.

She closed her eyes, and drugged sleep consumed her once again.

CHAPTER THIRTY

Wednesday, May 18
Utah
12:00 p.m.

JADE AWAKENED SLOWLY AND opened her eyes inside the darkened passenger compartment of the SUV. Eleanor Duncan was sitting quietly in the captain's chair beside her.

"What's happening to us?" she asked Eleanor, stretching cramped muscles. She pressed the seatbelt release button, but it remained securely fastened into the buckle.

"Save your energy. You won't get that seatbelt off. I've already tried," Eleanor replied speaking Thai. She'd learned Thai to communicate with the women she'd rescued all those years ago, and she had an excellent facility for the language.

Eleanor passed a bottle of water across the console between them. "It's not drugged. I've been sipping it for an hour."

Jade took the water and twisted off the cap. She sipped enough to soothe her dry throat. Taking her cue from Eleanor, she replied in Thai, too. "How are GiGi and the others?"

Eleanor shrugged and shook her head.

"So we've been abducted again?" Jade asked, her voice stronger now that her vocal cords were somewhat hydrated.

"I'm not sure. Could be something else."

"What do you mean?"

Eleanor leaned her head back against the seat. "Someone else was sitting in your seat before I passed out. An FBI agent."

Jade gasped. "You mean we're being deported? After all this time? We have papers. We shouldn't have been flagged anywhere. How did they even find us?"

"I have no idea." Eleanor shook her head. "My phone doesn't work, so I can't call for help. But it all seems rather high-tech for a run-of-the-mill kidnapping for ransom, doesn't it?"

Jade shivered. She had traveled many days in a comfortable shipping container and more long hours cramped into the back of a van with fifteen other women.

At the time, she'd been filled with happy anticipation. The trip was the most exciting thing that had ever happened to her. Strangely, those memories flooded through her as if they'd happened last week instead of years ago.

But this time, she felt anxious and afraid.

"So we're stuck here until we get to wherever they're taking us?" she asked, arching her eyebrows.

"Unless we can escape. They'll have to stop for gas, at least. Maybe they'll let us out to use the bathroom. I doubt they want us to urinate inside here," Eleanor said, her voice weary as if riding in a luxury SUV was far from the worst thing that had ever happened to her, too.

Jade nodded. "What about Reacher? Is he following us?"

She didn't know exactly what had happened to Eleanor back

in Nebraska, but she knew Reacher had rescued her friend somehow. Maybe he'd do it again now. She crossed her fingers and hid them in the folds of her clothes so Eleanor wouldn't see.

"Maybe he is. I haven't seen him. But the FBI agent, the one who got in here with me back at the bistro? She asked the same questions," Eleanor replied wearily.

"I see," Jade said, although she didn't understand. Not exactly. "Why would the FBI be interested in Reacher? How did they even know about him?"

Eleanor cleared her throat, and Jade handed the water bottle back to her. "Have you spoken to your brother since Sunday?"

Jade's hand flew to her mouth. "You think this is about Amarin? We've been taken because of what he did?"

Of course, it was possible. More than possible. Amarin worked for a gangster. He'd killed the fixer. Three days later, the bistro burns to the ground, and they're all kidnapped. It couldn't possibly be a coincidence.

"Karma's a bitch." Eleanor kneaded her temples with the fingers of both hands. "Look, this might not be your brother's fault. It could be mine."

"Your fault? Why?" Jade was bewildered.

Eleanor frowned and opened her eyes again. "Who is your brother's boss?"

"I don't know his name. Amarin never told me." Jade shook her head. "But what does it matter?"

"Gangsters have long memories. They're not forgiving, either."

"So he'd want revenge against Amarin," Jade said, frowning, still unable to grasp whatever Eleanor was trying to say. "But not us. We didn't do anything to him. I've never even laid eyes on the man."

Eleanor nodded. "He might want revenge against Amarin. If I were your brother, I'd be watching my back, for sure."

"But I've never met the man. Why would he steal all of us?" Jade asked. "He doesn't even know we exist."

Eleanor was a very strong woman, but she wasn't bulletproof. No human was. She inhaled deeply and held the breath for a full three count. It was something Jade had only seen her do when she was seriously rattled and trying to hold it together.

The silence lasted a while. Jade waited.

Finally, Eleanor said, "When I rescued you all back in Nebraska? They would consider what I did stealing from them. All of you were bought and paid for. Specifically, they'd paid my husband and his family a great deal of money to deliver you all from Thailand, unharmed."

Jade widened her eyes and blinked several times. Her breathing came in ragged bursts of pain in her chest.

"Strictly speaking, it was my husband and his family who handled the shipping from Thailand. And they're all dead now," Eleanor said. "But it gets worse."

Jade's heart was pounding now with fear, blood rushing in her ears. Her voice shook when she asked, "How can any of this be worse?"

"The men who paid for you have a grievance against Reacher, too. Reacher helped me escape. He helped you, too. Back then," Eleanor explained wearily as if revisiting old horrors was the very last thing she wanted.

Jade realized something she should have guessed before. Eleanor wasn't speaking in the Thai language on a whim. "Are they listening to our conversation right now?"

Eleanor shrugged. "Possibly."

Perhaps their captors could speak Thai well, but the risk was worth taking. Once again, Jade and Eleanor needed to work together to save themselves and the others.

Jade closed her eyes and tried to calm herself. Hyperventilating wouldn't solve anything.

She was a prisoner in this seat. Eleanor, too.

Her sister, GiGi, was a prisoner in the compartment behind her, along with the others. And the women in the van, the ones who worked at the bistro. Eighteen of them in all.

Eventually, this SUV would stop somewhere. They'd be released from these restraints. Which was when the fresh hell would start.

CHAPTER THIRTY-ONE

Wednesday, May 18
Unknown Location
12:30 p.m.

A NOISE IN THE distance jostled Kim awake. She opened her eyes and tried to moisten her lips with her dry tongue.

She cocked her head, attempting to identify the sound. Buzzing around, back and forth, up and down, like the world's largest bumble bee.

She grinned. Her brain fog had cleared enough to realize how silly that thought was.

So what was it?

Motorcycles? Off-road vehicles? Something like that. Which meant humans were having fun on motorized transportation. If she heard some, there could be more people close enough.

Perhaps she could hitch a ride.

Sound traveled far in the desert. The vehicles could be miles away.

Even if her feeble shouting could be heard across the distance, the whining engines would overwhelm any sound she managed to make with her voice.

But maybe hikers or campers were closer. Without the heavy background volume of the machines, an aural signal might reach them.

Kim dug her cell phone out of her pocket and located the specialized air horn application. She opened the app, maxed up the volume, and pushed the button to sound the horn.

The noise was loud. Really loud.

She listened for any sort of response. Nothing.

The riders were not focused on distress signals. They were probably wearing helmets with some noise-canceling tech inside, too.

The cell phone horn was probably not loud enough to capture their attention.

She waited, listening to the roaring engines accelerating, decelerating, coming, and going in the distance. They didn't seem to be headed toward her.

Kim tried the horn again. Twice. Same result.

A louder noise might work, but the only thing she had was her service weapon with a limited number of bullets, which she was reluctant to waste.

Hikers or campers in the area might have heard the horn's blast but had no means of response. She couldn't waste time on wishful thinking. She focused on the riders.

She needed a visual signal. Something they might see from a distance. The riders were watching the ground and each other. Enjoying the ride more than the scenery in the distance. She wouldn't squander this chance.

A road flare would probably do the job. If she had one. Which she didn't.

The reflection from a mirror could be seen for miles by land, air, or water rescue crews looking for survivors. Any normal woman would have a mirror in her purse. But Kim didn't have a purse. Or a mirror.

Her FBI survival training had been focused on urban warfare, but she'd been a Girl Scout once, and she grew up on a farm with brothers. She'd been camping lots of times. She knew the basics. And she understood technology.

Kim could sacrifice one of her three cell phones. She chose the burner that was her lifeline to Gaspar. She could always call him on one of the others when she made it to a cell tower connection.

She put the phone on the ground and stomped the back with her boot to bust it open. The reflective material on the back of the screen would be enough to reflect the bright sunlight and create an effective signal.

The engines were still revved and running off to the west. She held up the mirror to catch the sun and aimed it through extended fingers toward the riders. If they were looking toward her, they should see it. She hoped.

She held the mirror aimed in the right direction for a good long time, but nothing about the engine noises changed. If hikers or campers were in the area, they might have seen her signal by now, too.

Kim had been listening closely to the engines long enough to distinguish four distinct vehicles, revving up and slowing down at different intervals.

And then she noticed that two of the vehicles shut down. Only two were running now. The riders might be getting tired. Wrapping it up for the day.

If she lost this chance, it could be hours, or days, before another opportunity appeared. She could be dead from exposure by then.

She needed what her family, football fans all, called a Hail Mary. A desperate, last-ditch attempt to score with little chance of success.

If she combined the horn, the signal mirror, and a signal fire all at once, maybe one of the riders would notice. And failing that, she'd fire her gun.

For the first time in her life, she regretted being a non-smoker. A smoker would carry a lighter or a box of matches. Kim had neither.

What she had were three cell phones. All containing batteries.

It was the longest of shots, but one cell phone was already destroyed, and she could afford to sacrifice a second.

The off-roaders wouldn't stick around forever.

She was out of better ideas.

The first thing she needed was flammable tinder.

A woman with a purse might have a flammable spare tampon or hand sanitizer packet. Kim had neither.

The ground near her shady rock was bare and dry.

She found what she needed ten yards away on the other side of the big rock. Dry sagebrush. She picked up an armload. She shredded a few pieces into a finer nest that might ignite quickly if she could produce the right conditions.

Kim removed the battery from the destroyed cell phone and found a thin wire to create a hot short circuit.

She bent low to shelter the tinder and the battery from any errant breeze.

"You can do this," she rasped and then held her breath to steady her hands. She tapped the wire to the positive and negative ends of the battery terminal simultaneously.

The short circuit heated up and then, somehow, flashed a spark. *Yes!*

The spark ignited the tinder. *Double Yes!*

And the tinder began to burn.

She sheltered her small fire and added more tinder to keep it alive. When it was large enough, she added more dry sagebrush for kindling. Soon, she had a nice signal fire going.

She listened to the engines.

No change.

She stood near the fire, used the mirror again, and triggered the signal horn. All three at once.

No change.

She grabbed her service weapon and discharged two bullets. The ear-splitting blasts reverberated in her ears, drowning out the noise of the engines. But did the explosive roar travel far enough to grab anyone else's attention?

Kim bent to feed her fire with the last of the kindling she'd collected before she left in search of more. She didn't want to destroy another cell phone to start over. Easier to keep the fire going.

Starting fires was a felony in some places, especially when conditions were dry and breezy.

She'd put the fire out before she allowed it to get out of control.

But maybe, if she were lucky, some concerned outdoor enthusiast would see it from afar and report the fire to the proper authorities.

On the other side of the big rock she'd used for shade and shelter, she'd found the dead sagebrush earlier. She walked back there to collect the rest of it, wondering where she'd find more after this armload was consumed.

Her hearing was still impaired from the gunshots and dehydration. She couldn't distinguish the engines now. Were there still two? Or four? Did it matter?

Carrying an armload of dry sagebrush, she came around the big rock, headed toward the fire, and saw a four-wheeler idling on the leeward side of her fire away from the smoke.

A woman pulled her helmet off and killed the engine. "What kind of idiot are you? Fires like this can burn out of control in minutes. Acres of wildlife and habitat destroyed by your selfishness." The redheaded woman was furiously stamping on the fire. "What the hell did you think you were doing?"

Kim dropped the armload of sagebrush and hurried toward the Valkyrie on the quadbike. "Hoping to hitch a ride back to civilization. Any chance?"

CHAPTER THIRTY-TWO

Wednesday, May 18
Denver, Colorado
2:00 p.m.

GASPAR HAD DOUBLED DOWN on his effort to find Otto.
He didn't know if she had gone dark intentionally or whether she
was in trouble. Hell, he didn't even know for sure that she was
still riding in the black SUV she'd climbed into with Eleanor
Duncan back at the bistro. She might have climbed right back
out again at Denver Tower or somewhere else entirely.

The uncertainty was what bothered him.

He'd been able to find Otto 24/7 since the first day they'd
teamed up back in November. She'd become a part of his family.
She could take care of herself, but he felt responsible for her
anyway.

He knew she felt the same.

She had never deliberately tried to avoid him before. Was
she doing that now?

Possibly.

If it served her purposes, she would have deep-sixed her phones and failed to reconnect.

Perhaps he was unnecessarily tense about the situation.

Still, this felt different.

Gaspar flipped through the sequence of events again, searching for something he knew wasn't there because he'd done the exercise several times already.

It was as if Otto had fallen into some black hole when she'd stepped into that limo and never emerged. Which wasn't necessarily an indicator of the truth on the ground either way.

He'd poured yet another cup of Cuban coffee. The milk and sugar and caffeine had kept him on track, but he was no closer to finding Otto.

Gaspar's cell phone rang. "About time," he mumbled as he punched a button and spoke into his headset. "What's up, Burke? You still with the Audi?"

"Stayed with it until your guys picked it up. Figured you could follow it from there," Burke replied.

"Did you tell Cooper?"

"You asked me not to," Burke said, which wasn't exactly an answer.

Nothing Gaspar could do about it if Burke had blabbed to The Boss, so he moved on. "We may have results later today or tomorrow."

Reacher's DNA wasn't on file anywhere. Now that Gaspar's contacts had impounded the Audi to collect samples, they might have solid DNA evidence. It was only one-half of a matching equation. They'd need a known sample from Reacher, too.

But it was something concrete Otto could use in a case without solid evidence. Which was more than she'd had before.

Burke asked, "After they ditched the Audi, Petey Burns

probably stole another vehicle. His preference is German luxury cars, according to his rap sheet. Any BMWs or Mercedes reported stolen near where we found the Audi?"

"Nothing's turned up on the various databases so far," Gaspar replied. "But across the street from that shopping mall is a luxury apartment complex. Ten minutes before Reacher and Burns abandoned the Audi, he circled that lot. None of the video cams supply a good viewing angle for all of the parking areas, so it's hard to say what he found."

"Drove through slow like he was looking for a replacement vehicle, you mean?" Burke asked. "I'll go over there. See if I can chat up the manager. Maybe one of the residents left his car home while he went on vacation or something like that. He wouldn't know to report it stolen until he got back."

"Keep in touch," Gaspar replied and hung up. Then pulled up the video recordings of the black SUV and zipped through them at four times recording speed, just in case he'd missed something before.

The girl in Jade Chen's apartment, Mika, had overheard a conversation about Las Vegas. The stretch SUV had traveled west on the Interstate out of Denver. Could have been headed for Las Vegas.

The lead was tenuous, but it was the only lead he had. Following up gave him something to do instead of waiting for trouble to strike.

Drive time from Denver to Vegas was ten hours and forty-three minutes, according to his map program. The SUV had been on the road about eight hours since it rolled away from Denver Tower.

The video feeds Gaspar could access were more helpful when the SUV had been closer to Denver. As civilization thinned, traffic cameras did, too. He transitioned to downloading satellite feeds, which was a slower and more complicated process. Mostly because of government controls on the satellite feeds that he had to circumvent to hack into them.

He took a break from the screens and stretched his weary muscles. His leg was aching more than usual. He popped a couple of Tylenols and washed them down with the cold coffee. He didn't allow himself to take anything stronger.

Everything about this situation was too slow for his liking. Otto could be in total control of the operation. Which would be okay. Or she'd been abducted, which was definitely not okay.

Either way, Otto had gone dark inside that limo for too many hours. Was she alive and in control? Or not?

From personal experience, Gaspar knew human life could be terminated in the blink of an eye. Torture lasted much longer. Disposing of the body of an FBI agent was way more complicated.

All he knew was that every minute she remained out of touch was a minute too long. There was nothing he could do about it from Miami. Burke was closer to the limo now but not close enough.

"What's this?" he said as he rolled up on four hours into the video.

Near Grand Junction, Colorado, the limo had exited the Interstate.

"Probably getting gas. Maybe food," Gaspar murmured under his breath as he searched for the next traffic cam to pick up the limo on reentry.

The next time any available video feed showed the SUV was Fruita, Colorado, a town Gaspar had never heard of. From there, the limo continued west along Interstate 70 toward Utah.

He followed the SUV until it turned south on Interstate 15, headed toward Las Vegas.

Mika's guess was looking more likely.

His phone rang again. "Yeah, Burke, what do you have?"

"Good call on the apartment complex. I had to juice him up with two hundred bucks, but the manager says one of the residents has been working out of state for a couple of months. Drives a Mercedes SUV." Burke said. "The SUV is missing from its parking place. Got the plate number, too. Ready?"

"Yeah," Gaspar replied, jotting down the plate number. He ran it through the Colorado DMV. "Late model Mercedes GLC. A damned hybrid."

"Surprising. I figured Burns for a purist."

"With all the bells and whistles. Cardinal Red Metallic."

"Pricey," Burke said. "But the good news is you should be able to find it easily enough, right?"

"Depends. Burns disabled the trackable tech in the Audi and the Jetta and BMWs he'd stolen before," Gaspar replied. "The good news is that the Mercedes will stick out if you see it on the road. Can't be many of those floating around out there."

Gaspar was already searching the earlier video recordings near the apartment complex. He heard Burke start the engine on the rented Lincoln he was still driving.

"No point in stealing another car just to take a joy ride with Petey Burns," Burke said, as the Lincoln's big engine accelerated. "I'm gonna guess that Reacher went after Eleanor Duncan. He came to Denver for her because he thought she was in trouble. Her situation got worse with the fire. Now she's been kidnapped. He'll be on that like white on rice."

"We still need to find your partner. Where are you going?"

Gaspar asked, peering at the traffic on the screen, looking for a pricey red German SUV.

Burke said, "I'm entering onto I-70 west. Get a head start now that I know what I'm looking for. I've got fifty bucks that says Reacher is following the black limo. He'll be making better time, too. That big black tank isn't as fast or nimble as the Mercedes. When you find them, I'll be within range."

Gaspar was preoccupied working the keyboard when Burke's words sunk in. "Within range for what?"

CHAPTER THIRTY-THREE

Wednesday, May 18
Las Vegas, Nevada
3:00 p.m.

ROSSI HAD RETURNED TO his office. Two beer caps rested on the tray. He'd reviewed his various business matters and chosen a good book to read tonight after dinner. It was an old favorite. *Too Many Women.* Under the circumstances, the title amused Rossi as much as the familiar story, which he had read many times before.

Dolly knocked on his office door and opened it before he had a chance to object. She walked in and closed the door behind her, despite the nasty scowl he directed her way.

"Mr. Rossi, Alan Chen is here. He's demanding to see you," Dolly said in her real voice, which was octaves lower than her fake Dolly Parton. Her lip quivered. "I told him absolutely not, but he looks…well, he's absolutely terrifying."

"Call security, Dolly. And show him in," Rossi nodded.

He reached down and opened the second drawer on his desk where he kept a loaded Glock.

She nodded, blinking back tears, and opened the door. Chen walked in and she scurried out, closing the door behind her.

"Mr. Rossi," Chen said respectfully enough. He did not apologize. He stood in front of Rossi's desk, legs apart, weight balanced, hands folded in front.

Rossi pursed his lips and breathed noisily. Chen's impertinence could not be tolerated. No one showed up in Rossi's office uninvited. Never. He waited for Chen's inadequate apology.

"The two bodies. The ones they found in Jarbidge canyon. Who were they?" Chen asked, his voice gravelly as if he was holding his emotions in check.

Not even the most abject apology would have been sufficient, but Chen should have offered one. And begged forgiveness. He did neither. Rossi's anger mounted.

Killing Chen in his office would make a terrible mess. But he'd done it before. He had a cleaning crew on call, 24/7. Which meant he was fully prepared to take all necessary action at any time.

The Glock rested comfortably in Rossi's grip as he replied, "Why do you ask?"

Chen said calmly, "I want to see my family. I will not perform for you again until you allow me to see them."

Rossi cocked his head, his anger burning hotter. "Your family? You have no family."

"I have two sisters and two brothers. And a niece. You transported us from Thailand. You can deliver them here to me," Chen said as if he was in a position to demand compliance. Which he wasn't, although he didn't seem to realize the full import of his fragile position.

"You give me too much credit," Rossi replied through gritted teeth. "I can do many things but raising bodies from the dead is beyond even my considerable skills."

Chen resembled a crouching tiger, prepared to pounce and tear his prey apart with fast, vicious blows. His eyes widened and the muscles in his jaw flexed. He unclasped his hands and allowed his arms to fall to his sides, fists clenching.

Rossi relaxed further into his chair, left thumb tapping rhythmically on the buttery leather, and raised the pistol in his right hand. He held the weapon steadily and pointed the barrel toward Chen's torso.

"I've seen you kill many times, Chen. You're fast and you're strong. But you're not faster or stronger than the bullets from this gun," Rossi said, his cadence relaxed and his words delivered with steady precision. "From this short distance, I won't miss."

Chen glared into Rossi's fleshy face. "Those boys they found at Jarbidge…"

Rossi replied, barely moving. "They were your two brothers. You didn't care who they were. You never even asked. Not before you killed them and certainly not afterward."

Chen's stare never wavered. He didn't blink. His fists continued to clench and release, and his breathing was as tightly controlled as the rest of his body.

The door opened and two of Rossi's security team entered.

"Let's go, Chen," one of the burly men said as he grabbed Chen's arm.

Faster than even Rossi would have believed, Chen screamed as he lifted one leg and kicked the man solidly in the solar plexus with his full body weight and all the force of his impotent rage.

The man dropped Chen's arm and bent double, forehead to knees, holding his belly. Chen kicked him viciously in the head and he toppled to the side, hitting his head on a corner of the metal side table before he hit the floor. He landed in a widening pool of blood that would stop as soon as his heartbeat ceased.

The second bouncer advanced, pulling a gun from his belt. Chen chopped the weapon from his hand, breaking the bouncer's wrist in the process. The man howled with rage and pain as his hand fell limp. Bones broke through the skin and blood spurted everywhere.

He lowered his shoulder and rushed toward Chen, attempting to tackle him.

Chen stepped adroitly to the side and the big man stumbled past. Chen delivered a solid kick to his kidneys, knocking him to the ground, and kicked him again in the same spot, harder than before.

Then he stomped on the guy's neck and the bouncer stopped moving.

With both bouncers neutralized, Chen turned again to Rossi.

"Impressive." Rossi nodded, still holding the gun aimed toward Chen.

Then he fired two shots in rapid succession. One passed Chen's right shoulder, skimming the air near his sleeve. The other passed Chen's left shoulder half a moment later.

Chen didn't flinch. Instead, he continued to glare at Rossi.

"I could easily have hit you both times. You're still alive because I chose to miss," Rossi said, still holding the Glock pointed at Chen. "You are scheduled to fight tonight. We have important guests attending. They, and I, expect you to win. When you stop winning, you will no longer be of any use to us."

Chen stood as still as a redwood for another couple of seconds, glaring at Rossi with pure hatred.

"Would you like to stop winning right now?" Rossi inquired menacingly.

Without another word, Chen turned and walked out.

Rossi pressed the intercom. "Dolly, call security. Send up eight men."

"Yes, Mr. Rossi," she said, terrified and teary.

Rossi opened another beer. He'd downed half of it by the time the burly security guards arrived. He waved toward the floor. Four guards heaved and grunted to remove their fallen co-workers.

Rossi posted two men outside his office door. The last two were some of his best. Huge specimens who could quickly quell a riot with brawn alone.

"Alan Chen is reluctant to fight tonight," he said to the two guards as if discussing a misbehaving child. "Find Chen. Keep him in sight at all times. Deliver him on time."

"Yes, Mr. Rossi," one of the men replied. "What if he doesn't want to show up?"

"Whatever it takes," Rossi replied with a final nod. "And afterward, return him to his rooms and keep him there until I send for you."

"Understood," the other man said before they turned and left.

When Rossi was once again alone in his office, he reloaded the pistol and returned it to the drawer with the others he kept there. He opened another bottle of beer and swallowed half of it, licking his lips with appreciation.

"Such a shame," he said aloud as he studied his roster, checking the lineup for the rest of the week and the rest of the quarter.

Personnel would be shifted to meet demand. Three big fights were planned. Heavy bettors arriving from Asia had certain depraved tastes that only Rossi's stable could satisfy and for which they were willing to pay handsomely.

Chen had never failed to deliver the fatal blows to his opponents at the end of a death match, but tonight would be his last performance. Tomorrow, replacement killers would be installed.

This was the kind of problem Rossi managed with ease. He very quickly made the changes and drained the beer.

Chen was the best boxer Rossi had ever owned. But he wasn't the only one who could kill opponents with a single blow and bring in the cash from gamblers with gleaming eyes which craved watching strong young men die.

Rossi always had a plan B. For everything.

And no one was indispensable. Not even Alan Chen.

CHAPTER THIRTY-FOUR

Wednesday, May 18
Fruita, Colorado
4:10 p.m.

AFTER SHE'D EXTINGUISHED THE signal fire, Kim had persuaded the red-haired woman to give her a lift on the quadbike. They'd rejoined the woman's friends and then rode too many long, dusty miles. Eventually, they passed a sign that proudly welcomed them to Fruita City.

The place was bigger than Duncan, Nebraska, but it was still a small farming town located in the middle of a whole lotta nothing.

The miles of land between where she'd been dumped in the desert and where she climbed off the quadbike in Fruita could have been the end of her.

She'd been lucky to find a way out and to survive. Incredibly lucky.

Her new friends had been full of questions. They'd wanted to know how she came to be out there and what the hell she was doing hiking alone with no food or water and didn't she know she could have died, and so on and so forth.

Kim deflected the questions and thanked them profusely when they finally dropped her off and waved goodbye as they returned to their campsite outside of town.

She stood in the parking lot of the diner and watched until they were out of sight.

The quadbikes' lifesaving engines had been revving in her ears for hours, drowning out all other sounds. When they finally faded into the distance, she felt as if someone had pushed the mute button on the entire world.

Kim dusted herself off as well as she could and made her way to the Lapham Chuck Wagon, established May 1, 1884, according to the cracked stencils on the glass.

The date surely must have related to an earlier enterprise. Kim guessed the construction on this one had been completed sometime in the mid-1970s and it could certainly have used an upgrade.

She pulled the front door open and walked inside, standing for a moment to allow her eyes to adjust after the blinding sunlight.

The Lapham Chuck Wagon was organized like diners everywhere. A row of booths along one wall and a long counter with stools along the opposite side. The kitchen was in the back. The booths were covered in cracked red vinyl and the tables were flecked laminate, once white but now yellowed with age and use.

A middle-aged Native American woman stood behind the counter, dressed in a tan western-style shirt with a bolo tie held together by a large turquoise and silver arrowhead. Kim guessed the outfit was a costume and not normal attire for her.

"Been mountain biking?" She tilted her head toward the rear. "Restroom's back there if you'd like to wash the dust off before you eat."

"Thanks," Kim said, walking over the cracked linoleum floor until she reached the door with the unisex sign. She flipped on the combination light and overhead fan, slipped inside the tiny room, and closed the door.

She used the toilet and flushed. Then she stood before the damaged antique mirror and looked at her reflection. The image she saw amid the blotchy tarnished and oxidized spots on the glass was almost unrecognizable.

Her face was tender and sunburnt and covered in sandy dust, black hair, eyebrows, and lashes almost beige with it. She bent over the sink and splashed her face with several handfuls of warm water. She rinsed the dust from her mouth, too.

When she looked again, her image hadn't improved much.

She pulled her hair loose from the knot at the base of her neck and knocked out as much of the grit as possible. Then she quickly rearranged the bun.

Frowning into the mirror, she smoothed her eyebrows into place. She dampened a paper towel and used it to brush as much dust as possible off her black suit.

"That's as good as it's going to get without a dry cleaner and a shower," she said aloud in a still dry and raspy voice.

She tossed the paper towels into the trash and returned the way she'd come. The waitress behind the counter waved her to a booth by the window. Kim slid into the seat and the waitress brought a menu, a glass of water, and a small thermos of coffee with a brown plastic mug.

The waitress grinned, wrinkling the sunlines at the corners of her eyes. "Honey, you look like you been rode hard and put up wet."

"Um, thanks?" Kim offered a friendly smile in return. She'd never heard the expression before. Some kind of horse metaphor, she assumed. But she got the gist. And she couldn't argue.

"Most folks who come in here know me. Been working here all my life." The woman poured the coffee into the mug and set the pot on the table, along with the water and the menu. "I'm Abigail."

Kim nodded and took a big swallow of the water, which tasted better than anything she'd ever had to drink in her entire life. "Thank you, Abigail. What's good to eat here?"

"Everything's good. We wouldn't have stayed in business more than a hundred years otherwise. You hungry?"

"Starving," Kim said, because it was true.

"I recommend the cheeseburger and fries, then. That'll fill you right up," Abigail suggested.

"Sounds great to me. You have cell phone service here?" Kim asked.

"Honey, we got all the modern conveniences. There's only twelve thousand of us lives here, but we get tourists coming here from all over. They act like they'll die if they can't connect to the outside world," Abigail said with a grin on her way to put in Kim's order.

While she waited for her food, Kim drained the water glass and then pulled her phone out of her pocket. She'd turned it off to save the battery charge when she'd first awakened in the desert and realized it was useless. She powered it up now and waited for the promised connection to local cell towers.

Man, it was dry out there. She might never get rehydrated. Kim drank the coffee Abigail had poured, which was surprisingly great.

When the signal came in on her phone, she found several

missed calls from Burke but no messages. None from Gaspar or The Boss. Which wasn't surprising since both Gaspar and Cooper believed she had dedicated burners for each of them in her pockets.

She'd destroyed Gaspar's burner to make the signal fire. If he'd left messages there, she'd never be able to retrieve them.

Next, she checked Cooper's phone. No calls. No messages. Figured. He only contacted her when he wanted something. She could be dead for all he knew. Or cared.

Kim shook her head. After another hit of caffeine, she punched the redial on her personal cell to call Burke. After three rings, he picked up.

"Where've you been?" he said over a Bluetooth connection, probably in the Navigator. The window must have been open in the vehicle, too, judging from the wind noise.

"Not sure exactly. I can tell you where I am now. Fruita, Colorado. I need a ride," she said, as Abigail delivered a cheeseburger the size of a dinner plate, along with a bowl of shoestring fries.

Kim picked up her knife and cut the burger into quarters. She took a bite of juicy goodness and found her napkin to wipe the grease that ran down her chin.

"Maybe Gaspar can help you with that ride. Take me too long to get back there. I'm a couple of hours out of Las Vegas already," Burke replied.

Kim blinked. Did she hear that right? "Las Vegas? What for?"

"You need to catch up," Burke chuckled. "What did Eleanor Duncan tell you?"

"You want me to ask Gaspar for a ride? What happened to keeping him out of our business at all costs?" Kim frowned, dipping two crispy fries in mustard before she plopped them into her mouth and chewed.

"Right. Well, call Cooper, then," Burke said.

"What are you doing right now?" Kim asked before taking another bite of the burger.

"Following Reacher. Our job is to find him, in case you've forgotten."

She swallowed the food and chased it with the coffee. "You have eyes on Reacher? Right now? Where is he?"

"Not exactly," Burke replied.

"So what is it, *exactly*?" Kim said. "Give me the blow-by-blow."

"While you were doing whatever you were doing, Gaspar and I tracked Reacher down. He's still riding with Petey Burns. Headed toward Vegas," Burke said and then followed up with a brief recitation of the facts he'd been living since she saw him last.

When he finished, she gave him a quick rundown on her activities and then said, "I'll meet you in Vegas."

"Copy that," he replied. "And stay in touch this time, will you?"

"Aw, you were worried about me," she teased as she chewed another potato, although his answers bothered her.

The point of having a reliable partner seemed to be lost on him. He wasn't the Lone Ranger, looking for Reacher on his own. He should have had her back first and foremost.

"Nah. Just didn't want to be left out of the action," he laughed.

"Right." She disconnected and called Gaspar.

"Good to hear from you, Sunshine," he picked up immediately. He sounded relieved. He'd probably been frantically searching for her for the past several hours.

Which was Burke's job, whether he acted like it or not.

"I've missed you, too," she replied.

"Helo's on the way. You're about five hundred miles from Vegas. You'll get there after Burke, but air time is a hair under three hours," Gaspar said. "Finish your food. Pilot's landing in the parking lot to pick you up in twenty minutes. Maybe less."

"You're a lifesaver, Chico," she said bravely as she pushed the burger away.

Three hours in a helicopter, perhaps the most unstable motorized air transportation on earth. The rate of fatal crashes attributable to non-essential low-altitude operations like a quick flight to Vegas across the desert was too significant to brush off.

Low flying helicopters encountered obstacles like buildings, powerlines, or hills that appeared suddenly in the fog. None of that should happen in the desert. But once they reached the outskirts of Vegas, the risks would multiply exponentially.

But Gaspar was right. A helicopter was the best option. All she had to do was survive the trip.

"Do you have any idea where Eleanor Duncan is now, specifically?" Kim asked as she wiped the grease off her hands and swilled the coffee.

"Still working on it. By the time you arrive, I hope I'll have a solid location. Meanwhile, I've sent what I have on her employees in files to your secure server. They're plain vanilla. Nothing special. When you reconnect with Burke and your laptop, let me know what jumps out at you," Gaspar replied.

"How about the limo driver and his sidekick? You were following them on traffic cams, right?" she asked.

"Yeah. Haven't had a chance to do much with that yet," Gaspar replied.

"Can you get a couple of stills and run them through all the facial recognition databases? This abduction was a smooth operation. These guys know what they're doing."

"Which means they've done it before...gotcha," Gaspar said.

"We'll talk soon. I'll buy you a beer and enthrall you with my latest adventures," she smiled to let him know she was okay, even though he couldn't see her, and it wasn't strictly true.

Her abduction had rattled her more than she wanted to admit. She'd been lucky back there in the desert. But for those quad bikers, she'd have died. She knew it as well as she knew her own shoe size. It was a truth she didn't want to dwell upon too long. That way lay madness.

"Sounds like a plan," he replied before he disconnected.

She didn't try calling Cooper again. He had access to her entire conversations with Burke and Gaspar. Whatever he wanted to know, he could find out himself.

She dropped a twenty on the table to pay for the food, including a generous tip, before she went outside. Across the street was a drugstore. She jogged over and bought four new burner phones. By the time she made it back to the Chuck Wagon's parking lot, the helo was on the ground.

Kim bent into the rotor wash, letting the strong breeze brush the rest of the dust off her before she climbed into the passenger seat and prepared for takeoff, hoping she could keep her meal in her stomach.

She'd be out of contact for the duration of the ride. Cell phones could interfere with a helo's navigation systems, which was the last thing she was willing to risk. The ride would be harrowing enough.

Gathering more intel from Gaspar and Burke would have to wait.

CHAPTER THIRTY-FIVE

Wednesday, May 18
Las Vegas, Nevada
6:10 p.m.

SYDNEY ROLLED HIS SHOULDERS and stretched his neck to work out the tension. The problem presented by the FBI agent he'd unintentionally scooped up with Eleanor Duncan had weighed on his mind for the entire trip from Denver.

All the solutions he'd considered carried consequences worse than the problem itself. He'd made his choice hours ago, for better or worse, and there was no going back.

But he kept turning it over in his head, looking for gaps he'd missed.

Had he done the right thing?

He'd been tempted to kill the agent and never mention the situation to Rossi at all. That's what Little Tony would have done and declared the problem solved. What Rossi didn't know could be swept away that easily, Little Tony would have said.

But he'd have been dead wrong.

Killing a federal agent would have put a bounty on Sydney's head like nothing else he could do. Rossi's, too, once the feds learned he was involved. And there was always a snitch looking to make a deal with the feds. Always.

Carting the agent back to Rossi had been a non-starter, too. It was one thing to snatch up illegals and move them across state lines. They were illegal. Who were they gonna call? Nobody. And nobody would care if they died, either.

Kidnapping citizens was another matter entirely. They had rights. They had families. They had jobs. Too many eyes and ears were out there searching for them.

The only kind of citizen Sydney wanted to mess with were the ones already on the wrong side of the law. Like Eleanor Duncan.

And abducting a federal agent? A thousand times worse than an ordinary citizen.

Too much heat came with a national manhunt for a missing agent. If the feds got wind of it, Sydney would never breathe free air again. He knew it like he knew water was wet. No doubts whatsoever.

The only thing worse than killing the damned woman would've been to keep her in any kind of captivity. Because then she could be rescued. And then she could talk. Which was beyond unacceptable.

The last time some idiot had abducted and killed a federal agent, heads rolled. Many heads.

Sydney was beyond keen to keep his head attached, right where it was.

After mulling things over, he'd chosen the least terrible option.

When he'd made up his mind, he told Joey Prime the plan.

He didn't mention that the suit was a federal agent. He said she was a citizen. That was all Joey Prime and his cousins needed to know.

"Whaddaya mean, she's a *citizen*?" Joey Prime asked, his mouth slack, eyes wide.

"I heard her talking to Eleanor Duncan before I gave them the gas," Sydney said. "She owns a local business close to the restaurant or something."

"Oh, cripes," Joey Prime said, swiping the sweat from his brow. "Whadda we gonna do wit her? We kill her, we're in trouble with Rossi. We don't kill her, we're in trouble with Rossi. Either way, we're in trouble with the feds."

Sydney nodded. Joey Prime might be a bit dim, but he was smart enough to understand the problem. Which had made things easier because Sydney wasted no time explaining.

"We'll leave her in the desert before we cross over to Utah. She never saw our faces, and she won't remember much else because of the fentanyl gas," Sydney said. Which might not have been true, but he'd hoped it was.

"She'll die," Joey Prime replied, nodding agreement as he worked it out. "No water, no food, no one around. Won't take long, either."

"If we're lucky." Sydney shrugged. "You're usually pretty lucky, Joey."

"Guess we got no choice. But Little Tony ain't gonna like it," Joey Prime said, shaking his head slowly.

Sydney didn't care what Little Tony liked or didn't. Little Tony was paid muscle, several rungs down the Rossi organization ladder.

Rossi's orders had been to drive carefully on the return trip, obeying all traffic laws, arousing no suspicion. "Sneak into town with my inventory," he'd said.

"No harm to those girls, either, Sydney. Not so much as a mussed hair, you understand?" Rossi had ordered sternly. "They'll bring top dollar, but only if they're in pristine condition."

Until he'd discovered the agent, Sydney's plan had been unfolding perfectly.

He'd worried about leaving the interstate, which carried too much risk. Someone might've noticed. The black stretch SUV limo was distinctive. Witnesses might remember, it and it was too easy to spot on traffic cams if anyone were looking.

These days, someone was always looking.

You couldn't even go to the bathroom in private anymore.

Dumping the woman had been the best viable option Sydney had come up with. Which was what they'd done.

But had he done the right thing?

Whether it was the right thing or not, Sydney couldn't change it now. But the situation made him as uneasy as a long-tailed cat in a room full of rocking chairs.

After they'd stopped to dump the agent at McInnis Canyon, Joey Prime switched to a fake Utah license plate on the SUV and stuffed the Colorado plate deep into a dumpster.

Sydney kept to the backroads for a while and then reentered the Interstate near Fruita, Colorado.

Joey switched the plates again when they crossed from Utah to Nevada.

It wasn't a perfect solution.

The plates alone would throw up red flags if the right people were searching.

On top of that, no plate would ever match the SUV in any database because Rossi had eliminated the vehicle identification number.

All of which meant that Sydney might make it to Vegas without being stopped. Or he might not. And the long hours in the driver's seat had left his mind to ruminate on the problem with the federal agent.

As the sun waned, he was nearing Sin City, and he'd never been so happy to see its millions of lights in the distant sky. He picked up a secure cell phone and rang Little Tony.

"Yeah?" Little Tony said when he picked up.

"You know where you're going?" Sydney asked.

"Pulling up now." Little Tony rattled off the address of the safe house where Rossi kept his most profitable cargo for processing when it first arrived.

The area was north and east of town in a specially developed warehouse district Rossi's predecessor had funded a decade ago. Rossi paid authorities to look the other way, which also made the eight warehouses valuable lease properties for Rossi's partners.

Most importantly, civilians never wandered into the area by mistake or otherwise. Which made security as tight as it could be in a warehouse district, Rossi figured.

Little Tony had been to Rossi's safe house before. He knew how to get through the security gate and park around back.

"You still got all their cell phones in the blocking bag?" Sydney asked.

Little Tony replied snidely, "They're wearing pajamas. They don't got no cell phones."

"You checked when you picked them up, though, right?" Sydney's blood pressure rose and pounded in his ears. "People do grab their cell phones when they're awakened in the middle of the night."

"A course we checked. Whaddaya think, we're stupid?" Little Tony snarled.

"We'll see you in an hour." Sydney disconnected as his heartbeat slowed. He saw the exit up ahead and moved the lumbering SUV into the right lane, heading toward the safe house.

Eleanor Duncan should be awake now. Jade and the others, too, probably. Which could make them less cooperative when they reached the safe house but also easier to move around. They could walk on their own two feet. Carrying them in, one by one, would have been a chore, even for Joey Prime.

Sydney flipped the switches to open the intercoms between the cabin and the two passenger compartments behind the front seat. He could hear them talking softly to each other.

Briefly, he considered gassing them again. But he didn't. Two doses of that gas in less than twelve hours might be fatal to the tiny women for all he knew. Rossi would be furious.

He'd come this far. He didn't want to screw up now.

Sydney flipped the intercoms closed again. He didn't care what they were talking about. He only needed to offload them in one piece.

After that, the inventory was Rossi's problem.

Sydney took the familiar route from the expressway exit through the open desert. A few miles later, he reached the turn onto Flume Road, so named because the content in the eight warehouses fed out to all of Rossi's enterprises, one way or another.

The warehouses were set back off Flume Road, four on each side. The metal buildings all looked the same on the outside. Gray metal siding and darker gray metal roofs. Steel entrance doors in the front without windows, also gray. Loading docks around back.

They had high ceilings and seven of them were the same

size. About half the square footage of a typical big box store. Some had shelving installed inside to increase storage capacity, depending on the product.

Newer warehouses were bigger and fancier with more attractive exteriors. But Rossi said the Flume Road real estate was already the most valuable he owned. He had no desire to improve it.

The eight buildings were spaced about one hundred feet apart. The space was divided in half, granting fifty feet to each warehouse. One side of the warehouses was devoted to driveways and the other side was parking.

Floodlights illuminated the lots and chased the shadows. The lights could be shut off with a single switch when Rossi didn't want to risk certain activities being discovered.

Sydney drove the black SUV limo along the wide pavement to the safe house, which was the last warehouse on the northwest corner.

The eighth warehouse was smaller than the others and set apart. It also had an attached multi-level garage around back.

Like the others, this one was surrounded on all sides by an electrified ten-foot chain link fence. But beyond the fence were several acres of empty desert.

He pulled up to the gate, lowered the window, and waited for a voice from a speaker mounted on a pole.

"Who is it?" the disembodied male voice asked.

Sydney supplied the name of Rossi's mother, Rosalina, who had always been and was likely to always be the love of his life. Rossi often said Italian men were all the same in that respect. Maybe they were. Sydney wouldn't know. He was Irish.

"What did you bring?" the voice asked.

The second question had been added to the routine when

Rossi read about increasing cyber security using two-factor identification in one of his daily newspapers. He said it was safer to require two passwords.

"Lager," Sydney replied.

Sydney raised the window and waited for the wheeled gate to slide open. When the space was wide enough to accommodate the SUV, he rolled slowly into the lot and drove around the north side toward the back.

In addition to being Rossi's safe house, this property also housed his vehicle collections. His taste was eclectic since he didn't drive and rarely went anywhere. Mostly, the collection consisted of vehicles he'd won when gamblers lost big bets in his casino.

Which meant everything from boats, RVs, and vans, to Ferraris and antiques. Sydney had no idea what he used them for or even how many were parked here. Maybe fifty were spaced apart on the two floors of the garage. Give or take.

He pulled into the garage beside the safe house and parked in the covered loading zone on the first floor, close to the side entrance. It rarely rained here, but the cover prevented satellite and drone imagery from spying on visitors to the safe house, Rossi said.

Joey Prime asked, "Think she's dead yet? The civilian we left at McInnis Canyon?"

"If we're lucky." Sydney shrugged. "I hope we never hear another word about her."

Joey nodded and climbed out of the cabin. He stood, stretching his arms and legs like an athlete preparing for battle.

He pointed across the driving lane to a perpendicular row of luxury cars attached to charging stations on the first floor. "Rossi into electrics now?"

"Won them off some guy who couldn't pay his debts, would be my guess." Sydney shrugged.

Joey grinned. "Must be two million bucks' worth of wheels parked right there."

"At least," Sydney replied, attention focused on other things. "You take the cargo inside. Little Tony and Big Tony will help you get them settled."

"After that, want me to drive the van over to the storage lot? Get it cleaned up?" Joey Prime asked.

By *cleaned up*, he meant sanitized of all possible forensic evidence. It was a standard precaution after transporting human cargo. Rossi was an exceedingly careful man.

"Yeah. Good idea." Sydney nodded. "I'll drop off this limo, report to Rossi, and meet you back here."

"Better you than me." Joey Prime grinned. "You might want to tell him on the phone. Showing up in person could be hazardous. The Elephant's a surprisingly good shot, I hear."

CHAPTER THIRTY-SIX

Wednesday, May 18
Las Vegas, Nevada
6:45 p.m.

JADE WALKED DOCILELY WITH the others when the trio of
scary men brought them inside the warehouse from the SUV.
She scanned the layout.

The interior had been built out as living quarters, like a
spacious modern home in a cosmopolitan city. The front half
was an open floor plan with several common areas organized
into usable spaces.

The metal walls were bare, but large windows had been installed
near the ceiling. During daylight hours, the space would be
bright and probably hot as hell without sufficient air conditioning.

Otherwise, various lighting elements had been placed to
eliminate the cavernous shadows after sunset.

Bright rugs splashed the painted concrete floors like pools
of color in asymmetrical shapes. Upholstery and fabric dividers
added more visual interest and some sound absorption.

Perhaps as many as twenty or thirty people could comfortably fit here in the kitchen, eating, and sitting areas. A huge television was mounted on the wall in one corner. Images were playing on the screen, but the sound was muted.

"Who are you?" Jade asked one of the men politely.

"Little Tony," he said and then pointed to the others. "That's my cousin, Big Tony. This here's my other cousin, Joey Prime."

"Where are my employees?" Eleanor demanded, jerking her bicep from Big Tony's easy grip.

"Relax, Mrs. Duncan. No need to get your panties in a wad," Little Tony replied from the kitchen, where he'd leaned against the countertop while opening a cold beer he'd pulled from the fridge. "Everybody's fine. They're getting washed up. We're cooking food."

Jade saw the one called Joey Prime leading Jade's sister, GiGi, and the women from Jade's escort business down the hallway on the north side of the kitchen.

"Where are they going?"

"He's showing them to their rooms. We have one ready for you, too," Little Tony replied.

Big Tony grabbed a beer from the fridge and walked over to stretch out in an oversized leather recliner across from the TV. He released the mute and turned the audio volume up, which meant the sound reverberated off the metal walls and ceiling like being inside a tin can.

Little Tony seemed to be the leader of the three-man crew. He gestured toward two chairs at the dining table, suggesting Jade and Eleanor sit.

Eleanor demanded, "Who are you? Why have you brought us here? And where the hell are we, anyway?"

Little Tony ignored her questions. In his thick New York

accent, he replied, "Mrs. Duncan, Ms. Chen, please sit down. I'll get you some water."

His tone made it clear that he wasn't offering a choice.

Jade lowered herself into one of the chairs, but Eleanor remained standing, stretching her limbs as if she might break into a quick sprint out the front door at any moment.

Which was a preposterous idea.

Even if Eleanor could open the door and get out before one of the thugs tackled her, the building was surrounded by an electrified fence with barbed wire on top. She'd seen the fence on the way in.

Eleanor should have seen it, too. She could run no farther than a few yards in any direction, and she'd be stupid to try.

Little Tony shook his head but otherwise ignored Eleanor's defiance while he retrieved two water bottles from the refrigerator.

Jade took the water and drank greedily. Eleanor didn't. Jade sent her a pleading glance, but Eleanor shook her head firmly, just once.

"Can't have you dehydrated, Mrs. Duncan. I'd rather not force you," Little Tony said. "But I will."

Jade cleared her throat. "How do you know our names?"

Little Tony shrugged. "Don't matter."

"Who are you working for?" Eleanor demanded.

"That don't matter neither. You're here now. It's temporary. You'll be going somewhere else soon enough," Little Tony replied, raising his eyebrows and flashing a meaningful glare at Eleanor. "I wanna deliver you unharmed. But we don't gotta do it that way. You know what I mean?"

Jade sent a beseeching glance toward Eleanor. "How long will we be here?"

Little Tony shrugged. "Long as it takes."

"They're locked in," Joey Prime said, jerking a thumb over his shoulder as he returned to the open room from the long hallway. "I gotta go clean up the van. You be okay here without me?"

Little Tony nodded. "Oven's heating up dinner. Hurry back."

"Want me to bring anything else?" Joey Prime said, already walking toward the exit to the garage.

"Nah, we're good," Big Tony said as he returned to the kitchen. "The fridge is stocked. These girls won't eat much. We'll get more stuff later if we end up staying longer."

Jade cocked her head and studied both Tonys in the brighter kitchen light.

She nodded slowly. She recognized them. She was sure.

And she remembered exactly where she'd seen them.

At her brother's boxing match in the basement of the Snake Eyes Casino in Vegas. They'd been guarding Amarin, keeping fans and gamblers away, as well as his sister.

Which meant these two, and Joey Prime and the guy who drove the limo that brought them here, all worked for Rossi. Just like Amarin did.

So Rossi was the one who had abducted them.

He was probably responsible for the fire at Eleanor's bistro, too.

But why? Was all of this Jade's fault?

She nodded. Of course, it was her fault. Somehow.

Because she'd wanted to see her brother?

Or because Amarin had tossed Rossi's fixer over the Hoover Dam bridge?

She spent the next few seconds trying to avoid the obvious.

Gangsters were all about an eye for an eye, weren't they?

Abducting eighteen women because of one dead fixer seemed extreme. Even for Rossi. Didn't it?

And what did he plan to do with them, anyway?

Something else *must* be going on here.

Jade had simply wanted to see her brother again. Why would Rossi object to that?

She didn't know.

And she didn't want to make the situation even worse.

Perhaps she could offer herself to Rossi in exchange for the freedom of all the others. She knew he liked women.

She needed to talk to Eleanor. Alone.

Jade flashed Eleanor a warning glance, willing her not to object.

She turned her gaze to Little Tony. "We'd like to go to our room now. We need to freshen up. Before we eat."

Little Tony narrowed his eyes and studied her for a moment before he nodded.

"Right this way," he said as if he was a doorman at Rossi's casino hotel, and she was a high roller, entitled to extra courtesies.

CHAPTER THIRTY-SEVEN

Wednesday, May 18
Las Vegas, Nevada
7:00 p.m.

JADE FOLLOWED ALONG AS Little Tony led them down the hallway to the closest room. He opened the door and stood aside as they entered. "I'm gonna lock the door. But if you wanna come out, just knock. You're not prisoners here. You're our guests. Understand?"

Jade nodded and said nothing. But they were most definitely prisoners. Before he left, she inhaled deeply to steady her nerves. "My sister is in the other room. Can she join us here?"

"Yeah, sure. I'll bring her in. What's her name?"

"GiGi."

Little Tony closed and locked the door. Jade waited until she heard the echo of his footsteps headed down the hallway and then two sets of footsteps returning.

The door opened and GiGi rushed inside. Little Tony closed

and locked the door again. Jade heard his heavy shoes returning to the kitchen.

Jade hugged her sister and waited until Little Tony was far enough away.

"What the hell are you thinking?" Eleanor fumed, speaking Thai, pacing the floor, both hands on her head. "Now we're locked in here instead of having a chance to get away from out there."

Jade took Eleanor's arm and led her over to sit on one of the beds. Also speaking in Thai, she whispered, "They may be listening."

"So what if they are?" Eleanor replied, still outraged, although she did lower the volume.

Jade leaned her head close to Eleanor's ear and spoke softly. "I've seen these men before."

Eleanor's eyes widened. "What? Where?"

"They work for Roberto Rossi. He's a Muay Thai boxing promoter," Jade replied, trying to explain but not knowing where to begin or how much more to say about her brother.

Eleanor already knew Jade and GiGi were in trouble. Eleanor didn't need to know more.

Her eyes grew even wider. Her nostrils flared and her face flushed and she looked truly terrified. Her voice quivered. "*Rossi*? Are you sure?"

Jade took one of Eleanor's hands and felt the pulse in her wrist pounding hard and fast.

Eleanor raised the water to her lips and drank. Jade waited for her to find her voice again.

"My husband did business with Rossi back in Nebraska." Eleanor's voice was low and quiet now, as she confessed the whole truth she'd partially revealed to Jade earlier.

GiGi gasped and her hand flew to cover her mouth.

Eleanor blinked a couple of times and then looked into GiGi's eyes. "Rossi is one of the men who paid to bring you here from Thailand. The other men are dead now. Rossi probably thinks I stole you from them. He's right. I did."

GiGi placed her palms on her flushed cheeks. Her heart was pounding hard now, too. Her breath came in short gasps. "Are you sure?"

"My husband did a lot of business with Rossi and the others over the years. I didn't know exactly what the business was at the time. But Rossi was a ruthless killer, even then," Eleanor nodded, eyes wide, like a deer in headlights.

Jade gathered her sister in her arms. She felt GiGi's heart pounding. Her hands shook. They were overwhelmed. She couldn't take it all in.

Rossi.

Jade searched her memories for any mention of Rossi's name before she'd found Amarin again at that Vegas boxing match. She was sure she'd never heard the name before.

She shook her head because she didn't want to accept that what Eleanor said made sense.

The Thai handler who had facilitated their passage to America. A longtime friend of her father's. Her father believed him to be a good man. He'd said Amarin was the one the promoter wanted. For boxing.

Rossi's name had never been mentioned, but even if she'd heard it at the time, the name would have meant nothing to her.

Rossi wanted only Amarin, but her father had insisted his whole family be allowed safe passage to America as well. He loved his family. He believed they would thrive and prosper away from the poverty of rural Thailand.

Her father had never realized he'd actually sold them into a life of slavery. How could he have known? They were all too naïve. Too trusting.

As they were loaded into the shipping containers, they surrendered their passports and identification and what little money they'd saved.

From that moment, they were trafficking victims, even though they didn't know the fate that awaited them for many days.

Not until Jade, GiGi, and the others had arrived in Nebraska that cold night seven years ago had she partially understood the truth.

Amarin and the other men had already been taken away. The women and girls were separated and alone and destined for terrible, short lives to follow.

Eleanor and her friends in Nebraska had saved them.

Now Jade knew that she and GiGi and Mika and the other women were more fortunate than the men. They were alone, with no money, barely speaking English. They had no idea where they were or what to do next. Those who had homes to return to had no idea how to get back there.

The only thing they could do was make the best of where they'd ended up.

Since Eleanor Duncan had first rescued them, Jade and GiGi and the others had slowly come to realize the destiny that otherwise awaited.

As she walked her mind through these old realities, Jade's racing heart slowed and her reason returned.

She'd been a victim back then. But she'd moved beyond her fate long ago. She wasn't that helpless girl anymore.

Rossi might believe he had bought her and owned her, but he did not. He never had. And he never would. *Never.*

Eleanor cleared her throat. "We have to get away from here. As quickly as we can. Rossi will kill me. And what he will do to all of you...I don't even want to imagine."

Jade nodded, her throat tight, holding back tears. She leaned in toward Eleanor. "We need Reacher. Where is he?"

"I haven't seen him since he left the bistro." Eleanor shook her head, naked fear in her eyes. "I asked him to watch over you. He said he would."

GiGi whispered. "Is he a man of his word?"

"He helped me once before." Eleanor shrugged. "That's all I can say."

"Perhaps he is here, then. Even if we can't see him at the moment," Jade replied, thinking about what little she'd seen of their current prison.

She hadn't seen Reacher anywhere. Nor Petey Burns. No sign of their white Audi, either.

If Reacher was out there, he'd hidden himself well.

Jade nodded, placed a finger over her lips, and moved into a corner where she could shield her actions from prying cameras.

She reached down into her boot and pulled a burner cell phone she'd safely hidden in an interior pocket.

She said a silent prayer before she fired it up and dialed a number she had committed to memory. She'd never expected to use it again after that day on the bridge.

When he answered, speaking quickly and quietly in Thai, she told him how Rossi had kidnapped them all.

"Where are you now?" her brother asked.

"I'm not sure. In a warehouse somewhere in the desert north of Las Vegas, I think," Jade replied.

"I'll be there soon," Alan Chen said.

"You know where we are?" she asked breathlessly, tears of joy flooding her eyes.

"Not yet. Rossi will tell me." After a moment's silence, he added, "They won't harm you. Rossi will kill them if they do."

"Are you sure?" Jade asked, still worried.

But her brother had already hung up.

CHAPTER THIRTY-EIGHT

Wednesday, May 18
Las Vegas, Nevada
7:30 p.m.

WHEN THE HELO SET down at the landing pad atop one of the best hotels in Las Vegas, Kim was more than ready to set her feet onto the solid concrete and keep them there. She bent at the waist and hurried away from the helicopter's relentless assault on her hearing.

Once Kim was clear, the helo lifted again and flew away from the strip, like a bird released from a cage. Her stomach had been doing backflips for the whole three-hour trip. Not something she wanted to do again soon.

She needed a shower and clean clothes and then her laptop to access the files Gaspar had sent to her secure server.

In that order.

Which meant finding Burke and retrieving her bags from the Navigator as her first priority. She pulled her cell phone from her pocket, fired it up, and punched the redial.

Burke's phone rang several times before her call went to voicemail. She left a brief message telling him where she was and asking him to return the call.

Kim went into the hotel and took the elevator to the first floor, where she checked in. At one of the shops in the lobby, she found an outrageously priced black suit she could wear.

At the room rates this place charged, the hotel would certainly supply toiletries and a toothbrush, so she skipped those, but she added underwear to the pile.

As she signed the credit card bill, she grinned. The Boss would have a heart attack when he saw her expense report. Served him right.

Twenty minutes after she'd landed on the roof, she was standing under a showerhead the size of a dinner plate with her face turned toward a warm, pulsing stream. She felt the sand wash from her pores as her skin began to rehydrate.

Kim lathered up with an expensive body wash and shampooed her hair. The scent of jasmine filled the room. She was tempted to stay in the warm spray forever. This was possibly the best shower of her life.

When she stepped out of the rain room, she felt better than she'd felt in days. Humidity was a wonderful thing.

She toweled off and wrapped one of the hotel's luxurious robes around her and grabbed a bottle of water that cost more than her entire meal back at the Chuck Wagon. She swigged half of it, soaking up the lifesaving liquid like a shriveled sponge.

Kim walked to the bed where she'd tossed the contents of her pockets and looked at her phone. Burke had not returned her call.

Thinking about Burke, wondering where he was and why he wasn't answering, she sipped the water a bit more slowly as she placed a call to Gaspar on the new burner she'd bought for that specific purpose.

"That's some pricey real estate you're enjoying there, Suzy Wong," Gaspar said with a smile in his voice when he picked up.

"Never underestimate the healing power of a great shower and high thread count linens, Chico," she replied cheerfully and enjoyed hearing him laugh. "Where's Burke? Any idea? I tried calling. He didn't pick up."

"Yeah, he arrived about an hour before you. His working theory is that Reacher is following that limo, the one that abducted you and Eleanor Duncan," Gaspar said. "He's followed the SUV to a warehouse north of town and staked it out."

"Has he actually laid eyes on Reacher?" While they talked, she stuffed her clothes into a laundry bag and sent them off with the valet for cleaning. Later, she'd collect everything cleaned, pressed, and ready to wear.

"Dunno. Haven't heard anything since he got there," Gaspar replied.

She nodded, taking another swig of the water. The bottle was almost empty. "What about the facial recognition on the driver and the passenger in the limo?"

"Just came in. Looks like the driver is one Thaddeus Sydney. The passenger is Joey Prime Callo." Gaspar paused as if the next line of the report was serious, and he didn't want her to miss it. "Both men are known associates of Roberto Rossi."

"Roberto 'The Elephant' Rossi? Seriously?" Kim whistled low and slow and plopped down on the side of the bed.

"The very same."

Every FBI agent knew the name and criminal history. Roberto Rossi had been one of the top ten organized crime bosses on the most wanted list for years.

Law enforcement agencies were never able to charge him with serious crimes that would stick. But he was believed to be responsible for dozens of crimes they couldn't prove.

Kim mused aloud. "What would a mob boss like Rossi want with a Nebraska housewife like Eleanor Duncan and a bunch of Thai restaurant servers?"

"Could be anything. Gambling, drugs, ponies, sports, counterfeits. Who knows? Rossi's got his fingers in every illegal pie there is," Gaspar replied. "And with the internet being one big cesspool, recruiting a housewife in Nebraska isn't as difficult these days as it was twenty years ago, either."

"So, the trouble Eleanor Duncan was in, the thing that made Reacher rush to Denver to rescue her, that was Rossi. He was the problem," Kim said, thinking aloud as she drained the last of the water and tossed the empty bottle into the recycle bin next to the bed.

"Seems like a solid hypothesis."

"Which probably means Rossi was involved in whatever was going on with Reacher back in Duncan, Nebraska, seven years ago." Kim cocked her head. "Because that's where Reacher met Eleanor. The one and only thing they have in common."

"The odds on that theory are pretty short, too," Gaspar agreed.

"So, seven years ago, Reacher leaves South Dakota. He hitches a ride to Duncan, Nebraska. He gets involved in some big trouble with Rossi. That trouble leads to the usual murder and mayhem," Kim said, walking through the theory, testing each link along the chain.

Gaspar picked up the thread. "With Reacher's help, Eleanor escapes and leaves town. Moves to Denver. Opens a Thai restaurant. All is pot stickers and yum beef salad for seven years."

Her stomach growled when he mentioned her favorite Thai

dishes. She hadn't felt hungry before. A quick grin stole across her mouth and disappeared.

"And then Eleanor is in trouble again. Rossi's back. She gets word to her friends in Nebraska. They get word to Reacher," Kim said, still walking it through and taking a long breath when she got to a pausing point. "And Reacher's still pissed at Rossi. So he goes running to Denver to finish what he started."

"Could make sense," Gaspar replied. "Or not."

"Rossi is based here in Vegas now, right?"

"Last I heard. Hang on," Gaspar said, clicking the keys on his keyboard. "Yep. Owns the Snake Eyes Casino. Lives there. Runs his business operations from an office there."

"Rossi's been around a long time. His business interests are, as you said, wide-ranging," Kim said, still massaging the new intel, trying to fit the pieces together.

After she'd paused for a good long time, Gaspar said, "What are you thinking, Suzy Wong? I can hear the wheels turning in your head, even from Miami."

Kim pursed her lips and then she said, "Eleanor Duncan's life was quiet. Until something happened to kick off this whole Rossi thing. Got Rossi riled up. Sent him to burn down her bistro and then kidnap her and every employee she had."

"Right," Gaspar said, elongating the word the way his teenagers did.

Kim cocked her head. "What was that thing? The thing that got Rossi riled up?"

"Gangsters need a reason?" Gaspar replied. "Rossi's famous for long, cold revenge. Folklore has it. That's why they call him The Elephant. Because he never forgets a slight, no matter how minor, and no matter how long it takes."

"Right," Kim said, mimicking his elongated tone.

Gaspar laughed. "Okay. So maybe he finally got around to dealing with Eleanor. Or maybe he's been looking for her and somehow she came to his attention again. Something she did back then or something she's done lately. Who knows?"

Kim nodded, thinking about it. "Can you check the Nevada news reports for the past month or so? Look for anything odd. Not gangbangers killing each other or hookers arrested for selling sex in the few counties where it's not legal. But…"

"This is Vegas. Odd for the rest of the country is ordinary there, don't forget." The clicking keys came faster as Gaspar searched the news reports. "Sorry. I'll keep looking. But nothing screaming weird is jumping off the screen at me."

Kim cocked her head. "Try this. When you researched the background on all of Eleanor Duncan's employees, did you find anything noteworthy?"

"Such as?"

"I don't know. Maybe an ex-wife or girlfriend of Rossi's? An unusually rich waitress who might have ripped him off?"

"Nothing remotely like that. No evidence of illegal anything. The employees were eleven females, all of Thai ethnicity, around the same ages. Relatively new immigration visas to the U.S.," Gaspar replied. "But it was a Thai restaurant. So it makes sense that the workers would fit a similar profile."

"Yeah, everybody in this country immigrated at some point," Kim replied. "My dad brought my mother back from Vietnam as a war bride decades ago. Your family fled Castro in Cuba even further back. Nothing particularly special in that."

"Well, keep looking for a trigger. Something that set Rossi off. And I'll keep thinking." Kim nodded. "Meanwhile, I'm heading over to the Snake Eyes Casino. I'll have a chat with Rossi. See what I can find out."

"Rossi thinks you died in that canyon in the desert," Gaspar warned her sternly like The Boss would've if he'd been the one on the other end of the line. "He's not gonna react well when your ghost walks into his office."

"I'm not going into Rossi's office. I'll find him on the casino floor. He won't try anything out in the open. Too many witnesses with all those customers around," Kim said as if she could confidently predict any mobster's violent behavior. "I'll tell Burke where I'm going. The Boss will hear my message. He can send backup if I need it."

"Yeah, maybe that'll happen. Maybe it'll snow in my backyard in August." Gaspar's sarcasm carried all the way from Miami. "Meanwhile, I'll see if I can locate Rossi or his two known associates, Sydney or Joey Prime. Or hell, maybe I can find Reacher. If Burke's right and Reacher is around, there's gotta be a million cameras in Vegas. One of them could catch a glimpse of him."

"Lotta ifs in that plan, Chico." Absently Kim nodded as she disconnected the call, tossed the phone on the bed, and headed to the bathroom to get dressed.

She'd be faster than Rossi in a fight. He was slow and lumbering. She was fast and nimble. But FBI intel was that he always carried a gun and he knew how to use it.

Marksmanship was always the great equalizer for Kim when she fought against a bigger, stronger opponent.

But in a gunfight with a man like Rossi, they could both lose.

CHAPTER THIRTY-NINE

Wednesday, May 18
Las Vegas, Nevada
8:00 p.m.

ROSSI'S OFFICE WAS A bloody mess. After a quick call from Sydney, reporting that the women had been delivered to the safe house, he'd ordered Dolly to call in the cleaners. They would get rid of the blood, bullets, and bodies. They'd bleach all the forensics, too.

He didn't need to supervise. The cleaners were experienced. Dolly could handle the rest.

But the scope of the work had required several changes to Rossi's evening schedule.

He had planned to watch tonight's Muay Thai match from his office on the closed-circuit TV. The specially constructed private arena was one of the most sophisticated and secure locations in the building.

Casual tourists, vacationing gamblers, and everyone else never knew it existed. The basement of the casino was strictly off-limits.

Entrance to the arena was only allowed when accompanied by one of Rossi's security team escorts.

The audience was limited to fifty attendees, each of whom was carefully vetted. Admission was permitted by invitation only. The attendance fee for tonight was fifty thousand dollars, paid in advance. Gambling minimums were set for each fight and should top out in the millions. Rossi skimmed off the top and collected winnings for the boxers as well.

Muay Thai boxing to the death had become a bigger moneymaker for Rossi than sex trafficking the boys. He'd made the shift and never looked back.

All of which meant that Rossi rightfully expected to collect a significant profit tonight, even without the unplanned extras. He should have raised the stakes substantially.

The Asian gamblers paid big money to see Alan Chen fight to the death.

Tonight, they would get much more than they expected.

Chen's last and most spectacular knockout would terminate three of his opponents, as planned. He would socialize briefly with the customers afterward.

Those were the elements the gamblers paid big money to watch.

What they didn't know was that this would be the last time Chen entered the ring.

He'd had a good long run. Seven years at the top of the ticket was an exceptional career for a Muay Thai boxer. Many times, Rossi had expected Chen to die. But he'd never been bested.

Chen had proven himself to be the champion his Thai handlers had claimed all those years ago.

Rossi was well pleased with his investment. He'd been repaid many times over.

But all good things must come to an end. Rossi shrugged. Tonight, Chen would die.

Tomorrow, Chen would be replaced with Rossi's best up-and-comer. A fresh face. Fresh energy. Unknown to the gamblers. Unpredictable. The betting would be wild.

Rossi grinned. He would make at least a cool million tomorrow night, too. Maybe even more.

Which was as it should be. He took one hundred percent of the financial risk. Of course, he would collect the rewards.

Muay Thai boxing was lucrative, as pursuits enjoyed by those with baser instincts tended to be. Bloodlust was common among the patrons willing to pay Rossi's prices. They cheered while men brutally attacked each other with fists and feet and elbows and knees.

One or more ended up bloodied and dead by the end of the night. Which meant Rossi needed a constant stream of new boxers. His trafficking operation from Thailand had grown exponentially and focused more on the boys than the girls these days.

Rossi found the Muay Thai scene beyond distasteful. He kept a wide distance from the fights and the fighters. He never allowed the patrons who enjoyed the brutality to encroach any other areas of the casino. Definitely not his penthouse or the greenhouse. The boxing was not even available on closed-circuit monitors outside his office.

Which meant Chen's last fight would be recorded. Rossi would watch it tomorrow. And then the video would be destroyed.

He hated delayed gratification. His every whim was always satisfied instantly. But not tonight. Which meant he deserved a special reward for his patience. He would unwrap something he'd been saving for such an occasion.

Rossi retired to his rooms to delve into the wondrous world promised by a rare text he'd discovered last week. The engrossing history of the Roman province of Dalmatia, from ancient times to the dawn of present-day Montenegro awaited his undivided attention.

With delicious anticipation sending a thrill up his spine, he changed into his silk pajamas and robe, slipped his feet into fine lambskin loafers, and arranged four bottles of beer chilled to the perfect temperature on the chairside table.

Rossi opened the first beer, laid the rare book comfortably in his ample lap, and glanced at the clock. The evening's events in the basement were well underway.

Boxers of lesser skill would fight first. But the match with the best fighter and the highest money stakes was always last.

Alan Chen's fight was slated for midnight.

He would be dead before dawn.

"Perfect." Rossi nodded with satisfaction and opened his book, giving such vexing matters no further attention as he became immersed in fascinating ancient times.

Too soon, the house phone rang loudly next to his recliner, yanking his attention away from the Romans. After the obnoxious bell blared a third time, he accepted that the only way to make the intruder stop was to answer.

He scowled, stuck his beefy forefinger between the pages to mark his place, and picked up the receiver before the noise assaulted him again.

He held the receiver to his ear and waited for the rudely insistent caller to speak.

"Sir, it's Siegfried. I'm sorry to disturb you," his gardener said respectfully, as always.

Rossi waited, heavy breathing the only response Siegfried might have heard on his end.

"Sir, it's about your *Rhizanthella gardneri*," Siegfried's voice quivered as if he was too afraid to speak.

Ella. Rossi's breath caught. His prized Western Underground Orchid was in trouble. Siegfried would not have disturbed him for a minor disaster.

The gardener had captured Rossi's full attention.

"What's wrong?" he demanded.

"You'll want to see for yourself," Siegfried stammered as if he was terrified of Rossi's reaction. "Can you come?"

"On my way." Rossi groused, his scowl deepening as he replaced the receiver.

He carefully inserted a bookmark where his finger had been and laid the rare volume aside before hauling himself out of the recliner.

Without stopping to change into gardening shoes, he waddled toward the private elevator at his most rapid pace and pushed the call button.

He opened the drawer of the side table and palmed his .22. He pushed his right hand, still holding the pistol, into the pocket of his robe and stepped into the elevator car for the short ride to his rooftop greenhouse.

One floor up, the doors slid silently apart and Rossi stepped into the cool night air. He seldom ventured here after dark, but the rooftop was as familiar as his own bedroom. He could have navigated it blindfolded, even without tonight's full moon and cloudless sky.

The exit from the elevator lobby opened facing the north side of the roof. Rossi waddled to the exit and turned right.

CHAPTER FORTY

Wednesday, May 18
Las Vegas, Nevada
8:30 p.m.

THE SNAKE EYES WAS a relatively small hotel by Las Vegas standards. Only twenty-one stories high, the hotel contained fewer than 1,200 rooms.

The building's design tapered toward the top. Which meant the casino had 50,000 square feet of total gaming space, but the roof only totaled 10,000 square feet.

The rooftop was intended for air handling and other necessary equipment. Only the east side was otherwise usable. Which was where Rossi had installed his greenhouse.

He had considered creating a rooftop bar because the Snake Eyes offered a spectacular observation point for the strip and the night sky. Another venue for tourists to spend money was always a good idea, as his consigliere had reminded him.

He'd rejected the plan because he didn't want people up here. Rossi wanted to keep the view and the spacious feeling of the open air all to himself. Sometimes he came here simply to enjoy the wide-open sky above Nevada.

His decorator had created a seating area between the elevator shafts and the greenhouse on the east roof where Rossi could enjoy the views. The glorious space was exactly what he wanted.

Siegfried had turned the lights on inside the greenhouse. It looked like an enchanted forest under glass across the roof.

Rossi waddled in that direction. His heavy footfalls were muffled by soft leather soles on the artificial turf that covered the concrete.

He pulled the glass door open and stepped inside his climate-controlled greenhouse.

Siegfried was in the back corner, hunched over the space dedicated to Rossi's most precious purple orchid.

Rossi made his way to the back, passing gardening tools, bags of soil, hanging boxes, metal rods with pointed ends that Siegfried used for stakes, and so on.

As Rossi approached, Siegfried half-turned to face his boss, chewing his lip, tears welling in his eyes, a wretched expression distorting his features.

He stood aside with an open palm, directing Rossi's gaze to what had been the orchid's carefully prepared habitat.

Rossi gasped and stared in horror, unable to fathom the jumbled mess on the floor.

The specially designed table had been ripped apart and smashed to splinters. Soil and pottery shards were strewn atop the destroyed wood. Withered petals of the fragile orchid, torn to shreds, curled in death amid the chaos.

On top of the destruction of his office and his boxing, and the dead bodies found in the desert, this disaster simply a bridge too far.

Slow boiling rage began low in Rossi's belly the moment he'd seen the destroyed habitat. Heat rose up through his chest, into his neck, and flooded his face with hot, blotchy fury.

"What the hell happened!" he yelled at full volume, spewing spittle from his fleshy lips, blowing steam from his nostrils like a charging bull.

Siegfried shook his lowered head as the tears spilled onto his cheeks. "I-I d-d-on't know. I-I c-came up to check on her and saw this."

"Idiot! Didn't you lock up before you left?" Rossi demanded.

"I did, yes. I know for sure," Siegfried nodded rapidly. "Because I-I had to unlock the door before I could access the greenhouse when I came back after dinner."

"Then how? How did someone get in here and do this? *How*, Siegfried?" Rossi angrily insisted. He gripped the pistol in his pocket. "*You're* the only one with the key. *You're* the only one who knew *exactly* which of my orchids was the *most* precious to me."

"I don't know. I don't know," Siegfried wailed, shaking his head while grabbing his face with both hands.

Rossi's rage became cold-hearted certainty. "Why did you do this?"

He stared at Siegfried for a few moments more, waiting for an answer that made sense. The man offered nothing.

Rossi nodded. Then he lifted his hand from his pocket, pointed the .22 directly at Siegfried's head, and from two feet away fired one shot, directly between his eyes.

Siegfried's eyes opened to the size of saucers just before the hit. Then he crumpled to the floor on top of the pile of trash that just this morning had been *Elle*, the rarest, most extravagant, and beautiful orchid in Rossi's world.

Rossi moved closer and put a second bullet in Siegfried's left temple. Just because.

Seeing Siegfried dead on the floor didn't make Rossi feel better, so he kicked the body a few times for good measure.

Out of breath, still angry, Rossi stood over the ruined habitat for what seemed like a good long time.

After a suitable period of mourning for *Ella*, he plunged the gun into the pocket of his robe and turned to leave the greenhouse.

Which was the moment he saw two things he hadn't noticed before.

The first was an open backpack on the floor, three feet from Siegfried's body.

The open zipper revealed a glowing digital clock.

Rossi's imagination supplied the ticking that thundered in his head.

A thin bead of sweat appeared above his upper lip.

He recognized the backpack and its contents.

An improvised explosive device.

A bomb.

He knew exactly how the IED was constructed and, correctly deployed, the significant damage it would do.

Rossi widened his eyes and quickened his step, hurrying away.

If that bomb exploded inside the enclosed greenhouse before he escaped—he didn't want to go there, even in his head.

He had to get out of here. Off the roof. Away from the bomb.

As fast as possible.

He lifted his gaze and looked toward the greenhouse door.

The exit was blocked by a man standing calmly, feet apart, hands clasped in front.

Holding a cell phone.

Which could be used to trigger the bomb's detonation device.

Or not.

"Good evening, Mr. Rossi," Alan Chen said.

"You did this?" Rossi asked, the anger in his gut flashing back to life as he stopped, dead still.

"Only one of your orchids and Siegfried are gone. Two things you cared about deeply. Perhaps they were as precious to you as my brothers were to me." Chen nodded once, raising the cell phone to be sure Rossi recognized its importance. "It is within your power to save the others. Where are my sisters? I know you kidnapped them and are holding them hostage. Tell me where."

Rossi scowled. "What are you talking about?"

"Ying and Gamon Chen. You call them Jade and GiGi," Chen replied coldly as if Rossi's confusion were genuine when he fully believed Rossi was well aware. "Release them to me and I will allow you and your remaining orchids to live."

"If you detonate that bomb, you'll die here with me, Chen. Who will save your sisters then?" Rossi demanded, eyes narrowed, nostrils flared as he inhaled and exhaled pure animal rage.

"This cell phone will activate a timed explosion. I will leave you here. I will find my sisters, whether you help me or not." Chen shook his head and smirked. "When the bomb detonates, you'll die alone."

Rossi glared and said nothing.

"Last chance, Rossi. Where are they?" Chen asked, raising the cell phone to demonstrate.

Rossi pushed his lips in and out, hands still stuffed into his pockets, holding the pistol, vibrating with anger.

Chen waited a full ten seconds.

"Goodbye, Rossi." Chen pressed the redial button to trigger a delayed detonation.

The moment after Chen triggered the device, Rossi pulled the pistol from his pocket, aimed at Chen's center mass, and fired.

Chen immediately grabbed his belly after the first shot, pivoted to open the door, and moved out of the greenhouse.

Rossi fired two more shots.

CHAPTER FORTY-ONE

Wednesday, May 18
Las Vegas, Nevada
8:45 p.m.

KIM HAD WANDERED AROUND the Snake Eyes Casino, hoping to find Rossi on the floor where there were plenty of people around. No luck. Next, she'd tried his office but found it to be closed due to some kind of renovation. Workers had stripped the rooms down to the studs and replaced the drywall and carpets. Rossi was nowhere to be found.

Which meant there were only two more places to look. His penthouse. Or the roof, where she knew he tended orchids. She decided to try the roof first.

Kim elbowed her way through the milling casino crowds toward the hotel elevators. The place was busy for a Wednesday night. She had to wait a while for the elevator to arrive and the first one was too full.

Finally, she was able to enter the next one, which seemed to stop on every floor until the car reached its final destination.

The nineteenth floor was last. Kim stepped out behind the couple and turned in the opposite direction.

She waited around the corner, staying out of sight until the couple entered their room and closed the door.

With the corridor empty, Kim hustled back to the elevator lobby. Next to the two hotel elevator cars was a heavy steel door. The doorknob wouldn't turn, but when she pushed against it, the door swung open. Someone had jammed the locking mechanism.

She slipped into the interior elevator lobby and closed the door silently behind her.

Normally used by maintenance workers and hotel staff, the interior space was painted beige. The floor was bare concrete. Nothing else occupied the space except the entrance to the emergency stairs and two elevator doors.

Kim tried the stairwell first. The stairs led down only. Oddly, there were no emergency stairs here leading to the roof. Which had to be a violation of the fire code.

Both of the elevator doors required a key to unlock the call buttons. She punched the call buttons anyway. One door remained securely locked.

The second door slid open. The last person must have forgotten to relock it. Which would have infuriated Rossi. It was the kind of mistake Rossi would consider a terminal offense.

Kim stepped inside and punched the sole button, labeled "roof."

As the elevator car lumbered upward, she heard the unmistakable sound of two gunshots fired.

"What the hell?"

She pulled her weapon and listened for more gunfire as the elevator car bounced to a stop. She didn't hear more shots, which could mean almost anything. She could be walking into an active shooter situation.

Burke should be with her. The whole point of having a partner was that two sets of eyes, ears, and weapons were always better than one.

But he wasn't here.

She could call for backup. She shook her head quickly. For the moment, she was better off alone.

Solo-officer response tactics had proved overwhelmingly more effective against active shooters than waiting for additional law enforcement teams to arrive. Mainly because waiting gave the shooter time to kill others.

Which didn't lower the danger level to that first officer at all.

Yet she knew she was playing beat the clock. Rapid action by a solo officer was more likely to succeed simply because she was here already and they weren't.

She breathed deeply to steady herself.

The elevator doors opened and Kim stepped onto the elevator lobby on the roof of the Snake Eyes Casino.

She chose the north exit. She stood with her back to the wall and turtled her head out to look left and right.

The roof was carpeted in artificial turf and illuminated only by the moon.

Kim turned left and exited onto the west side of the building where HVAC and other equipment provided cover.

She heard no further shots. No indication of other people around, either.

Kim stayed in the shadows, crouching low, and moved carefully around the corner of the elevator shaft enclosure to the south side.

Again, she saw and heard no one nearby. No further gunshots sounded.

Where was the shooter?

The elevator lobby was the only exit from the roof.

Twenty-one stories was way too far to jump to the ground and survive.

Which meant there were only three alternatives.

Had the shots been fired from a gun while the shooter was on the roof of the Snake Eyes? Or did they come from somewhere else?

Gunfire could be heard, she knew, from a mile away, depending on the weapon.

Briefly, she closed her eyes and replayed the sound of the two gunshots in her mind, attempting to fix the shooter's location now that she had her bearings.

Kim nodded. What she'd heard had definitely been close enough to the elevator. Given the noise level, she'd placed him somewhere on the roof of this building rather than another building nearby or down on the street.

Echoes, wind, weather. All of these could also confuse the shooter's location.

She shook her head, gave up, and opened her eyes. Given all the variables, she couldn't pinpoint his position. Not from the sound of the gunshots alone.

He could have committed suicide with the second shot or by jumping afterward. Or he was still there.

Either way, to confirm, she'd need to get eyes on the shooter.

When she moved around the corner of the elevator shaft to the east side of the roof, she saw something strange. She blinked to reset her vision and then looked again to confirm.

Yep. She'd been right the first time. Occupying much of the northeast side of the roof was a super-sized greenhouse.

Rectangular shape. As big as a roomy three-car garage.

At least thirty-six-feet-wide and twenty-five-feet long. Brightly lit from the inside as if a party was going on or something.

She shook her head. What a crazy-ass location for a house made of glass.

The beating sun would superheat the interior every day of the year. The climate-control expense alone would exceed her annual salary.

A rooftop greenhouse in Las Vegas could only be a rich man's folly.

Roberto Rossi was a very rich man. He owned the Snake Eyes. His private apartment was one floor below. And he famously collected and cultivated orchids.

Given the open roof and the somewhat muffled sounds she'd heard, it was possible, but not certain, that the shooter was inside the greenhouse.

Was it Rossi? Or one of his enemies?

She had a clear view. Between her position and the greenhouse was mostly open space.

But the interior of the illuminated greenhouse was a jumble of plants and plant hangers and flat surfaces upon which more plants rested. All of which blocked her view.

From here, she couldn't see anyone inside the greenhouse.

Nor did she know what equipment he had.

Safer to assume that his weapon was superior to hers.

Kim was FBI. She'd had some of the most sophisticated tactical training in the world. In theory, she possessed stronger awareness, preparation, training, tactics, and skill than the shooter. She hoped.

Otherwise, if his equipment was superior to hers, her duty weapon wouldn't be sufficient to defeat him.

CHAPTER FORTY-TWO

Wednesday, May 18
Las Vegas, Nevada
9:05 p.m.

MAINTAINING HER COMPOSURE, KIM focused on what
was important now. She must not become fatally distracted by
the known physiological changes she was already experiencing
and would only get worse.

Kim regulated her breathing and slowed her heart rate.

She focused on the greenhouse, realizing she might be
wrong. He might not be inside at all.

Tunnel vision could lead her to misjudge distances and rob
her of the ability to apprehend peripheral activity.

Kim needed to find him before he fired his weapon again.

She needed to leave the shadows and run across the open roof.

Kim twisted her neck to look around.

The shooter could be anywhere. If she ran into the open
space where she had no cover, he could easily pick her off from
a well-hidden sniper's nest.

The distance to the greenhouse was too far to crawl on her belly. And he'd probably see her if she tried.

These situations were fluid and conditions could change rapidly.

Leaving was not an option. She inhaled another deep breath and held it for a count of three.

She had to make a choice.

Stay here and wait for backup.

Attempt to draw the shooter outside where she'd have a clear shot.

Or charge the shooter to potentially save lives before more officers could reach the rooftop.

Nonsensically, she said the first thing that popped into her head. "What would Reacher do?"

Before she realized she'd uttered the words aloud, she heard gunshots from the interior of the greenhouse.

Question answered.

The shooter was definitely inside.

And so were his victims.

Kim recognized the psychological effects of tachypsychia, which gave her the sense that time was slowing down as she ran across the open space and approached the threat.

Before she reached the greenhouse, the door opened and a man stepped outside. He closed the door quickly behind him, propped something against the lock to keep it closed, fell onto the artificial turf, and rolled away from the gunfire.

Was he a victim? Or a killer?

More gunshots were fired inside the greenhouse.

Kim continued running toward the man. He glanced up and saw her.

He jumped up, holding his belly, and bolted toward the elevators.

"Stop! Stop!" she yelled as she sprinted behind him.

He ignored her warnings and kept going. If he made it to the stairwell in the elevator lobby, she might lose him.

"Stop! FBI!" She fired a warning shot into the air.

He glanced over his shoulder. She was close enough to hit him and she had a weapon.

He stopped, turned, placed his feet firmly on the hard surface shoulder-width apart, and prepared to fight. His hands were straight with his forearms facing her. Elbows out slightly and hips facing forward.

Even within the shadows, Kim recognized the square stance of a Muay Thai boxer. She'd trained in the sport and learned enough to defend herself in a street fight against sloppy thieves and clueless muggers.

But this guy was something else altogether.

This fighter was skilled and focused. Prepared to shift his weight to deliver kicks, knees, elbows, punches, and clinches. He wasn't breathing heavily. The sprint across the roof hadn't winded him at all.

She raised her weapon and pointed the barrel at his chest. "FBI. You're under arrest," she said.

"For what? I haven't done anything. That guy's shooting at me. Go arrest him."

She steadied her aim. "Who is he and why is he shooting at you?"

"His name's Rossi. He kidnapped my sisters. Now he wants to kill me." His sentences were short and clipped and came quickly as if he couldn't get the words out fast enough.

"Why did he kidnap them?"

"Go ask Rossi. Make him tell you where they are," he said quickly, eyes totally focused on Kim.

"Tell me their names." Kim's breathing had returned to normal, but she didn't lower her weapon.

"Jade Chen. GiGi Chen." He glanced toward the greenhouse and returned his gaze to her. "He abducted them in Denver. He's hiding them somewhere here in Vegas. That's a federal crime, isn't it?"

"Okay. Let's go talk to Rossi," she said, tilting her head toward the greenhouse.

But she'd barely uttered the words when he rushed her, hands and feet flying faster than should be humanly possible.

He kicked the gun from her hand, giving her an extra moment to move out of the way of his next blow, which caught him slightly off balance.

She kicked him in the belly. Hard.

When the blow connected, he howled like a wounded animal. Blood gushed from an open gash in his torso that she hadn't noticed before.

She looked closer into the moonlight's shadows. His torso was covered in blood. At least one of the shots fired inside the greenhouse must have hit him. Maybe more than one.

"You're wounded. We need to get you to a hospital," she said.

Without speaking, he came at her again, this time delivering a swift but weakened kick to her left thigh. She fell onto the roof. While she was down, he turned and ran.

Kim pushed herself onto her knees. She scrambled to grab her gun off the ground and gave chase again.

A half-dozen steps before he reached the elevator shaft, Kim was ten strides away from grabbing him when she heard a single deafening explosion behind her.

"Take cover!" she yelled an instant before she opened her mouth, crouched, and raised her arms to shield her head, seeking to protect herself from fragments that become missiles after a blast.

The roar of the explosion muffled her hearing like noise-canceling headphones.

Pieces of pebbled glass, dirt, plants, and shards of plastic and wood pelted her body.

When the falling debris storm subsided, she looked back over her shoulder.

The greenhouse had burst apart from the inside, flinging glass and remnants of the destruction everywhere.

The contents that weren't blasted away were now consumed by a giant ball of fire.

No way anyone still inside the greenhouse when the bomb detonated had survived that blast.

Kim pushed herself up off the artificial grass and hurried over to the man she'd been chasing. He lay on his back, lifeless eyes open.

His torso was bloodier than the rest of his body. But what had probably killed him was the sharp metal rod gigging the left side of his chest, penetrating his heart and pinning him to the roof.

Kim's muffled hearing discerned sirens twenty-one stories below from what seemed like a great distance but definitely coming closer. She rushed over to the pile of burning rubble that had been the greenhouse, but the fire was too hot. She couldn't get close enough to rescue anyone that might have been still alive.

She pulled The Boss's cell phone from her pocket and pressed the redial. He picked up, for a change.

She cleared her throat and rasped, "Can you handle this?"

"Send me a close-up photo of the boxer. Nothing more for you to do. I'll deal with the fallout and locate the abducted sisters. Go now. Before you get caught in more red tape than either of us wants to handle," he replied.

"Where am I supposed to go?"

"Burke needs help. I'll text you the address."

"Copy that." She hung up, snapped a few photos of the dead man, and sent them off to The Boss.

She stood for a short while and took one last look as she shot a video of the devastation. She sent the video to Gaspar.

Then she holstered her weapon, hurried over to the emergency stairs, and headed down.

CHAPTER FORTY-THREE

Wednesday, May 18
Las Vegas, Nevada
9:15 p.m.

JADE HAD CALLED AMARIN for help two hours ago, but she didn't know her exact location. Amarin said he'd find out. Then he'd come for them. They only had to wait until he arrived.

Eleanor was skeptical. "Amarin might be your brother, but he's also Rossi's man. You can't trust him. Anyone connected to Rossi is bad news."

Jade had no illusions about Rossi. Eleanor was simply voicing the fears Jade and GiGi tried to ignore.

"What alternative do we have? You saw that fence outside. We can't climb it or break through it," Jade said, "We need a way to get out of here. Once we're free, we can figure out what to do. But for now, Amarin is our only option."

"Jade is right," GiGi had nodded her agreement. "Mika is alone. No one else knows she exists. No one will rescue her. If we don't escape…"

GiGi's voice trailed off. She'd been petrified since she awakened in the limo hours ago. Jade had tried to reassure her sister, but they both understood the situation all too well.

If Jade and GiGi didn't escape, Mika would never be okay again. GiGi couldn't deny the truth but dwelling on it wouldn't help.

"Trust me, there is no escape," Eleanor shrugged, defeated. "You have no idea who you're dealing with. Even if we get away again, Rossi will hunt us down and kill us. He already has good reasons. Not that he needs a reason to do exactly as he pleases."

"We have to be ready. We can't do that from inside this room," GiGi said, looking around again as if she might have missed something before. "We have no windows to climb through, and the only door leads into the main part of the safe house, where the men are waiting."

"They'll offer us dinner. When they do, we'll go into the main room. Remain alert for a chance to escape," Jade said. Gigi and Eleanor nodded.

After an eternity, Big Tony knocked on the door and invited them to eat pizza at the big table in the kitchen. Jade and GiGi readily agreed. Eleanor reluctantly came along.

The other women were still locked in their rooms in the back of the safe house. Jade had not seen them since they'd all arrived.

Big Tony and Little Tony were watching an excessively violent movie on television with the volume turned up so loud that conversation was impossible. Something about a guy with a dead dog and a lot of gunfire and explosions at ear-splitting decibels followed by screaming victims.

The noise reverberated off the metal walls and ceilings and

rumbled through her body, defeating all attempts at conversation.

Jade sat with her back to the sink, facing the front door. The television was to her right. The men were seated facing the screen.

The front door was directly opposite her chair. She found herself wondering if she could simply sprint out quietly. How long would it take them to notice? Probably the length of the movie, at least, if she could bring herself to pull off the brazen move. Which she couldn't.

Eleanor and GiGi were seated at opposite ends of the table. GiGi's back was to the television. Eleanor had a clear view of the screen and the front door.

Jade picked at the pizza, eating the vegetables off the top like a child, thinking about how to escape. She wasn't the least bit hungry, but if one of the men noticed she wasn't eating, they might lock her in the other room again.

At this point, Jade feared Eleanor was right. But instinctively, she felt they had a better chance of escape if they stayed in the common areas.

She worried that Amarin wouldn't be able to fight off three big gangsters at once when he arrived. The women needed to be ready to help.

Jade glanced at the clock on the wall above the refrigerator. Amarin should be here soon.

She pulled a few mushrooms off the pizza and stuffed them into her mouth, chewing each piece as long as possible. Every moment seemed to last another lifetime.

Suddenly, an ear-splitting crash, like a wrecking ball hitting the big fence out front, filled the room.

The steel gate, if that's what it was, screeched like a banshee for a long time.

GiGi looked up from her pizza, eyes wide and questioning. Eleanor's expression was wild as she whipped her head from side to side, seeking the source of the sound.

Jade shook her head, cautioning them to remain calm.

She thought the screaming had come from outside, but it could have been generated by the surround sound speakers on the television. The various sound effects from the movie reverberated off the metal walls and ceiling and so much that she'd given up trying to separate them from reality.

Finally, the ear-splitting noise stopped. The absence of the screeching afterward was almost worse than the noise.

The men remained engrossed in the movie. They never even looked up.

Jade waited, fingers crossed under the table, hoping Amarin had found a way to destroy the gate and get them out of here.

She didn't wait long.

Under cover of the movie's overwhelmingly loud sound effects, the front door burst open and Petey Burns rushed inside.

His eyes were rounded and his face was flushed with excitement or fear or both.

He hopped around like a wild rabbit.

Jade's mouth opened wide. Fervently, she hoped Reacher wasn't far away.

Petey was charming and clever, but they'd need Reacher to supply the brawn required to handle Big Tony and Little Tony.

Petey gave Eleanor a meaningful look and tossed his shaggy blond head toward the doorway. Eleanor nodded and rose from her seat.

Petey shared the same look with GiGi and Jade.

Big Tony was the first to glance up and notice the commotion.

When he saw Burns, he stood abruptly, dropping his empty beer bottle on the concrete floor. It shattered silently and shot pieces of brown glass in every direction.

"Who the hell are you?" Little Tony demanded.

"Joey Prime's outside. He's hurt. Come on!" Petey said, waving his arm toward the open front door.

"Go check it out," Little Tony said to his cousin.

"Damned Joey. Always screwing up." Big Tony said as he followed orders.

His footsteps pounded the floor, making the kitchen table and the chairs bounce with every step. He walked through the open door, leaving Little Tony and Petey Burns inside with the women.

"Again, who the hell are you?" Little Tony asked.

Petey stuffed his hands into his pockets and ducked his head shyly, but he didn't answer the question. He glanced toward Eleanor and gave her another wink. Then he turned and dashed through the open doorway, following Big Tony.

Little Tony pulled a pistol from his belt and ran after Petey, who was at least fifty pounds lighter, ten years younger, and a lot more nimble. Little Tony didn't stand a chance in hell of catching the intruder.

When the men were all outside, Eleanor said, "GiGi, get the others. We need to hurry."

GiGi ran down the hallway to release the women locked in their rooms and led them to the front of the building.

Eleanor headed toward the front door.

Jade said, "Is Reacher out there?"

"Maybe. I don't know." Eleanor shook her head. "But now's our chance. Look outside. The gate was destroyed. The van is out front."

Jade shouted over the movie's volume, shaking her head. "We must wait for Amarin."

Eleanor yelled back. "Let's get out of here while we can."

Gunfire sounded from somewhere. Maybe it was the raucously violent film blasting through the surround sound and reverberating against the metal walls, bouncing back from the metal ceiling to ricochet again.

Or the gunshots could have come from outside. All the noises were jumbled up. Jade couldn't tell them apart anymore.

GiGi had released the other women from their rooms and they ran into the kitchen and toward the exit.

Jade held back for a moment, but then she realized Eleanor was right.

She wiped the pizza grease off her hands, took a deep breath, and sprinted outside.

CHAPTER FORTY-FOUR

Wednesday, May 18
Las Vegas, Nevada
9:20 p.m.

KIM STOPPED THE DRIVER when she saw the Navigator parked two blocks from the safe house.

The driver turned around in his seat, pocketed her cash, and offered her a business card. "Call me if you need a ride back to your hotel. You won't get a taxi in this area tonight."

"I'm meeting a friend, so I should be okay." She tucked the card into her pocket. Always good to have a plan B. "But thanks."

Kim stepped out of the sedan and closed the door behind her. He turned around and headed back toward the strip. When his red tail lights were far enough away, she approached the Navigator and glanced inside.

She went around to the passenger side and opened the door. The interior lights came on. She scanned the cabin, half expecting to see Burke's body battered and broken. Because that would have been a good reason to explain his absence.

But he wasn't there.

Kim popped the hatch and hustled to the back to look in the cargo compartment. No body there, either.

Which didn't necessarily mean Burke was still alive. But where the hell was he?

She closed the hatch and scanned the area more closely.

The warehouse district resembled hundreds of others she'd seen in other cities. It had probably been built on spec and then sold or leased.

A row of generic warehouses was set back on both sides of the road and separated from each other by open space. A chain link fence along each property line created an equal amount of available land on both sides of each building.

The road between was wide enough for big rigs to pass each other, entering and exiting.

The driveways were blocked with gates on wheels, wide enough to accommodate a big rig. At each entrance, a steel pole with a speaker box mounted on it probably required some sort of entry code to open the gates.

Street numbers were attached to each warehouse. Some also had company signs posted at their entrances, but most did not.

Rentals. Smallish storage for newer, startup businesses, probably. If the business survived and outgrew the starter warehouse, they'd move on to something larger.

All of the warehouses seemed closed up for the night. No lights or vehicles or other activity, at least on the sides facing the road. She couldn't see the back sides from where she stood.

Gaspar said Burke had followed the black SUV here from Denver because he'd guessed that Reacher was also following the black SUV.

He'd set up a stakeout.

Not long afterward, he'd gone dark.

Kim had assumed Burke's stakeout position was inside the Navigator. Which would have been okay. But he wasn't here now and she had no clue where to look for him. Which was definitely not okay.

Even with the bright cone of light cast by the tall floods at each driveway, there were too many dark places around here to hide.

If Burke had been conducting a stakeout from the Navigator, something must have enticed him to leave the relative comforts of the roomy vehicle.

She opened the driver's side door and slid into the driver's seat.

"What did you see, Burke?" she murmured. "What lured you out there?"

Her gaze scanned the area. Without binoculars, she could see four warehouses on each side of the street. From this vantage point, he'd probably been watching the opposite side.

And he'd have hung back.

Which meant the place to start was two warehouses ahead, on the left.

She stepped onto the running board, which raised her eyes about fifteen inches, to get a better view. Nothing unusual seemed to be happening at the moment.

Kim jumped to the ground and closed the door on the Navigator, which turned off the interior lights and made the surrounding darkness seem blacker than it was for a few seconds. She waited for her eyes to adjust before she moved out.

Staying in the shadows as much as possible, she kept low and headed for the last warehouse. It was smaller than the others, which made it stand out. Since she didn't know exactly which place Burke had been watching, the last one seemed like a reasonable place to start.

The full moon illuminated the pavement too well. There were no windows in the warehouse buildings. But if anyone was looking, they'd probably see her, even as she did her best to avoid attracting attention.

When she reached the driveway to the last warehouse, she saw that the gate had been pushed in and demolished. That must have been what Burke saw from the Navigator that drew him out. Maybe he saw it happen in real-time.

If Burke thought Reacher was responsible, he'd have gone after him. For sure.

Kim pulled her weapon and hustled a little faster toward the entrance. A gray panel van was parked in front of the building's entrance. Otherwise, everything in the vicinity seemed quiet.

Kim swiveled her head and scanned constantly, but she didn't catch a glimpse of Burke. If he'd created an observation nest for himself, he'd done a good job of cloaking it.

A pair of headlights preceded a Jeep along the roadway, headed toward the warehouse. Kim took another quick look around.

The only viable cover on the front side of the warehouse was the gray van.

She ran toward the vehicle and slipped into the shadows behind it, moments before a Jeep's headlights flooded the entrance from the driveway.

The Jeep paused at the destroyed gate, giving her a chance to sneak around to the shadows on the opposite side of the van.

She took a few tentative steps and tripped over a big man lying flat on the ground. She landed on top of him and rolled off on the other side.

The Jeep's headlight beams cast a wide arc under and around the van, providing enough illumination to get a better look.

The man was splayed in the dirt near the front door. His body looked like he'd been hit by a truck.

His head was bashed in. His nose was a bloody mess of pulped collagen. His limbs were twisted in unnatural ways because his elbows and both knees had been crushed.

Kim checked his carotid pulse, which had stopped beating a while ago. His body was cool to the touch.

She noticed another body, slightly smaller, crumpled in a heap ten feet away from this one. His head had been blown away by gunshots. No need to check his pulse.

Kim raised her weapon, prepared to shoot, her back flat against the cold gray steel, breathing hard, as she waited for the Jeep to move.

CHAPTER FORTY-FIVE

Wednesday, May 18
Las Vegas, Nevada
9:30 p.m.

THE FIRST THING SYDNEY noticed as he approached the safe house was the gaping hole in the fence where the big gate should have been.

"What the hell?" he said, narrowing his eyes to stare.

Black tire marks on the paved driveway led up to the fence. Like the guy had accelerated while he braked, transmission wound up tight, tires screeching and smoking.

The kind of loud and unusual noises Little Tony should have heard from inside. Big Tony, too.

So what the hell were they doing in there?

The impact had mangled the gate all to hell and flung it back into the yard. The lock had busted and left the hasp still dangling.

It looked like a big SUV or a heavy pickup truck had rammed into the fence at full speed and kept on going, laying rubber, even after the gate was destroyed.

A blow like that would have done all sorts of damage to the front of whatever vehicle did the smashing. Shouldn't be too hard to identify the doer. So where were the vehicle and the maniac driving it?

He lowered the window to listen and swiveled his head to scan for threats. He saw and heard nothing alarming. Which was odd in itself, given the damage.

Sydney slowly moved the stolen Jeep he'd picked up at Rossi's car lot when he'd dropped off the limo for sanitizing.

He rolled past the security box, seeing it had been attacked with considerable force. The heavy metal pole was bent flat against the ground, and the box itself had been bashed into tiny pieces.

Which meant Rossi already knew about the destruction. The security team would have been alerted when the box was destroyed. They would have notified him.

So why hadn't Rossi called?

Sydney idled into the yard, continuously scanning for enemies. They had to be here. No question. But where? And who were they, anyway?

Rivals or enemies were the two likely options.

The locals didn't have the balls to hit Rossi. Which meant it had to be out-of-towners.

For a brief moment, Sydney worried again about the feds. They had the guts and the muscle to put Rossi out of business at any time.

Rossi paid big money to keep cops off his back. Usually it worked well enough. The relationship was mutual. Rossi conducted his business and left law enforcement alone. They returned the favor.

But that agent Sydney had dumped in the desert could have been different.

Earlier tonight, he had confessed the situation with the FBI agent to Rossi. He would have found out anyway. Joey Prime couldn't keep a secret for more than ten minutes without blabbing.

In the end, Sydney had decided it was smarter to confess and spin the situation to his advantage before Little Tony got in there to skewer him.

Rossi hadn't been pleased. But the agent was already handled before Sydney told him about her, so Rossi had said nothing.

Sydney wondered now whether the agent they'd dumped in the desert could have survived and come back here to demolish the place.

Not likely.

But possible.

Maybe destroying the safe house gate had been her doing.

"Nah. That's not it," Sydney said aloud, shaking his head to reassure himself.

This didn't look like the feds seeking revenge. They'd have moved in with teams and weapons and overtaken the place with force.

"They'd still be here. Feds can't get in and out this quick. Hell, they can't do anything quick."

Sydney shook his head slowly, baffled. Nothing he could think of made any sense.

Including the safe house.

How could it seem so normal with all the noise destroying that fence must have made?

Little Tony was a lot of things, but he wasn't deaf. Or stupid. And he had a very strong survival instinct.

"This is nuts," Sydney said under his breath.

The lights were on inside the safe house, which was a good sign.

But the gray van Joey Prime should have already moved to Rossi's car lot was parked at the front door, which wasn't a good sign at all.

As he rolled past the front of the gray van toward the garage, he saw the van's front end was in good shape. Which meant the van wasn't the vehicle that had rammed through the gate.

That bit of intel presented two more problems.

If the van hadn't demolished the front gate, where was the vehicle that did?

And the second issue. Joey Prime took the van to be cleaned a long time ago. Why did he bring it back?

Were they moving the women already? Rossi told Sydney he'd sold a few of the females. The others were going to one of Rossi's brothels in northwest Nevada. But they didn't know that yet.

Sydney shook his head. Moving the product. Nah, that's not it.

Rossi would have told Sydney if they were moving the Thais already. Because Eleanor Duncan wouldn't be joining the others. Rossi had other plans for her.

And even if the timeline for moving the Thais had accelerated, Joey Prime should have parked the van in the garage out back where they could load up away from any prying eyes or listening ears.

Sydney clicked his tongue against his teeth. Joey Prime knew better. He shouldn't have dropped the ball like this.

Where was Joey Prime, anyway?

The gray van appeared to be unoccupied. The engine was off. No one sat in the driver's seat or the passenger seat. All the doors were closed. So was the front door to the safe house.

Sydney picked up his cell and dialed Rossi. The phone rang on the other end a dozen times.

Maybe Rossi was involved in a top-level meeting, but that seemed unlikely. Unless it was some sort of emergency.

Rossi said Alan Chen was fighting his last bout tonight. He'd scheduled Sydney to dump Chen's body later.

Tonight's heavy bettors were already seated, waiting for the big finale. Maybe Rossi didn't answer because he was occupied with the boxing. Not likely. But possible.

Sydney gave up, disconnected, and called Dolly's number. Again, no answer.

His third call was to Little Tony. Sydney hated that prick. But he'd run out of options.

Little Tony's phone rang and rang, with the same result. No answer.

Sydney cursed and spiked the useless cellphone into the passenger's seat. It landed near his loaded Glock and bounced onto the Jeep's floor.

Whatever was happening here at the safe house, he'd have to handle it on his own.

"What would Rossi do?" he said aloud as he pushed the Jeep's accelerator and passed the gray van on his way around the building to the multi-level garage in the back.

As Sydney entered the garage, his headlight beams caught an old turquoise sedan the size of a small tank blocking the driving lane near the electric vehicle charging stations.

"What the hell?" he said aloud as he slowed and pulled up behind it.

CHAPTER FORTY-SIX

Wednesday, May 18
Las Vegas, Nevada
9:45 p.m.

SYDNEY STARED AT THE huge car, his mouth hanging open in slack disbelief. The sedan looked like a movie prop for a film shot in Cuba, where car designs seemed frozen in 1959.

The old boat seated at least six adults and a few kids. It had to stretch close to twenty feet, bumper to bumper. Heavy metal. Cast-iron block. V-8 engine. The gas tank held more than twenty gallons.

"Must weigh three tons or more," Sydney said, shaking his head. Definitely big enough and powerful enough to have shoved in the front gate. When he got a look at the front end, he'd know for sure.

The sedan was parked in the driving lane, parallel to Rossi's row of electric charging stations and perpendicular to the vehicles plugged into them.

Curiously, the sedan's four doors, trunk lid, and hood were wide open. Like a bunch of rowdy teens were conducting a prank, like a Chinese fire drill or something.

A moment later, while Sydney was still trying to make sense of the situation, a man dashed from the charging stations. He darted between two electric SUVs, running fast, full out as if the hounds of hell were chasing him.

Sydney shoved the Jeep's transmission into park and jumped out, brandishing his pistol.

"Hey! You! Stop!" Sydney yelled.

The guy was average-sized, and his long, blond locks fanned out behind him as he ran. He maneuvered adroitly, sprinting between parked vehicles, heading away from the sedan as if his life depended on it.

As the runner passed cars and SUVs, and trucks, he pulled doors open and kept running.

Sydney squinted and shook his head. "What's up with that? Trying to block the path of anyone chasing him on foot?"

Sydney didn't have a clear line of sight, but he aimed and fired at the man's retreating back anyway.

The bullet ricocheted off a concrete pillar.

He heard the ricochet strike something hard. Not the runner, for sure.

Then he heard crashing glass, sounding in a zigzag pattern, moving toward the ramp to the second floor.

The guy was busting out windows as he went.

"Dammit!" Sydney fired again.

The sound of gunshots inside the garage was deafening, but it didn't bring Little Tony or anyone else out of the safe house.

Before Sydney had a chance to worry about that, he heard a loud whoosh and felt the instant heat.

The sedan lit up from the inside, where all the stuff that's easy to ignite was installed. Carpet, seat foam, soft plastic, even windshield wiper fluid. All flammable.

The guy must have put an accelerant inside the sedan and started a slow blaze before he took off.

Flames burst from the front seat first. Followed quickly by more flames from the back seat. Next, the contents of the trunk caught fire.

What the hell? Call the fire department?

Sydney smelled gas. He scanned the area around the burning sedan until he spied the problem.

A trail of gasoline led from the sedan's trunk toward the electric chargers on the other side of the vehicles.

The flames that had flumed beyond the interior of the car danced along the fuel trail, broadening and gaining strength as they rushed ahead.

In Sydney's periphery, big clouds of heavy black smoke emitted from beneath four electric cars.

Where the lithium-ion batteries were located.

Batteries that had been known to catch fire and explode when deliberately sabotaged.

Understanding dawned. The running man must have been tampering with the batteries when Sydney rolled up.

The smoke and the fires and the gasoline combined with the breeze blowing between the open floors of the garage brought stinging pain to Sydney's eyes. He blotted his face with his forearm but failed to quench the pain.

The stench burned his nostrils and hurt his lungs as he tried to breathe through the thick smoke.

The black smoke expanded, spreading to the other vehicles. Quickly, a small SUV began to flame from underneath. And then the flame spread along the row, from one electric vehicle to the next, lightning-fast.

Too fast to believe, at least a dozen vehicles inside the

garage were aflame. He was surrounded by fire and smoke and the smell of gasoline.

Sydney stared, mouth agape, struggling to comprehend and defend.

A moment too long.

Something inside the big sedan's trunk exploded, pushing steel and plastic and metal outward.

Sydney was ex-military. Instantly, he knew this was no accident. The force of the blast could only have been caused by an improvised explosive device. An IED created by an expert.

The blast wave expanded outward from its explosive core.

Transmitted. Absorbed. Reflected by the garage and everything in it.

The first explosion was followed by four more, like a symphony's staccato punctuation with cannon fire during holiday fireworks.

Five explosions.

Four electric vehicles and the big turquoise sedan were now spectacularly ablaze.

The charging stations ignited next.

Sydney swiveled his head, widened his eyes, mouth agape. The scene was too spectacular to grasp.

The open-air breeze moved swiftly between floors to oxygenate the blazes.

Six minutes after Sydney's Jeep had rolled up behind the turquoise sedan, a wall of fire filled the garage, superheating it beyond any human's ability to withstand.

Sydney turned and ran, feeling the heat coming fast and hard at his back.

CHAPTER FORTY-SEVEN

Wednesday, May 18
Las Vegas, Nevada
9:35 p.m.

KIM HAD WATCHED FROM her position behind the gray van.
After a couple of minutes, the Jeep rolled through the open maw
where the gate had been. Headlights inched into the yard and
kept going. The driver passed the van slowly as if looking inside
the cabin before moving on.

She'd pushed herself upright, rose to her feet, and jogged a
few steps to the front of the van, watching.

The Jeep rolled past the van and around the opposite corner
of the warehouse. The extra illumination provided by the
headlights abruptly disappeared. The red tail lights went dark a
moment later.

After the Jeep turned out of sight, Kim inched away from the
front of the warehouse and around to the other side of the van.
She allowed her night vision to adjust and then scanned the area
again. No more bodies were visible from where she stood.

There was probably a back entrance to the warehouse or a back exit from the yard. Or both. Maybe more storage of some sort back there, too. Could be anything. To search effectively, she'd need backup.

Where the hell was Burke?

He'd come here looking for Reacher.

Was Reacher inside?

What about Petey Burns?

Half a moment later, she heard gunfire from somewhere in the back. The same area where the Jeep had disappeared.

As if her thoughts had conjured him, Petey Burns came running from behind the warehouse building.

Petey ducked around the front of the van, flung open the door to the warehouse, and ran inside, shouting, "Eleanor! Jade! GiGi! Round 'em up. Let's go!"

Kim had heard two of those names for the first time tonight from the man on Rossi's rooftop. They had to be Rossi's kidnap victims.

Was this why Burke was here? And what did Reacher have to do with any of it?

Kim saw that the side door of the van was wide open. Several women ran from inside the warehouse and piled into the van.

The last one was Eleanor Duncan, running fast. She pulled the driver's door open and lifted her leg to hop inside.

Before she could get settled into the driver's seat, Kim ran forward and yanked her out again.

Eleanor's eyes were wild. She fought hard to get away, but Kim subdued her, speaking urgently. "Eleanor! It's me! Stop!"

Eleanor jerked her arm, frightened.

Kim shook her again, harder this time. "Stop!"

Eleanor finally seemed to recognize her.

She tried to shake Kim's hold on her arms. "What the hell do you want?"

"I want you to tell me what the hell is going on," Kim demanded.

"We can't talk here. I have to go. Get into the van if you want to come along. Otherwise, get out of the way," Eleanor said.

Kim didn't move.

"Unless you want all of us to die."

Before Kim could respond, she heard the first explosion from the north side of the warehouse. It sounded like a bomb. Like the IED that had exploded on the roof of the Snake Eyes earlier tonight.

While Kim's attention was divided, Eleanor shook off her hold and ran the short distance to the front of the van. This time, she stepped up onto the running board, made it inside, and closed the door behind her.

Smaller explosions followed the first. Kim looked up. An orange glow lit the sky.

The last of the Thai women piled into the van and one shoved the door closed.

Eleanor yelled, "Jade! Get in!"

The woman ran around to the other side of the van and climbed aboard. "Go! Go!" she yelled to Eleanor as she slammed the door.

Kim knocked on the window. Eleanor lowered it.

"Where are you going?" Kim asked.

"Why would I tell you that?"

"Why wouldn't you? You're all kidnapping victims. I'm an FBI agent. We can protect you," Kim replied.

A hysterical laugh erupted from her mouth while Eleanor shook her head violently and attempted to raise the window.

Kim pulled one of the burner phones from her pocket and wedged it into the gap before Eleanor could get the window all the way up. She pulled her weapon and pointed it at Eleanor on the other side of the glass.

"I don't want to shoot you, Eleanor. But I will," Kim said, hoping the terrified woman wouldn't call her bluff. "Where are you running to? Where can I locate you?"

"Somewhere Rossi's men will never find us," Eleanor said, panting, fumbling with the controls.

"Rossi's dead, Eleanor. You don't have to worry about him anymore," Kim replied, trying to calm her and failing fast.

"Don't you get it? Men like Rossi never die. Someone else always takes over. We'll never be free of them. We have to go. Right now. You should go, too. While you still can," Eleanor said, sliding the transmission into drive and stomping the accelerator.

Kim jumped back from the van to avoid being hit by the moving vehicle.

Eleanor kept the accelerator flat against the floor, burst out of the fenced yard, and took a squealing turn onto the road. She headed toward the interstate as fast as the fully loaded gray box would carry them.

The explosions from the garage kept coming as if every vehicle in the garage was being systematically destroyed, one after the other.

Kim felt the heat blowing over her with the breeze.

Burning petroleum and other fumes she couldn't identify assaulted her nose and her eyes.

What would happen if he exploded the warehouse?

With enough force, every inch of metal on the building could become flying shrapnel.

When Kim glanced over her shoulder, she saw Petey Burns running like a fiend toward the opposite side of the yard.

"Burns! Stop! FBI!" she yelled, facing him and fully prepared to shoot.

Before she could get off a clear shot, he jumped into a red SUV and revved it up. He punched the accelerator and sped toward the exit.

Kim fired two rounds attempting to slow Burns down. The bullets hit the vehicle's back window in two places, but it didn't stop.

Burns kept going at full speed until the SUV was out of range.

She had to hope The Boss or Gaspar or Finlay had a bead on the vehicle.

There was nothing more she could do about Burns from here.

Kim was standing in the warehouse yard, out in the open, when she saw another man running from the garage. He was older than Petey Burns. Taller. Bulkier.

His clothes were rough. One pant leg was torn away from his boot, flapping in the breeze.

The back of his jacket was on fire.

The fire trailed him as he ran silently forward.

And he was armed. He carried a pistol in his right hand. His head swept back and forth frantically searching.

He didn't seem to notice her. She stepped back into the shadow of the warehouse building and waited as he came closer.

When he entered the cone of light from one of the big power poles, she saw his face.

The same face Gaspar had captured on the traffic cams.

The driver of the black limo.

The man who had abducted her back at the Orchid Thai Restaurant.

Thaddeus Sydney.

He seemed to realize his jacket was burning. He shrugged it off his left arm and then switched the pistol to his left hand so he could slip his right arm through the sleeve.

Which was when Kim made her move. While the right arm was still inside the burning jacket, she stepped into the light cone, raised her weapon, and yelled, "Stop! FBI!"

Sydney kept coming, right arm still encased in the burning jacket, eyes wild.

Time seemed to stand still as she watched him lower the pistol in his left hand, aim and shoot directly at Kim's center mass.

Half a moment before he squeezed the trigger, she dropped to the ground and rolled to his right, aiming her gun and taking her shot.

He went down. The burning jacket, entangled on his right arm, went with him.

The fire spread to his shirt and then his pants.

He rolled onto his back, trying to smother the flames, as he squeezed off two more rounds in her direction.

The fire consumed his entire torso and climbed toward his face.

He kept shooting.

Kim aimed and fired at him again.

Her shots hit the mark. His screaming stopped instantly.

Kim jumped to her feet and ran toward him, but she was too late.

He was already dead. All she could do was stare in horrified fascination as the fire intensified and devoured him.

Her perception of time returned when she realized the entire compound was exploding and afire.

The breeze had picked up to gusts in the past few minutes. Briefly, she wondered how long it would take for the blaze to spread to the other seven warehouses. The combined inferno would melt everything in its path.

There was nothing she could do for the three dead men.

She and Burke needed to go. Now. While they could still reach the Navigator.

Where the hell was Burke?

CHAPTER FORTY-EIGHT

Wednesday, May 18
Las Vegas, Nevada
10:25 p.m.

KIM HAD A CLEAR line of sight since Eleanor and the others sped away in the gray van.

She craned her neck to scan the area, not sure exactly what she was looking for or hoping to find.

Balls of fire leapt onto the roof of the warehouse and tumbled toward the back. For half a second, Kim wondered what was back there and how quickly it would catch fire and add to the massive conflagration.

The scene had already been deadly for three men on the ground. There might be others. They could be still alive. Needing help.

A moment's indecision.

Should she stay or should she go?

In the back of the warehouse, the roof caved in with a thunderous crash.

Total destruction of the building and its contents was speeding along with rapid and unrelenting passion.

Were there more explosives planted inside? Was the whole place booby-trapped and ready to flash?

As soon as the thought occurred to her, the fire whooshed toward the open front door, lapping up the oxygen outside.

The heat and the flames and the stench and the unrelenting noise were overwhelming.

Kim squeezed her eyes shut against the stinging smoke and opened them again to peer inside.

A man was limping toward the exit from deep inside the warehouse, holding something. Probably a gun. He was covered in soot.

There was so much smoke and fire between them that Kim couldn't see him well. Perhaps he could see her. No way to know for sure whether he was friend or foe.

She pulled her weapon and pointed in his direction.

The adrenaline rush flooding through her body had heightened all of her senses. Even as her heart pounded hard in her chest, she tried to slow her breathing and regain control.

She didn't call out. The effort was useless. He couldn't hear her anyway.

He kept coming.

She took cover, blinking and wiping her stinging eyes to clear her vision as much as possible in the continuing onslaught.

The man stumbled and fell onto the floor.

She waited.

He didn't get up.

She peered into the smoky interior, straining to see more clearly.

Repeated explosions in the garage, along with the roar of noise from the fires and the collapsing building, made it impossible to hear any human voices.

Kim moved closer to the door, shielding her face from the intensifying heat, narrowing her gaze to focus on the man down. She crept closer.

The heat and the noise and the wind gusting through the burning roof and across the flames terrified her.

She inched further inside, closer to the downed man. She knew she was moving swiftly, but it seemed to take an eternity to get there.

He might be dead.

Or he might rise up and shoot her.

She crept a few feet closer, still squeezing her eyes open and closed, still holding her weapon ready, watching for falling debris that might crush them both.

The heat, the smoke, the flames, the heart-pounding terror intensified with every breath she struggled to grasp.

But she couldn't simply leave him there to die. She'd seen enough death tonight already.

Another few steps toward his prone body, one more blink, one more swift breath.

And finally, she recognized him.

Burke.

Quickly, Kim holstered her weapon, covered her nose and mouth with her forearm, and rushed to him.

She leaned down toward his head and yelled to be heard.

"Come on, Burke. It's Otto. We've got to get away from here. Whatever is exploding on the other side is coming closer. Get up. I'll help you."

His clothes, hair, and face were covered in black soot combined with sweat. He stunk.

He was wounded. One hand was splayed across a wound in his side, applying pressure to stop the bleeding. No such luck.

Breathing heavily, Burke seemed not to recognize her at first. When he realized who she was, he said, "Reacher. He's gone. Get him."

"We will. But you can't help me if you're dead. Come on. Stand up." She helped to lift him as he struggled to push himself upright.

He put his arm around her shoulder, still applying pressure to his wound, and they managed to move, slowly, haltingly, inches at a time.

After what felt like a second eternity, they stumbled outside into the marginally cooler, clearer air.

Kim used the momentum they'd created to lead Burke away from the blaze as quickly as they could move.

Her gasping, halting breaths burned slightly less as they moved toward the road. Her eyes stung and watered and her vision clouded.

She kept going. Kept dragging him along with her.

What seemed like a third eternity later, when they finally reached the fence, she helped him to rest against it for support.

Kim slid his arm from around her shoulders, making sure he was as steady as possible on his feet.

She shouted, "I'll get the Navigator. You wait here. Lean against the fence. I'll only be gone a minute."

Burke nodded, which seemed to be all the strength he could muster.

She slipped his arm off her shoulders and ran.

Through the opening where the gate had been.

Down the driveway.

She turned onto the road and ran flat out along the wide, smooth pavement illuminated by the full moon's soft silvery glow.

Until she reached the Navigator.

CHAPTER FORTY-NINE

Wednesday, May 18
Las Vegas, Nevada
10:45 p.m.

KIM YANKED THE FRONT door open, stepped onto the running board, and jumped into the driver's seat. Sitting on the front edge to reach the pedals with her toes, she started it up. She pressed the accelerator as far as she could reach and raced the engine toward the exploding warehouse.

With improved perspective, she saw that the serial explosions were now igniting from the north side garage.

Each explosion was another vehicle catching fire.

Petey Burns knew how to steal cars. Made sense he'd know how to detonate them, too. Which wasn't as easy to do as popular fiction made it seem.

She drove the Navigator back toward the open gate surrounding the expanding fire, rushing to get in and back out to escape from what she feared would be a massive explosion when the heat and flames reached the warehouse itself.

Burke remained upright, leaning heavily against the fence. She backed the Navigator as close to him as she could get it. Then she hurried out of the SUV and ran around to help her partner get inside.

She opened the passenger door and threw his arm over her shoulders again. She cajoled him along and helped him lift his feet into the footwell. They struggled to get him inside and then she asked, "Anybody else back there we can save?"

Burke's eyes were closed. He shook his head slowly.

She closed the door behind him.

Kim ran around the back of the Navigator and climbed into the driver's seat again. She pulled away from the fence just as yet another blast propelled itself into the sky from the garage behind them.

She pressed the accelerator all the way and fought the big SUV from the driveway to the road, passing the first warehouse and then the next, heading south toward the road that would take them into the city.

As the distance between the Navigator and the warehouse slowly widened, she heard sirens coming fast. Fire trucks and bomb squads, she hoped.

She glanced into the rearview mirror, looking for the flashing lights atop the approaching first responders.

Half a moment later, the warehouse exploded high and hard and loud behind them.

The blast jolted the Navigator. It lifted off the ground and plopped back down onto all four wheels.

Metal shrapnel flew everywhere.

Projectiles pelted the Navigator as if it was taking incoming rounds from all sides.

Several of the windows broke and cracked and fell into the

cabin. She could only imagine the damage the roof was absorbing.

The headlights were shattered and stopped illuminating the road ahead.

One of the tires was punctured. Then a second.

Kim sat on the edge of the seat, both hands gripping the steering wheel. She kept her foot on the accelerator, heading away as fast and straight as the heavy SUV would travel.

The tires went flat quickly. Running on the wheels, the Navigator leaned lower and pulled hard to the right side. Kim struggled with the steering wheel to keep the heavy SUV on the road between the ditches.

Burke had strapped himself in and pulled his seatbelt tight. He held onto the handle above the window. Every bounce of the plush interior forced a heavy groan from his lips.

Kim glanced into the rearview mirror again. Flashing red lights and loud sirens turned south at the intersection behind her. More responders were approaching ahead.

She peered through the cracked windshield, looking for an ambulance. No one back at the warehouse could possibly need immediate medical attention. Burke did.

Before she could pull over to the side of the road to flag down the ambulance, a man ran out in front of the Navigator, waving his arms, asking her to stop, pointing something straight at her in case she didn't feel like stopping.

The damaged windshield refracted his body like a funhouse mirror.

Kim saw him at the very last second, not quite sure what she was looking at because of the distortions.

The thing in his hand was definitely a gun. From this close

distance, the chances of a successful headshot through the windshield were better than zero.

A quick thought ran through her head. Who was this guy? He had a gun. He knew how to use it. Had he killed the others?

She didn't have even half a moment to sort the situation out. If she didn't manage to stop the Navigator, she'd kill him and the vehicle, too.

No question.

Kim risked releasing one hand from the steering wheel to give him one final warning. She palmed the horn and planted both feet on the brake pedal and stood on it with all her weight.

Too late, he realized she couldn't stop within the short distance.

He fired off two rounds that went wildly over the roof just above her head.

He tried to fire again, but he was out of bullets.

Kim jerked the wheel to avoid mowing him down.

The big, heavy SUV slowed and wobbled and skidded, slewing toward the right side of the road.

The man leapt sideways toward the west shoulder at the same time.

The Navigator collided with him while he was still in mid-air.

The left front of the SUV slammed solidly into his torso.

A hard, loud blow bounced him to the ground.

The gun flew from his hand.

The Navigator kept rolling, right over his body.

Panting and delirious, Burke yelled, "You've killed Reacher!"

Was that Reacher?

Kim couldn't believe she'd killed him. Pulsing shock waves ran through her body. Her stomach churned like a thrashing swamp creature determined to jump out. She pursed her lips to hold it back.

Her constant pressure on the brake seemed to take hours instead of moments to stop the big SUV.

She slid the transmission into park and jumped out.

She left the door open and ran to check on the man, glancing back once more at the warehouse.

The blazing structure sent gales of sparks and gasses outward. Big, curled flames tumbled free, burning in the air, dancing and splitting and distorting the air with their heat. They hurled themselves up and up and up higher as if reaching for Heaven itself.

When she found him in the dark ditch, even from above she could tell the man's body was battered beyond repair. He lay on his belly, face down in the muck at the bottom of the trough.

Kim didn't expect to find a pulse, but she slid down the side of the ditch, stumbling and flailing.

When she reached his corpse, the adrenaline surging through her body gave her enough strength to heave him sideways.

Dead eyes stared straight ahead.

She checked his carotid artery just in case.

Life no longer pulsed in his veins. The big Navigator had pounded it out of him.

She patted his pockets, looking for ID. She didn't find any. She had no idea who this guy was. But she saw enough to know one thing for sure.

He wasn't Jack Reacher.

Kim stood on the bank of the trench for a few more moments, allowing the truth to sink in. Willing her heart to slow and gasping to control her breathing, forcing her nerves to settle.

She wiped the sweat from her face with her sleeve and then jammed her hands into her pockets to control the jittering.

The Navigator rested sideways on the shoulder. It was not drivable. Burke couldn't walk anywhere.

There was nothing more she could do for the man in the ditch. Burke needed medical attention. There were medics on the way.

Kim stood, watching the fires in the distance, waiting for an ambulance.

She walked around to the Navigator's open door, leaned in, and found the emergency flashers. She pushed the button to turn them on, hoping they still worked. The last thing she needed now was to have one of the rescue vehicles plow into the Navigator because they didn't see it.

The noises from the sirens and the fires and the explosions in the distance roused Burke from his stupor once again.

He opened his eyes, twisted his head to scan the interior cabin, looking for Kim.

He struggled to talk, but no words emerged from his dry throat.

Kim found an old bottle of water she'd left in the cup holder, twisted the cap off, and handed it to Burke.

He took a couple of deep swigs, swishing the water around in his mouth before he swallowed. Then he cleared his throat a couple of times.

Finally, he managed to rasp, "Is Reacher dead?"

CHAPTER FIFTY

Wednesday, May 18
Las Vegas, Nevada
11:30 p.m.

THE FIREFIGHTERS AND EMS units and local law
enforcement vehicles began to arrive at the scene. Sirens wailing,
lights flashing, zooming past the Navigator where it still rested on
the shoulder.

One of the units stopped to offer aid while the others rushed
toward the blazing warehouse. The EMTs checked Burke out
and then rolled him on a gurney into the ambulance.

Kim expected him to be admitted for treatment. Whatever
had happened to his torso would take a while to fix.

In response to her questions, the EMT said, "He'll be in the
hospital at least twenty-four hours. Maybe longer if surgery is
required."

"When can I see him?"

"It'll be a few hours, at least. Probably not until mid-morning," the EMT replied as he closed the back doors, leaving Kim standing on the shoulder.

Watching the receding tail lights on the ambulance as it headed back to downtown Vegas, she patted her pockets until she found the ticket the driver had given her on the way out to the warehouse. She called him to pick her up.

They transferred her bags and Burke's stuff from the Navigator to his SUV. The first responders were overwhelmed with issues down at the warehouse. Someone would notice the Navigator and come around asking questions at some point. The Boss could deal with all that.

She settled into the backseat and closed her eyes, content to let the driver handle traffic as they left the chaos at the warehouse behind.

Twenty minutes later, the driver dropped her off at the hotel she'd checked into earlier. She didn't need a mirror to know she must look like an escaped refugee who had clawed her way out of a pile of rubble.

The bellman met the SUV at the hotel entrance. He flashed odd glances her way before he worked up the courage to suggest that she might want to *freshen up*, as he put it before she entered the casinos.

"Thanks. That's my plan," Kim replied. That dinner-plate-sized shower head was calling her name.

"Would you want to ride up in the back elevator with me?" Which she took as a request instead of a suggestion.

She nodded. "Yeah. One moment."

When she returned to pay the driver, adding a generous tip, he said, "Keep my card. You may need another ride while you're in town."

She didn't bother to argue. After all, he'd been right before.

The bellman delivered Kim and her bags to her room and backed out, thanking her profusely for the second large tip she'd delivered tonight. It was only money. Cooper's money. And he owed her.

Kim emptied her pockets onto the bed. Three cell phones, some cash, a fresh roll of antacids, and not much more. She pulled off her weapon and tossed it onto the bed, too.

The clothes she'd sent to the laundry earlier had been returned to her closet.

She stripped off the now revolting new suit and stuffed it into a second laundry bag, trying not to gag when the stench of sweat, smoke, dirt, and whatever else was at the bottom of that ditch back at the warehouse assaulted her senses.

Kim closed the bag up tightly, using the elastic band from her hair, and dropped the whole mess into the trash can. No laundry on earth could ever make those clothes wearable again.

She spent the next thirty minutes under the shower's dinner-plate-spray. She'd soaped up her hair and her body and rinsed until her fingers were wrinkled prunes before she turned off the water and stepped out.

Housekeeping had brought fresh towels and another luxurious white robe. She dried off, slipped into the robe, and padded into the bedroom. The mini-bar yielded two small bottles of red wine, two bottles of sparkling water, and some mixed nuts. There was a wine glass, too. And a room service menu.

She gathered it all up and carried it to the bed and plopped down, cross-legged, to prepare dinner. She twisted the top off one of the wine bottles and poured it into the glass. Then she ripped the mixed nuts open with her teeth.

After she'd taken a sip of the red wine, which was actually not too bad for mini-bar booze, she saw The Boss's burner phone jumping around on the bed where she'd tossed it earlier.

She munched and sipped and watched the vibrating rings bounce the plastic phone around for a good long while before she punched the answer button and put the call on speaker.

"Burke will be in the hospital overnight," was the first thing he said. "He'll be discharged tomorrow, ready to go."

"Uh, huh." While he talked, she thumbed through the room service menu. The copywriter had done an excellent job describing the food. Her mouth was watering and her stomach was growling already.

"He's got a nasty gash on his left side. Fortunately, whoever slashed him with whatever it was didn't hit any vital organs."

"Good to know."

"He's got soot in his lungs, probably exacerbated by the dry air out there. But the docs expect it to clear up on its own after they give him some oxygen. If he stays hydrated."

"He's lucky. Could have been a lot worse." She read through the entrees. The crab cakes and grilled asparagus sounded perfect.

"What's wrong with you?" Cooper demanded, noticing her lack of engagement. Normally, he didn't care about her at all. For some reason, tonight he did. Odd.

"Took you long enough to ask," she replied, definitely adding the gourmet mac and cheese. And a nice bottle of red wine, too. She wasn't going anywhere else tonight. Might as well splurge on Cooper's tab.

Cooper ignored her sarcasm and carried on with his report on her partner. "Burke says he fought with Reacher. He says Reacher wounded him."

"And you believed that?" She leaned back against the pillow, sipping the wine.

Cooper's exasperation made him snappy. "Why wouldn't I believe it?"

"Seems unusual, is all," she said, pulling the house phone off the side table to order her meal. "How many people have we come across who were *wounded* by Reacher? Lots of dead people. Not too many wounded ones walking around."

He paused. After a moment, he said, "You think Reacher wasn't at that warehouse tonight."

"I'm fairly sure he was there, actually. The scorched earth levels of damage done to the place, not to mention the dead bodies, has 'Reacher' written all over it."

"So what's your point?" He'd run out of patience.

Kim had tired of the game and was ready to order dinner. "My *point* is that Burke had no business being out there in the first place. He left me alone in the desert. He's my *partner.* He's supposed to have my back. But he didn't. We're supposed to work as a team. But we don't. Why is that?"

"You're the team leader, Otto. You tell me. Your team's dysfunction is your problem, not mine," he snapped and disconnected the call.

Kim swiped the phone off the bed and sent it flying across the room. The cheap plastic hit the wall and busted, sending bits of plastic flying, which made her grin.

CHAPTER FIFTY-ONE

Thursday, May 19
Las Vegas, Nevada
1:05 a.m.

DESTROYING COOPER'S PHONE HAD been a childish thing to do, but it was satisfying in the moment. And it was a short-term solution. He'd deliver another one soon enough. He always did.

She picked up the house phone and dialed room service. Delivery was promised in thirty minutes.

Before she had the chance to check in with Gaspar, the third burner, one of the new ones she hadn't even turned on, vibrated on the bed.

She picked up the phone. The caller ID was blocked. Not many hackers could activate a burner phone remotely and place a call like that. Only three she could think of, including Cooper.

"Yes," Kim said.

"Good evening, Otto," Lamont Finlay replied smoothly. His deep voice was one of his best features. "How are you tonight?"

"Getting better," she replied. She didn't bother to ask how he'd acquired the number. He wouldn't have told her anyway.

"Sounds like you've had a busy time lately."

"You're calling because you think I got too close to Reacher tonight," she replied.

"Not exactly, but yes. Much too close." His upper-crust Boston Brahmin accent supplied his words with heavy gravity.

"I will find him. You know that."

"You may. When he's ready. Not before."

A few moments of silence filled the gap. She glanced at the clock. Her dinner would be here soon and she wanted to enjoy it while the food was fresh and hot.

"So what is the reason for your call?"

"I'm worried about your new partner," Finlay replied.

"What the hell? Burke will be fine. Cooper just told me they'll be stitching him up and giving him some oxygen. Doctors say he'll be right as rain by tomorrow," she said. "Why is everybody so worried about Burke?"

Finlay chuckled and covered the speaker, but she heard him say that he'd be done with this call soon.

When he came back, he was totally serious. "I'm not worried about Burke's health. I'm worried about you. Burke is not Gaspar. Watch your back, Otto."

"What do you know that concerns you?" She felt the familiar anxiety begin to hum in her veins, her body's warning system fully reactivated by his simple admonition.

He was quiet and she realized his attention had been snagged by someone else. When he came back this time, he said, "I'm sorry. I have to go. We'll talk again. But don't forget what I said. Be careful out there."

Before she could reply, he'd hung up.

A loud rap on the door made her jump. "Room service," a female voice called out.

Kim let the woman in. She set up the table and opened the wine and Kim signed the bill. The food looked amazing and smelled even better. But her stomach was in no state to appreciate it all at the moment.

What the hell was Finlay warning her about? She paced the room, seeking clarity and finding none.

Her glance returned to her meal, ready and waiting.

Resting on the table was a padded manila envelope, puffed up with the new burner cell phone from The Boss. She shook her head. The guy wasted no time.

The sight of it spoiled her appetite.

She carried a glass of water over to the bed, opened her laptop and wrote her personal report, sending it off to her secure server. Paying her insurance premium, she called it.

Next, she wrote a sanitized version of the past few days for The Boss and sent it off to him. She included all the ancillary loose ends, like Petey Burns and the Thai women and Eleanor Duncan.

She identified four bodies. All were known associates of Rossi. Thaddeus Sydney and three cousins in the Callo crime family—Big Tony, Little Tony, and the one who shot into the Navigator's windshield trying to kill her, Joey Prime.

She mentioned the Thai women and the connection between the man impaled on the rooftop and his sisters who had been abducted along with Eleanor, Jade, and GiGi. Kim still had no idea what the connection was between the Thais and Reacher. But her gut said the link existed.

Cooper would follow up or he wouldn't. Either way, the women weren't her responsibility. After she kicked all of that upstairs, she wasn't required to do more. She had problems of her own to deal with.

Finally, she downloaded several files from Gaspar. He'd included more intel he'd gathered on Burke. She read through it quickly, frowning as she finished each paragraph.

By the time she'd written all the facts that had been swirling around in her head, her appetite had returned.

Kim stifled a yawn and glanced at the clock on the bedside table. The morning was well underway in Miami. She called Gaspar while she sipped the wine and nibbled on the crab cakes, which were, as advertised, worth dying for.

"Hey, Chico."

"Talk to me, Suzy Wong," he said in his easy, unflappable style. She could almost smell the Cuban coffee from here.

CHAPTER FIFTY-TWO

Thursday, May 19
Las Vegas, Nevada
3:15 a.m.

KIM REPORTED EVERYTHING TO Gaspar like she would
have if they were still partners, slipping into the familiar pattern.
She imagined she could see steam coming out of his ears when
she told him about her conversation with Finlay, and she
grinned.

During the call, she opened the padded manila envelope
from The Boss. She dumped the new burner phone and the
encrypted flash drive onto the table.

Gaspar held his questions, but she could hear him clacking
keys on a keyboard the whole time.

When she'd brought him up to date and finished the first
crab cake, she washed it down with more of the amazing wine.
Her stomach had stopped thrashing and she was starting to feel a
bit mellow, which was probably more about the wine than
relaxed anxiety about Cooper or Burke or Reacher.

"I located the Mercedes GLC that Petey Burns drove out of the warehouse lot. He ditched it at a shopping mall and picked up a boxy black thing. Meaning a black G-550. Reacher was still with him, like you thought," Gaspar said, still clacking his keys.

"Where's the G-550 now?" she sipped and munched and waited.

"Lost them somewhere in downtown Las Vegas. Burns has probably ditched the G-550 by now anyway. I'll keep looking, but don't get your hopes up. Lots of people and lots of vehicles in Vegas. Finding them again won't be easy."

She grinned. "Of course not. If it was easy, anybody could do it. I wouldn't need high-priced talent like you, Chico."

He laughed. "Flattery will get you everywhere, Suzy Wong."

"I'm counting on it," she replied good-naturedly. After a brief pause, she broached the subject that bothered her most. "The Boss believes Burke engaged Reacher at the warehouse."

"Yeah?"

"Burke says the fight was close and personal. And Reacher walked away."

Gaspar said with a dry chuckle, "The only way Reacher loses a fight is when at least three burly guys hold him down while two more wail on him."

"Exactly. So if this fight actually happened, why would Reacher leave Burke alive?" she pondered aloud.

"You think Burke is lying?" Gaspar said slowly, trying the idea in his head.

"Not totally. I think Reacher was there. I saw Petey Burns, and we know they've been together for a few days. Which means Reacher was probably there, too," Kim said. "But why engage Burke?"

"And if Burke was the aggressor, why fight him and then

leave Burke alive…" Gaspar's voice trailed as if he was
considering the possibilities and wasn't happy with the options.

"What?" Kim asked.

Gaspar blew out a long, frustrated breath. "The only thing
that makes sense to me is that Reacher believes Burke has vital
intel."

"Vital to whom?"

"Dunno," Gaspar said.

"Intel Reacher already knows?"

"Don't know that, either."

Kim ran her hand through her hair and shook her head.
"Doesn't make sense. Reacher's got my number. He's called
before. If the intel was all that vital and he already knew it, he'd
tell me himself. Wouldn't he?"

"Hell, Sunshine. Maybe. Maybe not. Maybe he just has a
hunch, and he needs you to dig up the dirt. I don't know. No
point in guessing. Let me sleep on it."

She nodded and moved laterally to a slightly different topic.
"And what about Burke?"

"What about him?" Gaspar said lazily. "He's done you a lot
of favors here, Suzy Wong."

She grinned, feeling slightly better, more normal. "Such as?"

"Better the devil you know, right?"

"What do you mean?"

"Now you know you can't lean on Burke. You also know
he's a glory hog," Gaspar said.

"How so?"

"Seems to me he wanted to find Reacher on his own. He
doesn't want to be the junior member of the team, subordinate to
your success."

"Or Burke followed Petey Burns, got to the warehouse, ran

into Reacher, and couldn't leave," Kim replied, somewhat surprised to hear herself defending Burke's behavior tonight.

But he was on her team now, for better or worse. And he was impulsive. So it could have happened that way.

Until she had a chance to ask him, she'd give him the benefit of the doubt.

"Doesn't matter *why* he went there," Gaspar growled. "What's important to remember is that he left you to fend for yourself and never looked back. You could have died when Sydney dumped you in that desert. Burke wouldn't have even known about it. Your body could still be out there. Vulture food."

"That seems a little harsh, don't you think?" Kim shuddered because Gaspar was right. "At least let me talk to Burke and find out why he went ahead without me. He's my partner. I owe him some loyalty, too."

"Look, Otto, he's a guy. Guys are just not that complicated. He washed out of the hostage rescue team," Gaspar replied, one logical step after another as if the situation was obvious. "Cooper's giving him a chance to prove he's got what it takes to stay employed. Burke's pulled out all the stops to please Cooper."

"It's friendly competition."

"Not that friendly. Burke's out to prove he's better than you."

"You think?"

"Hell yes. You've been on the hunt for Reacher for seven months. If Burke finds Reacher quickly before you do, he gets the glory. And he gets his job back." Gaspar paused and swigged the coffee and then wrapped up. "He shows you up. And you get screwed. Again."

Maybe it was that simple. She nodded again, eyes closed, thinking it through.

But Gaspar's theory didn't feel right to Kim. Tomorrow, when her head was clear, she'd figure out why.

"What about Eleanor Duncan?" she asked, deflecting, moving to a less controversial subject.

She had finished the food, poured another glass of wine, and carried The Boss's encrypted flash drive over to the bed. She slipped the drive into her laptop and waited for it to load up.

Gaspar replied, "What about her?"

"Looks like Reacher came to help Eleanor for some unknown reason. And this was the second time he's rescued her. Seems like she'd want to express her gratitude, doesn't it?" Kim asked while she opened the files on Cooper's flash drive.

"Maybe she's used up her quota of Reacher's goodwill now," Gaspar replied. "They'll go back to Denver to collect the girl, Mika. They could rebuild the restaurant. Jade's escort business will continue to thrive. There's an endless supply of customers. They could stay."

"Or they could move on and start over somewhere else. They've started over before," Kim said, skimming her new orders from the Boss.

They didn't talk for a few minutes.

Kim finished her wine.

Gaspar was probably sorting through images, looking for Burns and Reacher and Eleanor, while he consumed mass quantities of sweetened coffee with milk and pastries.

She grinned. Honestly, Gaspar should weigh three hundred pounds. It was unfair to women everywhere that he didn't.

After a bit, she heard Gaspar's son crying in the background. He said with a chuckle, "I'd better go. He's got quite a set of lungs on him, my boy. Maybe he'll be a singer when he grows up."

"One more thing," Kim said, even as she heard Juan's relentlessly demanding wails.

"Yeah?"

"Eleanor Duncan strikes me as a woman feeling a lot of guilt."

"Maybe. So?"

"What's all that guilt about?" Kim asked, tapping her finger absently on the wine glass. "And how is Reacher involved in it?"

She could feel his shrug across the miles. His all-purpose gesture. Could mean anything.

He said, "Does it matter now? Reacher saved all those women. Twice. That's all that's important to Eleanor and the others at this point."

Kim cocked her head. "Would he look at it that way?"

Gaspar had always been her secret weapon where Reacher was concerned.

Understanding the quarry was the first rule of hunting. Gaspar thought like Reacher. They'd had the same background and experience until Gaspar joined the FBI.

After the army, their paths diverged.

Gaspar chose to become a devoted family man.

Reacher became a lonely drifter. At least, that's how it looked from the outside.

But the Eleanor Duncan situation proved that Reacher was more concerned about the people in his life than he liked to pretend.

Which made sense of The Boss's strategy, too. Cooper had been sending Kim to people and places where Reacher had gone before.

Gambling that Reacher would come back when those people were in trouble.

Sometimes Cooper had engineered the new trouble. Other times, he'd committed a hundred crimes to discover it.

Either way, he'd been right too often.

Like with Eleanor Duncan.

The baby cried louder, insisting now.

"I gotta go or he's gonna wake up the entire household," Gaspar said.

"Give my love to Marie and the girls," Kim replied.

Then he offered one last warning before he signed off. "Don't get all hung up on Reacher's motives, Kim. He'd say he never saved those women at all. Luck and happenstance saved them. Reacher just happened to be in the right place at the right time. That's what saved them. He probably never even saw their faces."

Yeah. But it turns out Jack Reacher has a heart after all.

Kim was tired. Sleep when you can, Gaspar would say. Reacher would say that, too, probably. It was good advice.

She turned off the lights and settled deeper into the luxury of high thread count sheets and lightweight down comforters.

For now, she closed her eyes and allowed the wine to hasten sleep.

She'd collect Burke from the hospital tomorrow. He was still her partner. If he really had engaged Reacher and survived because he possessed vital intel, Burke was more valuable to her now than he'd been before.

Orders from The Boss on the flash drive had included two plane tickets to Chicago.

As usual, the orders were terse. No explanations. She didn't know why he was sending them to Chicago or where they were ultimately headed, or how Cooper had acquired intel sufficient to issue the orders.

The mission remained the same: Find Reacher.

And now she knew things about Reacher she hadn't known before.

She had Burke and access to whatever vital intel he possessed.

She also had at least one viable lead: Petey Burns.

FROM LEE CHILD
THE REACHER REPORT:
March 2nd, 2012

The other big news is Diane Capri—a friend of mine—wrote a book revisiting the events of KILLING FLOOR in Margrave, Georgia. She imagines an FBI team tasked to trace Reacher's current-day whereabouts. They begin by interviewing people who knew him—starting out with Roscoe and Finlay. Check out this review: "Oh heck yes! I am in love with this book. I'm a huge Jack Reacher fan. If you don't know Jack (pun intended!) then get thee to the bookstore/wherever you buy your fix and pick up one of the many Jack Reacher books by Lee Child. Heck, pick up all of them. In particular, read Killing Floor. Then come back and read Don't Know Jack. This story picks up the other from the point of view of Kim and Gaspar, FBI agents assigned to build a file on Jack Reacher. The problem is, as anyone who knows Reacher can attest, he lives completely off the grid. No cell phone, no house, no car…he's not tied down. A pretty daunting task, then, wouldn't you say?

First lines: "Just the facts. And not many of them, either. Jack Reacher's file was too stale and too thin to be credible. No human could be as invisible as Reacher appeared to be, whether he was currently above the ground or under it. Either the file had been sanitized, or Reacher was the most off-the-grid paranoid Kim Otto had ever heard of." Right away, I'm sensing who Kim Otto is and I'm delighted that I know something she doesn't. You see, I DO know Jack. And I know he's not paranoid. Not really. I know why he lives as he does, and I know what kind of man he is. I loved having that over Kim and Gaspar. If you haven't read any Reacher novels, then this will feel like a good, solid story in its own right. If you have…oh if you have, then you, too, will feel like you have a one-up on the FBI. It's a fun feeling!

"Kim and Gaspar are sent to Margrave by a mysterious boss who reminds me of Charlie, in Charlie's Angels. You never see him…you hear him. He never gives them all the facts. So they are left with a big pile of nothing. They end up embroiled in a murder case that seems connected to Reacher somehow, but they can't see how. Suffice to say the efforts to find the murderer and Reacher, and not lose their own heads in the process, makes for an entertaining read.

"I love the way the author handled the entire story. The pacing is dead on (ok another pun intended), the story is full of twists and turns like a Reacher novel would be, but it's another viewpoint of a Reacher story. It's an outside-in approach to Reacher.

"You might be asking, do they find him? Do they finally meet the infamous Jack Reacher?

"Go…read…now…find out!"

Sounds great, right? Check out "Don't Know Jack," and let me know what you think.

So that's it for now…again, thanks for reading THE AFFAIR, and I hope you'll like A WANTED MAN just as much in September.

Lee Child

ABOUT THE AUTHOR

Diane Capri is an award-winning *New York Times*, *USA Today*, and worldwide bestselling author. She's a recovering lawyer and snowbird who divides her time between Florida and Michigan. An active member of Mystery Writers of America, Author's Guild, International Thriller Writers, Alliance of Independent Authors, and Sisters in Crime, she loves to hear from readers and is hard at work on her next novel.

Please connect with her online:

http://www.DianeCapri.com

Twitter: http://twitter.com/@DianeCapri

Facebook: http://www.facebook.com/Diane.Capri1

http://www.facebook.com/DianeCapriBooks